the
Time
Weaver

Shana Abé

BANTAM BOOKS • NEW YORK

The Time Weaver is a work of fiction. Names, characters, places, and incidents either are the product of the author's imagination or are used fictitiously. Any resemblance to actual persons, living or dead, events, or locales is entirely coincidental.

2011 Bantam Books Mass Market Edition

Copyright © 2010 by Four Rabbits, Inc.

All rights reserved.

Published in the United States by Bantam Books, an imprint of The Random House Publishing Group, a division of Random House, Inc., New York.

BANTAM BOOKS and the rooster colophon are registered trademarks of Random House, Inc.

Originally published in hardcover in the United States by Bantam Books, an imprint of The Random House Publishing Group, a division of Random House, Inc., in 2010.

ISBN: 978-0-553-59123-1

Cover design: Eileen Carey
Cover images: © Brand New Images/Getty Images (hand)

Printed in the United States of America

www.bantamdell.com

9 8 7 6 5 4 3 2 1

Bantam Books mass market edition: June 2011

PRAISE FOR THE NOVELS OF SHANA ABÉ

THE TIME WEAVER

THE TREASURE KEEPER

QUEEN OF DRAGONS

"*Queen of Dragons* . . . succeeds as well-written fantasy."
—*The Denver Post*

"Abé's graceful storytelling and evocative details make this a good choice for adult fantasy collections."
—*Library Journal*

"Romantic fantasy fans are sure to look forward to further installments in this winning series."
—*Publishers Weekly*

"There are few more alluring creatures than Abé's shape-shifting *drákon* with their imaginative stories and pulse-pounding adventures. This talented author has perfected the legend and created a sensual world of magic and desire that truly soars."

—*Romantic Times*

"*Queen of Dragons* is a gorgeous story. The words flow in near lyrical prose . . . A Perfect 10."
—ROBIN LEE, Romance Reviews Today

THE DREAM THIEF

"As thrilling as it is magical, as passionate as it is adventurous and as memorable as *The Smoke Thief*. The story has an indefinable, haunting quality that lingers long after the end. Surrender to Abé's remarkable ability to bring magic to life and soar with the dragons."
—*Romantic Times*

"*The Dream Thief* reads like an evocative fairy tale, filled with the sights, scents and tastes of life and love . . . The prose flows like a lyrical dream and the story will steal your heart, earning *The Dream Thief* a Perfect 10."
—Romance Reviews Today

"Abé is a multiple RITA finalist, and the reasons are clear—*The Dream Thief* is a heady, fast-paced, heartbreakingly romantic story rendered in hypnotically beautiful language."
—BARBARA SAMUEL, *BookPage*

"Another stunning example of a unique and absorbing paranormal historical romance . . . This engrossing story kept me glued to the pages. An excellent read!"
—TANZEY CUTTER, *Fresh Fiction*

THE SMOKE THIEF

"Shana Abé has a rare magic. I was completely captivated by this beautifully written novel."
—JANE FEATHER, *New York Times* bestselling author

"Abé pulls out all the stops in this 'catch-me-if-you-can' story. It's ripe with romance and a legend so intriguing you'll believe every word. Abé brings a new dimension and new possibilities to the genre in an enthralling tale that breaks down boundaries."
—*Romantic Times*

"Spellbinding, dazzling, *The Smoke Thief* is pure magic from start to finish. I simply couldn't put it down. Abé is an immensely gifted storyteller."
—KAREN MARIE MONING,
New York Times bestselling author of *Faefever*

"Adventure, romance, and thrills galore. I was swept away by Shana Abé's wondrous imagination and lyrical prose. *The Smoke Thief* crosses many boundaries of traditional genre fiction. Just call it an absolutely terrific read, and get started."
—MICHAEL PALMER,
New York Times bestselling author of *The Last Surgeon*

By Shana Abé

THE TIME WEAVER
THE TREASURE KEEPER
QUEEN OF DRAGONS
THE DREAM THIEF
THE SMOKE THIEF
THE LAST MERMAID
THE SECRET SWAN
INTIMATE ENEMIES
A KISS AT MIDNIGHT
THE TRUELOVE BRIDE
THE PROMISE OF RAIN
A ROSE IN WINTER

Books published by The Random House Publishing Group are available at quantity discounts on bulk purchases for premium, educational, fund-raising, and special sales use. For details, please call 1-800-733-3000.

For Nita Taublib, whose guidance and wisdom have been invaluable, and always appreciated.

My most sincere gratitude also goes to my awesome agents, Annelise Robey and Andrea Cirillo, and all the fantastic folks at Jane Rotrosen. And, of course, to Shauna Summers, who totally rocks, and Jessica Sebor, the go-to gal!

My love to my mother and sisters and brothers, everyone. *Moltes gràcies* to brilliant Sean. A special hello to MaKayla, Brianna, Braeden, Bailey, Nathan, Mallory, and MaKenzie. To Jules and Jax: It was a mosquito with a French fry, I swear!

And to Daddy. I miss you so much.

What if everything you loved, and everyone, suddenly vanished?

Your parents, your children, your friends. Your home. Your town.

Your species.

All the living beings that defined your world, that gave your heart reason to pump the blood that animates your flesh, that caused you to wake each morning and open your eyes and turn your face to your window to witness the new sun in the new sky; laughter and love and meals around the table and running games in tall grasses, snowball battles in winter; gentle hands holding yours, warm kisses on your lips—all that gone.

What if it were your doing?

Your future unfurled before you like a map marked with a thick black arrow drawn irrevocably, relentlessly straight toward Extinction. You never knew. You never guessed, until the end.

What would you sacrifice to erase that map?

PROLOGUE

Imagine a place empty of souls.

Imagine it lush and green and fertile, a land dripping with moss and dew, streams flowing like glass across peat and smooth dark rocks. Wild roses weep petals into the streams, sending them down and down hills into lakes that glitter sapphire and gold beneath the sun.

Pebbles of copper and silver live in the silt at the bottom of the lakes. Occasionally long speckled trout flick by, the fans of their tails stirring the mud into storms; fish do well in this place. They never hear the sad, persistent songs of the silver, the ardent copper, and there is no one above the water left to hunt them. The fish thrive.

Beyond the water the land is not yet so easy with itself. The scent of the creatures who used to dwell here still saturates the air. The decaying homes, the fallow fields, the deep tangled woods. The abandoned manor house on the knoll, still shining with windows, surrounded by grass and aspen and willows: everything smells of them, and all the little animals who would normally flourish in this green silence remain missing. It will take many years before any of them dare to reclaim the land.

Birds will appear first. Then rodents. Then badgers. Hedgehogs, red squirrels, moles, foxes, rabbits. And deer too. Along with the rabbits, deer will come last.

But they're not here yet, not even the smallest of larks. For now, all that may be heard is the water rippling over the rocks, and a scattering of insects hiding beneath ferns or under the bark of the trees in the forest, chirping and breathing.

This place was named Darkfrith, for the woods and the water. The beings who dwelled here—who built the cottages and the mansion and the mines and mills—were called the *drákon.*

They were dragons, of course.

There are none left now. But once—oh, yes, once upon a time, they ruled this empty place.

Beasts of brutal beauty and cunning, they had learned to blend with the Homo sapiens of the more ordinary world, to mask themselves as them, to conceal their true resplendence. Centuries past they had been driven from their homeland in the Carpathian Mountains, but in their flight these particular dragons had discovered the woods and lakes—heard the silver calling to them from the buried veins deep inside the earth—and decided to settle here. In England.

For a while, they managed it very well.

Darkfrith is a secret ripe corner at the northern edge of the country; remote, timbered and undulating, it offered nothing remarkable to tempt tourists or even common travelers. Occasionally a few would venture in anyway.

None of them lingered long.

By day they would discover a scene of idyllic perfection: lustrous-cheeked girls and strong, comely lads. Neatly tilled fields, Roman-straight orchards spangled with apples and pears, peaches and plums. Emerald hills that hugged the heavens, that invited the clouds down low for foggy kisses. A flock of black-faced sheep. That manor house, seat of an ancient noble family, gleaming with wealth. Silver mines. A bustling village. Everyone smiling and happy.

However, should he look more closely, the Traveler might notice how the smiles of the villagers never quite warmed their eyes. How there was but that lone drove of sheep, not nearly as many as the meadows could support. And how those sheep bolted from their keepers over and over again, even though they were herded only by children.

What the weary Traveler might perceive more quickly was the fact that Darkfrith had no inn. Not one. And the people of the shire—nearly all of them blond and pale and handsome—somehow never had a single room to spare, not even a bed of hay in one of the barns.

He might take coffee in the tavern, or ale, should he prefer it. He might admire the clean cobblestone lanes and elegant limestone architecture, the aroma of spiced tarts or *soufflé au chocolat* from the bakery, the books displayed in the bowfront window of the circulating library. But as the day would fade and dusk slowly darken into blue, the Traveler would begin to feel an uneasy sort of itching settle between his shoulder blades. A restlessness. The urge to press on.

For all their smiles, the villagers would make certain of that.

Because by night, Darkfrith became a very different place. By night, the smiling fair people were gone, and any Travelers left on the shire roads would have done well to duck their heads and move faster.

The skies writhed at night. The stars trembled, the moon shrank. The beasts took flight then, commanding the dominion of heaven: great, glimmering bands of dragons, curling and coiling and streaking through the dark. From over five leagues away, farmers would shiver and cross themselves for no reason; their wives would pull the shutters a little tighter against the unnatural moaning of wind carved by wings rising beyond the hills.

Everyone local knew not to venture to Darkfrith at night, even if they did not know why.

For sixteen generations the *drákon* thrived in this little pocket of the world.

By the time the seventeenth took their first toddling steps, it was done.

Here is the story of how they perished. Or perhaps it's the story of how they did not.

You'll see.

CHAPTER ONE

Dear Honor,

I leave this letter for you knowing you'll find it in the Year 1782, at the age of nearly fifteen, right before your Gifts begin to fully emerge. This is going to sound mad, but you must believe me.

I am you, eleven months and four days from now.

Keep reading. This is not a jest.

You are a Time Weaver. You are the only Time Weaver born to the *drákon*. It's just as it sounds: You will have the ability to Weave through time when you wish it—and sometimes, when you do not.

As it is when the rest of the tribe Turns to smoke or dragon, you will not be able to bring anything not of yourself with you when you Weave. You will reemerge in each new time exactly the same as you left the last, and (unless you Focus upon it very fiercely), in exactly the same place. However, you will be nude. You will have no jewelry. No weapons. Nothing left in your hands.

~~I am working, though, on a way.~~

I've not discovered what happens to all those things, because apparently they're not left in the previous time or place, either. They're Vanished. For now, don't Weave wearing anything you especially like.

When- and wherever you go during a Weave, however long you spend there, inevitably you will be drawn back into your Natural Time. It's rather like a *pull* inside you that grows stronger and stronger, until you can no longer resist it. Picture a strand of india rubber stretched long and thin and then snapping back to its normal shape. The strand connects you to your Natural Time. You always come back. And it's always the exact amount of time later *there* that you spent during the Weave.

That's another thing that's Vanished: the time you've spent away from your Natural Time. Once you Weave away, you can't touch it again. I've tried.

In a few nights, on July 6, a human man is going to come to the shire in secret for you. His name is Zane; you will recall he's the London Thief befriended by our Alphas, the Marquess and Marchioness of Langford, until he was banished for wedding their daughter. He will have with him some shards of a blue diamond once known as *Draumr*. He will summon you from your bedroom at Plum House, and you will go with him.

I know that at this point in your life, you've never heard of *Draumr*, so I will briefly explain: *Draumr* was a stone from our ancestral home in the Carpathian Mountains, and once upon a time it was guarded by, and belonged to, our cousins the Zaharen *drákon*. Its name means Dreaming Diamond, and it has a very long and unpleasant history relating to our kind. It enables whoever wears it or carries it (or its splinters, for that is all that is left of it in your Natural Time) to command the *drákon*. We have no choice, we must obey it.

Please do not attempt to resist it. Zane will not harm you.

He will take you to a safe place. *Your life is in danger in Darkfrith. You must not remain there. Zane is coming to save you.*

To convince you I am who I say I am, I offer you the following:

1. The second plank under your bed is loose, and there is a space beneath. You keep all your romantic novels Father thought he tossed away there.

2. Your first kiss came from Lord Rhys Langford, when you were eight and he twenty-two. He kissed you on the chin after Wilhelmina Grady pushed you down yet again, this time in front of the silversmith's shop.

3. You hunted Wilhelmina later that night, waited until she was alone, then threatened to cut off all her hair if she continued to hurt you.

4. You would not have cut off her hair (she did have a lot of it, though). Wilhelmina has always been extraordinarily large and short-tempered. But you were convincing. She never called your bluff.

5. Your secret tree in Blackstone Woods is an ash. You keep charms in its hollow; it's where I left you this letter.

6. Your favorite butterfly is the Brimstone. Your favorite wildflowers are harebells.

7. Here's the best bit: Approximately one week past, on a Tuesday, you lost an entire three hours. You were in your bedroom, feeling sleepy and reading (*The Decline of Lady Pamela*) whilst the hall clock was striking half past noon.

And then all at once you were there on the bed cold and unclothed (you remember *that*) and the clock finished its chimes at half past *three*.

You told no one about it, which was wise. You decided that you had fallen asleep, that you must have walked and disrobed—even the blasted corset—in your sleep. You were wrong. You never found that gown again, did you? Nor the book.

That was your first Weave, Honor. Eventually, the memory of it will return to you. (Hint: You went to a river.)

The rules of the shire are indisputable. You know what will happen to you if anyone discovers you're Gifted, especially since it's so rare these days for females to display Gifts of any sort. Yes, I realize you've daydreamed about being special, special enough to be given like a prize to the Alpha and his family to better their line. But believe me, your life with them will not be the stuff of dreams. You cannot Turn into a dragon; your Gift is unique . . . and, some might say, dangerous. The Alpha and his Council would never have permitted you the Freedom of your Gifts. At best, you would have been kept in chains and darkness. You would have been wed and bedded as a prisoner, for all the rest of your life.

There is a much, much better future awaiting you. There is a prince, I swear it. A real one.

Put this letter now in your apron pocket. Burn it after tea today. The drawing room is always deserted then, and no one will see. Remember everything I've written here, but don't speak of it to anyone. Even Zane!

Don't be frightened.
—H.C.

Second Letter

(I need to keep track, I think. This is the second letter I've written to myself Over Time.)

Honor,

By now you're in Barcelona, living with Lia Langford, and sometimes her husband, Zane. Yes, I know he's still a criminal, and a human. But she's like you, Gifted and apart. Please listen to her counsel. She wants only the best for you and all of us.

You're surprised to discover that you miss Mother and Father, and even Darkfrith. Well, the woods at least. I'm four months ahead of you, so I know it can be difficult. Dreadful, even. But Lia, more than anyone, can help you understand what it's like to venture into the future, to wrest control of it. You *need* her. Not only is she one of the last few females who can Turn into dragon, she alone has the Gift of Dreaming Ahead, and she's seen what's to come. Perhaps she seems too strict sometimes; perhaps she seems unfeeling. She's not, though. I'm certain she misses Darkfrith too. Remember, she's a Lady, the youngest daughter of the Marquess and Marchioness, of powerful blood. And yet she's been vanished from the tribe since she was a young woman herself.

She'll teach you Control. She'll teach you Responsibility. You Must Learn These Things.

You're fifteen, so by now you know about Sandu. Stay away from him. He's not ready for you yet.

—H.C.

Third Letter

The lovely heat. The white-salt scent of the Mediterranean floating inland, gentle against your face. *Pa amb tomàquet, sangria*. Festival dancers in the streets, laughing boys with black hair. Yellow sunlight and ripe oranges spraying sugar as you peel them open, fresh flowers all the year long. Oh, Honor . . . there are many things to recommend Spain.

I know you feel ready to burst at the seams. I know you're Sick Unto Death of Catalan and watching the traffic on Carrer del Bisbe pass by from behind the glass of the bower, that particular warp in the pane that somehow always remains level with your eyes. Trapped. Pinned inside the apartments like a butterfly to a board. But you promised. You mustn't leave. You're not nearly skilled enough yet to control this Gift.

Do not Weave in secret to Sandu's castle. Don't seek him out again. And don't go home either, not unless you want to tempt fate. We're too young to die.

You're nearly sixteen, you're smarter than that. Be more careful. The English cannot know where you are. They cannot even know you're alive. You'd risk everything by Weaving back to Darkfrith, even for a moment.

I'm a year and a half ahead, and I'm *still* struggling to master this Gift. Listen to me.

—H.C.

Post Script: I know you're thinking of finding me in the future and the past. Don't. It won't work, you can't come anywhere near me. We cannot interact that way. That's why I'm hiding these letters for you to find.

Fourth Letter

I can't really believe how incredibly stubborn I am. You, Honor X. Carlisle, are an idiot.

STOP spying upon Sandu!! Are you mad? Are you trying to start a war with the Zaharen? If they discover you there they'll instantly think the worst—the worst for Darkfrith, I mean. Is that what you want? Tensions between the two tribes are serious enough. The last thing anyone needs is for the Zaharen to accuse the English of sending an infiltrator, or the English to accuse the Zaharen of kidnapping you.

However much the Zaharen look like us, however much they act like us and speak and eat and fly and hunt—oh God, Honor, they're *not* us. These are a kind of dragon that are *pre*-Darkfrith. Imagine our tribe before the ancient split. Imagine the most primal, untamed versions of our kind, and there they are, still thriving in the highest peaks of the Carpathian Alps. Alone. Untouched. They have no human checks or balances, they have nothing of the Others to impede them. And they definitely have no reason to follow all the silly little rules of our shire. Why bother?

They're accepted exactly as they are by the peasants of the mountains. Their castle, *Zaharen Yce*, has been perched upon its crest as far back as human memory stretches. In the hamlets all around, the Zaharen *drákon* are welcomed as guardian spirits. Feared as devils. They hide nothing of themselves from the Others, whilst we hide all that we are, just to survive.

You come from a Time of Enlightenment. You were born to a tribe of civilized monsters, dragons who are devious enough to wear satin and taffeta and powder their hair and never, ever *whisper* a hint of their true selves to the outside world.

The Zaharen skipped Enlightenment. Oh, they have their own fine satins and wigs and jewels, but it's all purely for their pleasure. They gain nothing with pretense. In nearly every way that matters, it is still a feudal society.

The most obvious commonality between us is that they *do* follow an Alpha, but he doesn't even have a Council to co-govern, as ours does; ultimately he acts alone in all his decisions. And the Zaharen *drákon* comply, no matter what. It's in their blood.

Yes, our Sandu is their Prince Alexandru. Yes, he's been chosen as their Alpha. And he's strong and beautiful and—confound it, just stop Weaving to him. You don't have enough control yet to Weave back in case of disaster, and you know it.

Look here: see how my hand trembles, how the ink splotches and my sentences quiver across the page? Tonight I was nearly caught. Tonight could have been the end of everything. I ended up in a *ballroom*. During a *ball*. ~~And he looked at me like I~~

Oh, dear. I write you this letter knowing you haven't even made my mistakes yet. But you're going to. I want to change the future, but it's like pushing a boulder up a mountain. I never win. What I will in retrospect never matters. The future simply rolls right over me, no matter what.

Keep all this from Lia and Zane. Burn it, burn it. They will not understand.

Five hours ahead,

—H.C.

Fifth Letter

You're nineteen. You're desperate to know what happens. You're desperate to know even just a little of what will be. I recall that Lia seems acutely reluctant to share your future. Has it not occurred to you there's a good reason for that?

Yes, you will be married to him. There. Now you know.

Stop Weaving for practice. You're paying a price for it, one you haven't even noticed yet. But I have. Please stop.

Remember what the legends of our kind tell us: None of the Gifts are free. None of the glory comes without sacrifice. Our particular sacrifice is rather horrific.

Save the Weaves for emergencies. Settle your heart, and look ahead with clear eyes from your Natural Time. Do not be so eager to touch the future. Savor your today.

I wish I believed my words would make a difference. I wish I could change myself, and what is to come. I've tried so hard to put things right. I don't even think you're going to get this note. I don't know, I don't know, I can never tell.

Twenty-five years ahead,

—you

CHAPTER TWO

At the age of fourteen, I was kidnapped from my home by a pair of infamous outlaws.

Infamous to my kind, at least. And I suppose that, truthfully, the word *kidnapped* might be an exaggeration. After all, I knew it was going to happen, and I was fully prepared to comply. I'd warned myself days in advance about Zane, and about *Draumr*. Still, I have to admit I was secretly shocked when it actually occurred.

I'd been waiting, fully dressed, sitting upright upon my bed because somehow it didn't seem very dignified to greet one's kidnappers prone. I'd said my good-nights to my parents hours earlier that evening, as required, kissing the air by their cheeks—Joséphine always carefully scented of lavender; Gervase of pipe tobacco and harsh silver, his face angled away from mine—and neither of them had noticed anything amiss. It was hardly surprising. Neither of them ever seemed to notice anything amiss with me. They certainly never spoke of the numerous bruises or bloody scrapes I tended to acquire. My mother's cool hand lingered on my arm a few seconds longer than usual, perhaps, but that was all.

I withdrew to my room, packed my case, and waited.

Plum House was a fine Elizabethan mess of a place. The main structure had been commissioned by the Alpha of our tribe long ago to lodge the gamekeeper of the shire, and the remaining two wings and solariums had been added helter-skelter by various ancestors since. The Carlisles had always been the gamekeepers of the tribe, and so the House was always our home.

Of course, the job of gamekeeper for Darkfrith had a different meaning than it did for the rest of the world, for the Others. The challenge was not to keep the rapacious animals out of the confines of the shire, but in.

Still, we were gentrified enough by the time of my birth that the title was largely ceremonial; there were very few attempts at escape any longer. We were beasts, yes, but beasts who enjoyed the luxuries afforded us by maintaining our human façade. My father's actual employment was the management of the tribe's vast silver mines. It meant that while he was absent from Mother and me a great deal, we had the means for three young housemaids from the village and a cook, which pleased Joséphine very well. She and the staff rattled around the halls, polishing the dark Tudor panels and all the narrow-paned windows, shaking dust from the tapestries, concocting meals and teas and elegant soirées to which the Marchioness of Langford, the wife of our Alpha, would occasionally come.

Whenever the marchioness came to tea, my presence was required. I would sit in silence and not toy with the ribbons on my gown, and not breathe very deeply because of my corset, and nibble at tiny frosted cakes and crustless sandwiches, and all the *drákon* ladies would remark upon my fine manners. My mother would incline her head graciously.

The truth was, I was too petrified to speak. My mother, with her icy kohled gaze ready to find fault with me; the marchioness, with her daunting haute couture and imposing French wigs; all the simmering, contained ladies of the shire who beneath their imported satins and bell-beautiful voices burned to be as vicious as the menfolk were allowed to be—every single one of them frightened me, and always had. I had been born a timid gray mouse into a den of starving lions.

I did not belong. I was nothing like any of them. It didn't astonish me in the least to learn that my life was in danger; it had seemed apparent to me since I was a small child that, sooner or later, one of the real *drákon* would end up killing me.

I didn't even resemble the rest of them, not really. We were a clan of mostly fair, blond beauties, and although I had inherited my mother's blue eyes, my own hair wasn't the color of wheat, or sunshine, or summer flax. It was a shade caught between red and ginger, a little of both, not quite either. I was pale like all the girls, but while their skin shone with the translucent clarity of fine alabaster, my complexion looked to me more like chalk. I was scrawny, timid, and not very tall. A certain cadre of the village children found it persistently amusing to refer to me as *the runt*.

As in, *Look, it's the runt. Let's show her what hap-*

pens to the weakest of the litter, shall we? Oh yes, let's.

So on that sweltering summer night of July in 1782, I felt little more than wonder that somehow, for some reason, all of that was about to change. I was leaving. I was Gifted—I would be—and I was leaving.

I was a Time Weaver, apparently. Whatever that meant.

My bedroom's sole window faced north, so it was always one of the gloomiest chambers in the house. I was comfortable in that gloom, seated at the edge of my bed, listening to the cockchafers whirring in the woods nearby, the soft perfume of the honeyed wax the second maid had rubbed into the armoire that morning wafting sweet against my face.

Generations past, one of the young brides of the House had planted love-in-a-mist outside my sill. The flowers bloomed in a tangle of pink and mauve all summer long and spilled petals with the slightest hint of a breeze; they, too, were scented of honey. If I concentrated hard enough, I could hear the drifting petals *tip-tap* the spaded earth where they landed.

It was hot. I was wearing my best apricot silk dress with a buffon for modesty and a mobcap that dripped Irish lace to my shoulders. Eventually I removed the buffon from my bodice; it was far too warm to be wrapped in a muslin kerchief up to my neck. Despite my resolve not to nod off . . . I did. I only realized it when I lifted my head, because there was a sharp new twinge in my neck, and the slow, pensive music of the dream I'd been having did not fade.

I turned toward the sound, pushing back the lace from my cheek. Yes, there were notes floating around me, simple and haunting notes, a tune so familiar and yet not . . . like a lullaby with words you can't quite remember.

The dreaming part of me thought, *That's a diamond?* Because it was unlike any I'd ever heard before. Most gemstones sing to our kind, metals too, but diamonds sing strongest. They surround us with melodies that are always clear and keen, sparkling with life. We *drákon* love diamonds. Young or old, every female of the shire had at least a glittering pair of earbobs or a handful of fiery-cut rings. During my mother's especially stylish assemblies, the din from the ladies' necklaces and charms could drown out entire conversations.

Yet *this* song slipped over me like a cloud, dulcet and eerie, devouring my senses. It made me feel at once both happy and languorously indifferent. It made me want to close my eyes and release my very last breath.

Then came the voice, whispering between the notes.

"Honor . . ."

It was no natural voice. It was sly and gentle and chilled my skin.

"Honor Carlisle. You alone will hear me. You alone will sense me. Come to me."

I was on my feet before I'd realized I had moved. Layers of skirts and petticoats rustled back into place, brushing the tops of my slippers. The case felt suddenly light as air in my arms.

"Come."

And the music wrapped around me so completely that I practically glided out my door.

It was well after three in the morning. Everyone else

in Plum House was asleep. Mother, Papa, the maids, and the cook, who snored. No one heard me leave. No one but me heard the brass latch of the front door give its low amiable hum as my fingers closed about it. No one but me saw the starlight sketching the grass of the front lawn, or heard the press of my footsteps through the blades.

There'd been no rain for weeks, and the lawn was turning brittle. I'd leave a path here, I knew that, but it didn't matter.

"Hurry, Honor."

I reached the edge of our estate. Should I turn right, I would meet the road that led to the village, to the august mansion that housed the Alpha and his kin. Should I turn left, I would enter the thick black forest that surrounded my home, crisscrossing trails soon lost to peat and bracken and streams, and eventually a wide, churning river.

The notes, the voice, were coming from the forest. So I went left.

I knew my way through these woods. I'd grown up here, after all, and had claimed even the densest thickets as my own. Maidens without friends tended to spend hours exploring alone. And maidens who made enemies needed places to hide—I had plenty of those.

Blackstone Woods welcomed me with its familiar heady fragrance, rich and loamy, but even that was dulled beneath the uncanny notes of the song pulling me onward. The moss cushioned my steps; feathery ferns brushed my ankles; twigs crunched and leaves sighed and the voice had gone silent, but that was all right, because I knew where he was now, the man who had come for me.

He was on the river. He was in a boat on the River Fier, standing alert beneath the dim starlight, one hand lifted before him, a faint sparkle of blue shining from his open palm.

I should have been afraid. I was afraid nearly all the time, afraid of my parents, afraid of my species, afraid of myself. I was afraid of the dark, and of mirrors, and of the Council, of the strange smiles of the village boys and the casual cruelty of the village girls. I definitely should have been afraid of this notorious thief who was going to do who knew what with me.

Yet I was not.

Because of *Draumr*. I felt it from yards away, the music growing stronger and sweeter, drugging my senses. I floated forward and thought blissfully, *This is what it's like to fly. This is how it must feel when we Turn. Finally I understand. This is flight.*

The River Fier was never asleep, and the skiff rocked gently with the tugging of its currents. The man held his balance easily, lean and shadowy against the steel-gray ribbon of water beyond him, his shirt ruffling with the small breeze, his hair a long braided plait that swung all the way down to his waist. He watched me approach without another word. When I was close enough I was able to make out the color of his eyes: a wolfish amber, so clear and bright it seemed nearly inhuman. But he *was* human. I knew that much about him. He reeked of human sweat and musk.

"Get in," he said. His fist closed around the sparkle

of blue, and I felt a rush of pleasure so intense my eyes nearly rolled back.

"For God's sake," muttered the man, and grabbed me by the arm. "Spare me the swooning spells of adolescent girls. Bloody damned diamond. Honor Carlisle, I presume? Get in. Now."

The notes echoed him, *yesss, get in*, but I took a slow, river-scented breath. "Where are—"

"And do shut up," the man said pleasantly. "Aside from the fact that I'd rather leave this place with my head still attached to my shoulders, I doubt there's anything you could say to me I would find of interest."

That was my introduction to Zane, the Black Shadow of Mayfair, the Secret Worm of the *Sanf Inimicus*—and my new father.

It was his wife, Lady Amalia Langford, who had planned the abduction. It was Lia—who also grew up in the shire—who knew the surest way to smuggle me out of it was by water, where scents were swept quickly away, and no physical traces were left for the hunt.

I settled with my case upon the damp bottom of the skiff and watched Zane row, the flexing muscles beneath his shirt, fresh perspiration glinting along his chest and forehead, his gaze constantly searching the horizon. He steered to hug the shore, floating beneath the branches of the river oaks when he could, mottled shadows of charcoal and ash skimming over us both. Every now and again a different sort of shadow would flit across the surface of the water—swift and sinister, slim as a snake before vanishing against the trees. The air above us then would give the barest,

barest groan as it was sliced apart. It was the only discernible sound beyond the diamond and our breathing, and the soft splash of the oars cutting into the Fier.

Zane looked grim. He should have. Had one of those dragons soaring overhead happened to notice us, it would have meant his head indeed.

That is, I supposed, unless he managed to bespell the dragon first with the stone. He'd put the blue sparkly thing in his pocket but I still heard it. It swathed me in a song of contentment, and I didn't think I could be any happier to be kidnapped by a rude, smelly human and whisked away down a river to the unknown.

~~∞~~

We met Lady Lia in Harrogate two days later. Harrogate was a spa town, stinking of sulfur from the natural hot springs that bubbled up from the earth, with hotels and restaurants all faced in creamy pale marble, and people of every sort of fashion and station crowding its streets.

It was raining by then, not a little rain, but great sheets of water falling from the sky. It was warm still, nearly tropical, I imagined, although I had no real idea what *tropical* might feel like; it was merely a word I'd read in books, as distant and foreign to me as *Chinaman* or *polar bear* or *freedom*.

The rain fell and fell and swirled eddies of garbage and filth along the curbs, and flooded the meager storm drains, and soaked through my new oiled cotton cloak that Zane had purchased for me, since I had brought no cloak of my own.

But the rain was little help with the constant stench of sulfur rolling about the town in acrid curls of mist. Passing through one was eye-watering. Were it not for the shards of diamond Zane still carried and used on me—*stay with me, keep quiet, you're my daughter if anyone asks, a London tailor and his daughter on holiday*—I would have turned around and slogged back to Darkfrith, no matter how my life was endangered. But the pieces of *Draumr* never ceased their song, and so I managed only to cup a hand to my nose and mouth as we traversed those streets, trying not to inhale very deeply.

It turned out that the fragments of the diamond were embedded in a ring, something like a signet. He wore it day and night now with no gloves; I remained a few steps behind him as we walked, so I could follow the pale blue sparks of it with the swinging arc of his hand.

I had never before been around so many humans. There were fat ones and thin ones, many with grime darkening the folds of their pocked skin. Some had wooden teeth and some had no teeth at all. They wore homespun and brocades and wigs hopping with fleas. They shoved by us without apology, bellowing and belching and farting through the rain, and I was more profoundly grateful than I could say when Zane tugged a handkerchief free from the cuff of his sleeve and handed it back to me, so I could crumple that to my nose instead.

He threw me a look from beneath the brim of his tricorne. Water fell in a straight silvery line down the center fold, missing his nose by inches.

"The sulfur will throw them off" was all he said, but I understood him completely.

I skipped over the corpse of a rat that had washed up to the sidewalk, finally able to breathe. The kerchief was linen and lace, perfumed with pleasant spices. I discovered later that Lia had commissioned that perfume for him herself, had it made in small batches by nuns in the south of France and delivered every Christmas.

I could certainly understand why. Lady Amalia lived with her husband in this human world. Yet she was both nobility and *drákon*, one of the most pureblooded of us all. She would need every defense she could muster.

I'd never known her in Darkfrith. She was well over a decade older than I, and had vanished from the tribe entirely when I was just a young child. Even had we been of a closer age, we would not have mingled. The children of the Alpha were privileged enough to leave the shire and live with their parents in London for the season, learning their glamorous human ways, establishing themselves as the aristocracy the human kingdom required. They seldom mixed with our village society until it was time to choose mates.

Lady Lia hadn't even made it that long. She'd chosen her mate from this sea of Others, and it was enough to end her alliance with the tribe.

Not officially. Officially, she was still *drákon*, and the hunt for her had never ceased. She was considered a runner, someone who had committed one of the most egregious of all tribal crimes, and should she ever have been caught, her punishment would have been dire. It was why she and Zane lived in careful anonymity, far from the shire. It was why he and I slunk about now, on the bustling, pungent streets of Harrogate, with our shoulders rounded and our heads down as we made our way to the hotel she had procured for us.

I felt her at once as we entered the lobby. It was nearly as crammed with people as the lane fronting the hotel, but the men and women here wore no simple homespun. The Coppice Court catered to the *ton*, mostly those traveling to and from the hunts in Scotland, and even the plainest frocks to be seen were layered with fringework and beading.

Gentlemen and ladies minced across the checkered marble floor. They prefaced each deliberate step with walking sticks of cherry or ebony topped with ivory, and carried small china cups of what appeared to be muddy water. Their faces were powdered; their lavish wigs were powdered; their lips and cheeks were painted uniformly red. They chirped at each other in civil tones that sounded a bit too pinched to me . . . perhaps it had something to do with those cups of sulfur water.

Zane abandoned his slouch as if it had never been, shedding rain from his cloak in an impressive ring along the floor. With his pale amber eyes and tanned face and his braided rope of tawny hair, he looked abruptly like a corsair barging into a tea party. Several of the elaborately bejeweled women nearby gave gasping little twitters and snapped open their fans.

He paid them no mind. His gaze had gone instantly to a figure only half visible behind a green granite table spilling over with flowers and piles of fruits in crystal bowls. She wore a gown of coral, low cut, a wide sash of Prussian blue tied around her waist with the ends left to drape behind in a fashionable flutter along the polonaise of her skirts. Her hair was also powdered, her lips were also painted. Were it not for two wildly unusual discrepancies about her, she might have blended in seamlessly with this clutch of silk-cinched, cane-tapping humans.

One was her face. She was beautiful. Beyond beautiful. Beneath the dusting of flour I knew her hair would be golden. I remembered that of her. Her eyes were deep brown, barely lined with kohl. Her skin was flawless, her teeth were white and straight and she showed them in a smile as she caught sight of her husband, turning to us fully. And when she smiled, it was startlingly clear that she was nothing like any of the other females around her. She *glowed*.

The other discrepancy was far more subtle, and far more ominous to me. It was a delicate glitter of blue from a heart-shaped pendant around her neck, a pendant that hung from a black velvet ribbon.

Lady Amalia, it seemed, had her own version of *Draumr*.

Zane handed his hat and cloak to a doorman without looking at him and strode away. It was clear I had ceased to exist.

I watched them reunite with an unabashed curiosity. I'd been traveling for days with this man, who'd barely spoken more than a handful of sentences to me. He'd been curt and brisk and sharp-tongued whenever I displeased him, but he'd always ensured that I ate well, that I slept enough. That I was comfortable and clean and not afraid. He'd told me that at least four times: Don't be afraid.

He'd given me his handkerchief in the street.

Lia met him with her hands outstretched. Her smile was truly melting. Zane took her hands in his and bent over her fingers with an elegant bow. I could smell his pleasure and hunger and relief even from all the way by the main doors, even through the horrible wafting sulfur. Lia dipped her chin and pulled him closer and murmured something too low for me to catch. Zane gave a ragged sigh. He brushed his lips to her cheek, and then to her mouth.

I stood there soggily, dripping water, openly gawking. For all that they were both fully dressed and standing with a good foot between them, it was like they were making love to each other right there in the foyer. A white-hot heat seemed to envelop them both, sealing them away from all the rest of the people in the chamber.

My parents would barely even touch fingertips in public. I'd never seen adults act anything like this. It was rawly intimate, and I felt a spear of pure envy stab through me.

For the first time in my life, I thought: *That. I want that. I want to be that loved.*

A liveried footman carrying a tray of empty cups bumped into me, apologized over the clatter of china, and when I glanced again at Zane and Lia, they were both looking back at me. A pretty flush now stained her cheekbones—not rouge at all.

"Honor," she said warmly. With her hand still clasped in her husband's, she came to me by the doors. "Honor. I feel as if I know you already, but how happy I am to meet you now."

I gathered myself. I averted my gaze from her face,

from that too-entrancing wink of blue at her throat, and gave my best curtsy. It was a little shaky.

"I'm very pleased to . . ." I began, but trailed off, because despite all my mother's rigorous lessons in social discipline, I didn't know how to finish the sentence. *I'm very pleased to be abducted by you? So sorry that I don't know you in the least?*

Men and women swished back and forth across the lobby. Their voices were birdlike, their jewelry offering sporadic bursts of song that washed bright and loud through the air.

Lia released Zane's hand—not before giving his fingers a quick squeeze, I noticed—and took up both of mine. When I lifted my eyes again, her smile had returned. I couldn't help but begin to smile back.

"Dear girl," she said. "My dragon-girl. How would you feel about coming to live in Spain?"

Yesss, Ssspain, the fragments of *Draumr* whispered, from him and from her.

"What is in Spain?" I managed to ask.

"Your future," said the Lady Amalia simply. "I've dreamed it."

A runner and a thief. Fugitives, the both of them, with such prices on their heads that would make even Blackbeard shudder. They stood before me and offered me what no one else ever had, a chance to live beyond the rigid rules of the shire, beyond bruises, beyond my own deep-tendriled fears that had bound my every breath.

"Yes," I said, relieved. "Spain. Thank you."

CHAPTER THREE

The first time he saw her wasn't in a fashionable Viennese opera house, or strolling down a street in Bucharest, or framed in the glass window of a carriage. It was in the middle of a spring-swollen river in the mountains. He was eighteen, and she was crouched alone upon a rock, stranded.

Sandu noticed her hair first. It was the only thing about her that moved. He was high above her, very high, gliding along a jet of northern wind, enjoying the brisk cold bite of it that whistled along his scales and rushed tears to his eyes.

He'd been practicing kiting most of the morning, winging high into the luminous center of the sky until he found the perfect upsweep of air to support him. With his wings spread and his legs extended, Sandu would hover in place like a solitary fragment of midnight, fixed to the heavens.

It took mastery and stern concentration, an instinctive *knowing* of the gusts that would flip him if they could, slam him back to earth. The winds that howled along the spines of the alpine gorges would like nothing more than to turn Prince Alexandru of the Zaharen into a fine smear of blood upon the dirt below.

But he was better than that.

He was, in fact, better than anyone he knew at flight, and he took a secret pride in that. Although he'd been born a human-shaped child, it was a distant memory to him now. Without his will, without his even trying, he'd shifted into Something Else as he'd aged: more than just a man or a prince or even a dragon. Sometimes he thought it was like he'd snared a thread of blue from the heavens and swallowed it, and it had enwrapped his heart.

They were joined now, Alexandru and Sky, perfect reflections of each other. Up here, alone, he could at last be himself. He could be free.

His people, human or dragon alike, would gather in the hamlets and all along the crenulated edges of his castle when Sandu chose to soar. Those who could would sometimes follow him; day or night, every *drákon* of the mountains burned to fly.

But on that particular morning, he had been unaccompanied. He'd slipped out before dawn without any fanfare, restless and eager to escape the formality of the day he knew would come. Stretching his wings was a necessary solace.

When the mists caught between the highest eastern tors had lifted from pink into pearl, he knew it was time to return home. Duties awaited him. Papers, plans. All the winds of the world would not spare him from that.

Then came that flag of color beneath him that had snared his attention. It was bright, much brighter than the dark rock around it, or the raging green-and-foam river that had carved its path through the granite of the canyon. The flag glinted in shades of copper, dancing above the rapids.

He passed it, circled back, staring. A woman's hair.

He'd made another full loop before his mind accepted what his eyes were showing him. Yes, there was a woman *in* the river, hunched low upon a drenched rock with her arms around her knees, her face upturned to him. She seemed without clothes.

The wind shifted and her hair blew across her eyes. She lifted one arm—white skin, a quick and nervous push of her hand along her forehead to clear her vision—and stared back at him.

Sandu Turned to smoke. Instant buoyancy, all resistance to the wind gone, all the mechanics of flight and angles and gravity rendered moot. There were times when being smoke was even better than being dragon.

Smoke could maneuver down to the river in a way a dragon could not. Smoke could twine as thin as a whip against the channel of air that rushed atop the water, regroup without effort into the thickness that resembled his human shape. Smoke gave him weight upon the rock in front of her, feet that found a reasonable footing against the slick stone, a body and head and a face, inches from hers, because, honestly, it wasn't much of a rock and there was hardly any room.

The woman had stood too, staggering a bit to find her balance as he Turned to man in front of her. She gazed at him with wide blue eyes. *Very* blue eyes, dark as a bruise. She was pale and thin and much younger than he'd first realized—not a woman at all. A girl still. A maiden.

And *drákon*.

It was the second-most obvious thing about her, after that streamer of hair. It washed over him now in pretty little sugary waves, that sense of one of his own, a pulse that throbbed and matched his heartbeat, his blood. Electrical. Unique.

Even with her youth, she felt strong, stronger than most. The people of the mountains had mingled for centuries with the Others, and so their talents waxed and waned according to the whims of their ancestry. But this girl's power thrummed over his skin.

She didn't look like anyone he knew. The *drákon* ran the gamut of colors in their human shapes, but he'd never seen anyone in the castle or any of the villages with splendid hair like that, copper and rose and gold.

Still, she'd know *him*. She had to. All the peasants knew their prince.

Sandu smiled down at her, benevolently, because her eyes were still so wide. He offered her the traditional greeting her blood entitled her to. "Gentle One. What are you—"

The girl shoved him off the rock.

The surprise of it kept him whole, and when his back hit the water he went all the way under, thrashing like a fish. The river flowed from the glaciers lodged in the basins above and was shockingly cold, a frigid slap all along his senses. He actually inhaled a mouthful before managing to Turn back into smoke, wisping free of the torrents.

As a cloud he lifted, found his bearings and the rock and no girl.

He Turned to man atop the stone—dry again, his long black hair snapping in the wind; nothing remained on them from Turn to Turn—raised a hand to his eyes and scanned the waters.

There. A flash of copper, a pair of arms splashing helplessly as the currents tumbled her downstream. The spring runoff was high and she was already halfway to the falls.

Sandu sighed. It didn't look like she could swim at all.

He caught her at a bend, where she was hanging on by the tips of her fingers to another rock jutting above the froth. For an instant he debated about which would be more efficient, plunging in as a beast or a person, but there was really no question: Four clawed feet beat two human feet slipping over mossy stone.

He took his shape midstream, creating an instant barrier that fountained the rush of water into lather, splashing into his eyes. Alexandru lifted his chin and curved his neck to glare at the sodden girl. He couldn't speak or even growl, couldn't make a sound in this shape, and so only gave a jerk of his head to the ebony wing he held outstretched toward her, the river boiling up white between them.

Take it.

She was gasping, tendrils of hair tangling across her face and arms, her lips bloodless. She looked from him to the wing. Without warning, she let go of the rock.

He didn't know if she meant to slide under him or catch hold, and didn't give her the opportunity to choose. The open spread of his wing dipped down and caught her. She was scooped into a clumsy weight that mashed against his ribs.

She began to struggle. He closed his wing to hold her tighter. With the girl pressed to his side, he lumbered up the steep stone-and-mud bank, talons digging deep into the earth.

At the first stretch of level ground, he released her. She collapsed, still gasping, and curled into a ball on her side. Her body trembled, all that pale skin now tinged blue, very striking against the hair.

Sandu Turned again.

"One of us," he said, standing over her with his arms crossed, "appears to be rather stupid. Can you guess who I think it is?"

She rolled over, found her feet, scrubbing the muck off her palms and thighs. She backed up a few paces, glancing around them, stumbled over something and came to a halt. Her gaze met his, dropped down to his unclad body, and twitched up again to his face. Panic sketched across her features.

"Oh, yes," he drawled, unmoving. "Excellent notion. After all that fuss, I'm quite in the mood for a bit of fun. Besides, you must be all of twelve years? Thirteen? Kindly don't insult me. I have plenty of *women*," he gave the word a delicate emphasis, "who like me well enough not to drown me, anyway."

"Get back," squeaked the girl in a high, wavering voice—in English. "Get back! I'll hit you, I know how, I swear!"

Sandu blinked. He understood English, understood it very well, in fact, but it was hardly his native tongue. He'd been addressing her in the patois of the mountains, a lilting combination of Romanian and Latin, a touch of Hungarian thrown in, the language everyone from the gentry to the masses used.

As far as he knew, none of the commoners spoke English. Not more than a few words, and definitely not in that unmistakable, patrician accent. And she wasn't a royal of the Carpathians. He could count all the noblewomen on two hands.

"Who are you?" Alexandru asked flatly, also in English.

"Who the bloody hell are *you*?" she countered, still squeaky, and skipped back another step when he uncrossed his arms.

"I'm not going to hurt you," he said, impatient. "Look here, child. I'm turning my back on you, yes? I can't see you, you can't see me. We're both properly modest now. Just don't—"

"—run," he finished, as he heard her scrambling away.

He rolled his eyes to the sky, went to smoke, and funneled down in front of her at the brink of the forest, catching her by the shoulders with both hands.

She hadn't been lying. She did know how to hit, a flurry of punches aimed wildly at his face and chest. And for all her skinniness, she was still a *drákon*. He'd have bruises tomorrow if she kept this up.

"Stop it. Stop. Girl, you need to—damn it!" He freed her with a small push, wiping the blood from his lip. "*That* one hurt. *Don't* run." He examined the slick of red across his fingers, then glowered down at her. "If I'd wanted to harm you, don't you think I would have by now?"

She only stood there, panting.

"I could have just left you to the river," he added. "And ruddy good riddance."

"Where am I?" the girl demanded, all hint of the squeak gone.

He lowered his hand. She was yanking her hair across her shoulders and down her body now, trying to cover herself, but it was still dripping water, and not long enough. He made certain to look straight at her face.

"There are exactly two tribes of *drákon* in the whole of the world," Sandu said, slightly sharper than he should have, but his lip stung like the devil. "Where do you think you are? And don't bother to deny your heritage. I feel you. I know you feel me."

Her mouth dropped open. "This is . . . these are . . . the Carpathians?"

"Very credible. Did they choose you because you can act so well?"

"Choose . . . what?"

"The English," he said, and ran his tongue over his upper lip. "Your Alpha, Langford. Your Council. It seems a bit desperate, even for them, to send a little girl to spy upon me in the midst of hostilities, but then your ways have always struck me as odd."

"Spy? Hostilities?"

"This is going to get tedious. You needn't repeat everything I say."

"Why, you—you—ruffian!" The words seemed to burst out of her. She drew herself fiercely upright. "I'm not *little*!"

"Oh," Prince Alexandru said, smiling a cool, unpleasant smile, one that had been known to drain the blood from the cheeks of grown men. "But you *are* a spy."

A frown crinkled the pallid forehead; she clenched both hands above her heart. The wind returned and stirred the drying strands of her hair. She was a wet skinny twig of a child with a halo of coppery rose and flesh covered in goose pimples, as unlikely a scout as he'd ever seen.

But she was here, and she was *drákon*, and she was English. What else could it mean?

He held her eyes, now welling with tears. He was struck, once more, by the intensity of their blue.

"I'm l-lost," the child said. Her lips pressed into a quivering line; her voice came small and broken. "Please, sir. I'm lost. Can you help me get home?"

Before he could open his mouth to reply, she vanished.

She was there and then she wasn't. No smoke or dragon. Just the empty air, the silent woods. The roaring river. Sandu was left astonished, standing alone. If it weren't for the little-girl footprints pressed in the mud beside his, he would have sworn he'd dreamt the whole episode.

But they were there. They were.

That had been the first time.

A fortnight later he'd been asleep in his bed in the castle. The official royal chambers had once been the solar of the ancient fortress, modified and restructured over the centuries so often and by so many hands that by the time Sandu was to claim his place there, the space was a cluttered confusion of gilt and diamonds, crammed with artwork and imported furniture, everything to the touch slippery fabric or cold stone or dark-grained, heavy woods.

He'd spent exactly one week in the solar. After that, Sandu had discovered the tower room at the western end of the keep, and it had been his sanctuary since.

It wasn't precisely unadorned. But it was simple. Large, square, and echoing, it held a canopy bed, a mahogany *secrétaire*, a Renaissance table of mother-of-pearl inlay, and padded chairs. The fireplace had been rimmed in precious stones, and there were Turkish rugs strewn about for warmth. As Alpha, he'd made only a single major, modern improvement to the tower. He'd added a water closet, and liked it so much he'd commissioned ten more for the rest of the castle.

But the very best part of his private chamber was the view.

Eight glazed windows had been set in the walls, each one reaching nearly from floor to ceiling. Their beveled lozenge panes flared with sunlit prisms or the milky moon. From this lone, high tower, he could gaze in almost every direction, see nearly every corner of his realm. By day the rugged crests of the mountains greeted him, snow-kissed, clouds sweeping down their flanks to caress the green valleys and walled villages below.

By night he slept amid the stars, suspended in their brilliance; it was almost as perfect as flight through the purple-velvet heavens.

So, he'd been asleep. He thought he'd been asleep, because he was burrowed beneath his covers, and the fire in his hearth had dwindled to occasional sparks and embers. He frowned at them from his pillow, wondering what it was about them tonight that seemed different. The fire was lit every evening, even in the summer months. *Zaharen Yce*, the Tears of Ice, was a castle actually composed of quartzite and music and very chilled air, and no change of seasons would alter that.

But the embers seemed different. After a while—he wasn't certain how long—a new spark flowered and broke apart, and that's when Alexandru realized that their difference was not in color, or heat, or even their small lazy rustlings.

Their difference was that there was a naked woman standing to the right of the hearth. Beyond the post of his canopy, he could just see the outline of her leg, her calf and thigh and the curve of her hip. The bare russet glow of her skin.

He sat up. He stared at her from the soft trap of his bed.

Surely it wasn't the same maiden as two weeks ago. She didn't look quite the same. She was older, for one thing. Her hair was longer. She stood taller. Yet she might have been that child's sister: same coppery mane, even more glimmering by the light of the dying embers. Same long-lashed blue eyes glancing back at him.

And she was *drákon*, and she was nude. Just like that girl had been.

"I know this place," she said slowly. She spoke in English, solemn words, trailing a hand along the rubies and emeralds and topazes embedded in the mortar around the marble mantelpiece. Her face turned back to the embers; her profile was orange and dark. "I know these gems. I know their music. I've heard all this before."

Sandu made certain not to move; he only cleared his throat. "Have you?"

"And I know you." She shot him a look. "Don't I?"

"No," he said.

"But . . ." Her brows drew together; he saw then that he'd been fooled, just like the first time—she wasn't *much* older, probably barely as old as he. She crossed her arms to her chest and took a step forward, and the window behind framed her in stars. "Your face. I know your face."

"Did you Turn to get in here?"

She shook her head. "No."

"Not even to smoke?"

"No . . ."

"Then if this isn't a dream," he said carefully, "I'd appreciate an explanation."

"As would I."

She didn't smell like a dream. She didn't *smell*— but she was scented, very close to how that little girl had been. Yet it was warmer, more feminine now. More like flowers and honey than simple sugar. And strength. Still that.

Perhaps she sensed the change in him, his sudden unexpected arousal, because she eased back into the shadows. One finger tapped a topaz at the corner of the mantel, sending it into arias.

"How do you sleep with all this noise?"

"It's not noise." He inhaled through his teeth, slowly pushing back the covers. "It's beautiful."

"They're loud."

"They are soothing."

She seemed about to add something else, then lifted a shoulder in a shrug. "As you like. You do seem to sleep very soundly."

He could Turn to smoke. He could be before her in an instant, in less than a heartbeat. He could touch her and verify that she was real—

"You know, I'm not . . ." The woman dropped her hand, gave a small, embarrassed laugh.

"Not what?" One foot free. The other. He slipped from the bed.

"Not certain why I'm here. Or how."

"Let us talk then, English. Let us unravel it together."

"No, I'm not—" She started again, earnest, but vanished midsentence, a blur of tarnished light and dark that melted into empty night.

And she'd been telling the truth. No smoke.

This time he had no proof. This time he realized it might well have been a dream. A strange dream, of a strange female, and he should stop drinking spiced wine before bed, because clearly it was having a deleterious effect on his slumber. The first thing he did the next morning was ask to be served sherry instead.

But in his heart, Alexandru knew she'd been no illusion. The copper-haired girl was either a spirit set to haunt him, or else real.

Either way, it seemed like ill news.

He kept her to himself. It would not do to instill unnecessary fears into his people; his hold over them required their absolute confidence, and life here was difficult enough. The sharp-edged mountains, the stark terrain. The long, brutal winters that shriveled

crops and souls until spring cracked open all but the
meanest of the thick turquoise ice. It was a land saturated in legends and violet shadows, where a wolf
howling from the woods became a man-eater, a baby-
stealer, and the sweet dew found on edelweiss was
said to be fairy's broth, poison to all pure hearts.

Where the dragons that lanced across the moon at
night were either protective demons or avenging angels, depending on who was asked.

There were humans who hunted them, and a distant clan of kin who craved to conquer them. Surely
those were problems enough.

He would not deliberately add to the shadows by
speaking of this girl. He would not endanger his
reign.

Yet three times more, he'd glimpsed her. They did
not speak again; there was no opportunity. In each instance she was there mere minutes or seconds, still
unclothed, still pale, appearing somehow each time a
little older or a little younger . . . perhaps that was
nothing more than a trick of the light.

He began to wonder, rather seriously, if he were losing his mind.

He found himself searching around corners, examining empty spaces. Scrutinizing even the smallest
flickers of movement around him, ready to pounce.

And this is what Sandu saw:

She was a nymph in a field of August grasses, duck-
ing behind a pine just as he was Turning to dragon for
flight.

She was sudden color against the drab inner wall of
the granary, wheat chaff whirling in a tempest between them, because he and the servants were hauling

out bags of grains rotting from a leak in the roof they'd just discovered that must have been there at least a year.

She was a ghost in a ballroom, standing poised and naked for a brief, amazing fifteen seconds against the mural of gods decorating the eastern wall.

It was the harvest ball, a festival of darkness and jewels, tables laid out with all the fruits of their hard year's work: apples and pears and gaudy-striped gourds; braided breads and mulled wines; enormous haunches of seared meat; poached fish from the lakes; soured cream and cheese from the cattle. Sugared almonds, crepes, chocolate. Iced cakes trembling with glasshouse flowers, dusted with flakes of silver and gold.

Champagne. French. Because Sandu insisted upon that.

It was a chance to give his people a taste of true wealth and they reveled in it, nobles and peasants alike. Thin- or thick-blooded, they were *drákon*, and this was their night. And if, as the hours flowed like the wine, the laughter grew too loud and the violins too frantic, if eyes flashed and glowed and followed him as he moved, searching for the least sign of weakness in the Alpha of this ragtag, elegantly savage tribe—at least Alexandru had the champagne to cool him.

He savored it, every drop. The bubbles burned in crystal fire along the roof of his mouth.

He'd been seated alone at the head table, sprawled back to eye the sinuous beast that clung to the eaves high above them all in silence and shadow, bloodred wings fanned open, a gaze of bright goblin orange surveying the chamber below.

He wondered idly who it was this year. The nobles took turns up there; it was considered a rite of passage of a sort. He supposed someone had told him whose turn it was but he—

A woman shrieked. A platter fell.

Sandu turned only his head, already discerning the nature of the shriek—startled, high-pitched, not panicked—and the food that spilled—berries in cognac, the platter a ringing pewter—and from across the chamber, through the slippery candlelight and dancing shades of his kin, he found her.

Like he was suddenly staring at her from the end of a telescope, his senses honed. His blood began to hum.

She was older again, like him, long hair. Frozen. Pale against the wall, pale against the vivid formal clothing of everyone else. Eyes gone to round, astounded blue.

The beast at the ceiling shifted, leaning down closer, wicked claws digging into stone. The girl's face jerked upward to take in its abrupt orange interest.

From his gilded chair, from his linened table, Alexandru could clearly see the white of her fingernails on the hand pressed to her throat. Hear her stifled intake of breath.

But even as the serving maid who'd dropped the tray gave a second shriek and pointed, the copperhaired girl was gone. Blurred away, just like all the times before, with no trace left behind.

At least she'd been seen. At least, at last. The maid had seen her, the guests standing nearby had seen her, the dragon in the eaves. So he *wasn't* mad, and she was real.

Somehow real.

And then had come the letter from Spain, and everything changed.

CHAPTER FOUR

I had a secret.

Considering who and what I was, declaring that I had a secret was nothing more extraordinary than saying, *I breathe. I am.*

My life was a basket woven of secrets, it seemed. I was a secret from the shire of my birth. I was a secret from the fine people of Barcelona, where I now lived. I was a secret from my real parents, Gervase and Joséphine, and a secret from my false parents, Zane and Lia.

I was nearing the age of eighteen, and every day I ate and drank secrets like candy, like wine. If I tried to repress them, if I tried to mash them down under the relentless light of the Spanish sun, they squeezed up again through the cracks of night. They haunted my dreams.

The greatest one, of course, was *him.*

The prince.

Alexandru.

I knew that was his name, because I'd heard the *drákon* surrounding him call him that. Not many did—I supposed it was because he was royal and they were not—and it took me over a year of Weaving to him before I was able to sift through the strange foreign words enough to recognize the syllables of his given name. Sometimes he was Alexandru, and sometimes just Sandu, which I definitely liked better.

Prince Alexandru of the Zaharen was an Alpha with gray chill eyes and a fine mouth that never smiled. He was pale and lean in the most charismatically feral way of our kind, with straight long hair so deeply black it shone blue, and cheekbones sculpted sharp like his mountains. His voice was nearly always unnervingly gentle; when he spoke, it felt like electric shocks along my skin. Prince Alexandru sat on a throne in a sumptuous Great Room of green damask and hammered gold and watched the shadows and the light like a shark waiting restlessly for a little fish to swim by.

And all the little fish gave him a very wide berth indeed. Even the servants who brought his chalices of wine and finger bowls of lemon water avoided his gaze when they could.

Prince Alexandru was a leader locked in a silent, frigid war, although it took me a very long time to realize that, and even longer to realize with whom.

Sandu, though . . . Sandu was a man who slept. Alone. In a solitary tower chamber, with nothing to comfort him but a few blankets and stars and the songs of all the diamonds and colored gemstones pressed into the walls.

In sleep, his body relaxed, his face relaxed. In sleep, I could imagine him smiling. His hands atop the covers of satin and fur, long, strong fingers stroked with firelight. His hair unbound, smooth as ink across the pillows.

I'd watched him brush it out once early one winter morning, the strands crackling, his gaze distant, an emerald ring flashing on his thumb. I'd Woven to a far corner holding my breath but when my back touched the cold wall I think I must have released it, just a tiny bit; I hadn't meant to. He'd paused, head cocked, frowning at his reflection in the small mirror before him. Before he finished twisting around, I was gone again.

Stolen moments. That was how I knew Sandu.

I wasn't certain if it was Sandu or Alexandru who commanded his animal side, the huge gleaming black dragon who'd once plucked me from a river. He'd been both merciful and cruel, so perhaps both.

And I wasn't certain which aspect of him intimidated me more. I'd grown up with an Alpha heading my tribe, and I had a healthy respect for their power. I'd learned very quickly in life that the strongest ruled the weakest, and if you weren't prepared to be ruled, then you'd better fight or run. Alpha males not only fought, they won. If they had to kill to win, so be it; those were our ways. The shire of Darkfrith had an entire field devoted to the charred bones of those who had chosen to contest the rules of the tribe.

One glance into this prince's pale gray eyes and I could easily envision his own field of bones.

And yet . . . there was that sleeping man. The curve of his lips. The twin straight strokes of ebony brows, so peaceful. Sable eyelashes, thick and spiked. He never slept with a nightshirt on, not that I could tell, not even during sleet or snow. His shoulders were broad and muscled, ivory skin, a V of short curling hair winnowing down his chest. When the fire was bright enough, if he rolled over, if he shifted or moved his hand or parted his lips on a sigh . . .

Oh, those nights. I found it so hard to Weave away.

Back then I had no choice, though. I couldn't control my Gift. I'd be sitting at the kitchen sideboard peeling apples, or walking through a park, or reading at my desk. And then I'd simply be somewhere else. Some*time* else.

Nude.

That part was always awkward, to say the least. Usually the first jolt of realization that I'd completed a Weave would be someone screeching at the sight of sudden, unclad me appearing from nowhere.

With Lia's encouragement, I began to cloister myself in the suite of apartments we rented in one of the old palaces of the Gothic Quarter. We agreed it was far easier for me to duck behind a table or a curtain there than to hide in public. The few servants we employed were silent and stone-faced and paid exceedingly well to avert their eyes from anything unusual; I was not the only *drákon* in the residence with unexpected Gifts. My Weaves typically placed me about a year or two in the future, as far as I could fathom, but almost always in the same place I'd just left.

So, for the sake of modesty, my bedchamber became the safest location. Within weeks, I had memorized every plastered inch of it.

At first I hated Weaving. I hated the nauseating, pulling *lurch* of it in my stomach. I hated being clothed one moment and not the next. I hated that all I had was a half second's warning it would come, like that feeling that rises through you just before you vomit, and you know there's nothing you can do to prevent it. You're enslaved to the whims of your own body.

That was Weaving.

And then, when I started to go to *him* instead of to my bedroom, it became even worse.

I was young and afraid. Of course I was afraid. I didn't know who this dark young *drákon* could be, or why I kept ending up in his proximity. The Weaves were a compass and he became my North. I just kept going back. I discovered later that in our Natural Time, Prince Sandu was only a little over a year older than I. But in the Weaves I usually leapt ahead, and he was much older.

After the sixth Weave to him, I told Lia everything; I had no reason not to. I trusted her. I even loved her. Then she told Zane.

And I think *that*—that moment, that conversation for which I wasn't even present—was the beginning of our end.

I remember five days passed, uneventful. The evening of the fifth day the three of us were seated on the stairs of the *Catedral* in the *Barri Gòtic*, enjoying the soft spring twilight. There were street vendors hawking food and glass-windowed shops selling baubles. It was crowded: young couples with stern *dueñas* in ebony lace hissing and trailing behind them, families with children bickering over sweets, everyone ambling the narrow, cobblestone streets to take in the balmy air, the rising moon. We three were pretending—Lia loved to pretend—that we were also an actual family, appreciating the descent of the lemony blue night.

Zane only did it for her. I knew that.

A pair of gray-whiskered men were on the stairs below us, strumming *havaneres* on their mandolins for the passersby, singing sea-songs in wavering, graveled voices. A few tunes in, Lia rose to toss a handful of coins into the hat placed beside them.

Zane merely watched her go. I should have known then something was off. Whenever he was in town—which wasn't often—he stuck to her side like a burr.

He was peeling apart a dinner pastry with his fingers, one he'd purchased from a cart a few streets away. I'd been following the process surreptitiously; I'd already eaten mine. Flaky bits of roll littered the stairs beneath, the scent of sautéed chicken and onions from the stuffing making my stomach grumble.

He no longer wore the signet with *Draumr*. I'd been wondering where it was, but hadn't worked up the nerve to ask.

He spoke softly, without looking up at me. "Are you still Weaving to *Zaharen Yce*?"

I sucked in a breath with my surprise. I hadn't mentioned the name of the castle to Lia. I'd only just learned it myself that morning, during another involuntary Weave.

"If you tell her about it again," he said mildly, after a pause, "I'll have Nemesio flog you. I mean it."

Nemesio was our manservant. I doubted that was all he was, as he was large and scowling and only barely willing to do any sort of work around our home. His arms were roped with muscle and scars.

He kept a knife in the waistband of his breeches—it was steel. I always heard it crooning when he was near.

"Frankly, Honor, I don't care if you Weave to the castle or Fleet Street or the sodding Macaroni Club," Zane was saying to the pastry, still in that quiet way. "But my wife does, very much. So leave her out of it. You're giving her nightmares."

"Yes," I choked. "Fine."

"Fine," he agreed, and handed me a piece of roll.

Zane was one of the strongest strands in my new life of woven secrets.

⌖

Her dreams had always been blind. It was one of the restrictions of her Gift, Lia supposed, that she could hear what was to come but not see it. During the dreams it never bothered her. It was only later, after waking, that she would worry and guess and try to imagine colors and shapes and vistas to match all that she'd heard.

Lately she'd not wanted to imagine any of it. Lately she'd wanted only to erase it from her mind; she prayed to erase it, but like an evil wish turned inside out, it shone extra clear to her.

Perhaps it was because she missed home so much, the trees and lakes and people of the shire. Perhaps it was because her childhood had been so idyllic—gemstones and meadows and splendid animals in flight—a perfect painting fixed in her memory, and what she was dreaming now was so terribly opposite.

She could smell the sun-heated grasses, the bouquet of late summer.

She could hear the crickets tucked away in the woods, their rhythmic sawing. A few beetles. The wind shifting invisible clouds far, far above. Leaves clattering on the trees.

Skirts rustling. The faint squeak of a window being opened and the crickets getting louder; the scent of lilies swept over her with the breeze.

The voices. The man and the woman, and the girl.

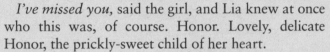

I've missed you, said the girl, and Lia knew at once who this was, of course. Honor. Lovely, delicate Honor, the prickly-sweet child of her heart.

Yes, said the man.

There was a pause. The sound of liquid being poured into a china cup; the hot wafting fragrance of black tea.

Did you miss me? asked the girl, hesitant.

Yes, said the man again. *Of course we did.*

Of course, echoed the third person in the dream, the woman.

I've so much to tell you. There's so much to say.

But no one said anything for quite a while. There were only the leaves sighing outside, the tiny random clinking of flatware against bone china. That scent of tea and lilies.

I wanted to say first that I'm sorry, continued the girl, determined. *Sorry that I left without word. Sorry that I worried you.*

Silence.

And that—that I've met someone. A man. A drákon, *I mean.*

Oh? said the woman, muted.

*A prince, actually. I . . . he's . . . he's really quite
wonderful. In fact*—the girl took a deep breath—*I
love him. So much.*

Another cup, my dear? asked the man.

*What? No. No, thank you. Did you hear me, Papa?
I've found my mate. It's Alexandru of the Zaharen.*
Another pause. *We're engaged.*

Ah, said the man.

I live in his castle . . . we have a little . . .

Yes, whispered Honor's mother.

. . . you'll be so . . . pleased . . . she's . . .

Close your eyes, said the man.

. . . what's . . . Mother . . .

Just sleep, said the man.

A muffled thump; perhaps a cup falling to a rug.
Silk rustling again, a great deal of it, and then the
woman's voice came to life, low and fervent.

*Tell us the truth, Honor. Tell me. Are you involved
somehow with the* sanf inimicus?

. . . mmm . . .

Honor! Tell me!

But the girl said nothing.

Lia heard breathing, ragged and soft. She heard the
sound of silk again, the footsteps of the man crossing
the rug. A door opened. Someone new entered the
room; she could not hear whom, she could not smell
whom. The person made no sound whatsoever. But
the energy changed somehow—instantly, violently. A
shiver crossed her in the dream.

I'm sorry, murmured the new person, a male. And
then: *It will be swift. But it's best if you go now.*

And Lia only understood what her eldest brother

meant when the door closed firmly again, and the woman beyond it began to weep.

∽

"Beloved."

Amalia came awake feeling utterly composed, as if she'd never closed her eyes, never laid back amid the cool sheets of her bed, caught in the cradle of her husband's arms. Never slept.

"Another one?" he asked, his voice a breath in her ear.

She didn't answer. She didn't need to. He knew her so well, knew all about her—just as she knew him. They'd been wed a dozen years, a lifetime. He was accustomed to her nightmares.

"Which one was it this time?"

"The tea."

"Ah."

His hand found the top of her head, began a slow stroking down her hair to her shoulder. She turned her face toward his and his lips touched her brow.

Aside from the constant low ripple of human conversation, Barcelona was quiet for a city at night, surprisingly so; the most obvious sound beyond that of a few horses and mules trudging along the streets was the pulse of the sea striking the shipyard bays, a few miles distant. When Zane spoke again, it was a bare brushing of words against her skin. She heard every one.

"Your brother was there?"

"Yes."

"And he still . . ."

"Kills her. Yes."

She swallowed, and swiped at her eyes with one hand even though they were dry; she was done crying over this particular dream.

"It's never changed, after all these years," said Zane, still softly stroking. "She goes back. Says she's engaged. Drinks the tea."

It wasn't a question, but she answered it anyway. "Yes."

"Snapdragon." His fingers paused. "I know how you feel about her . . . but if it's meant to be . . ."

"It doesn't *have* to be," Lia hissed, angry suddenly, sitting up. "It doesn't. I've changed the future before. I refuse to believe she has anything to do with the *sanf*. How could it even be possible?"

He let his hand fall to the covers, silent. His eyes met hers, a pale wolfish gleam, visible even through the gloom.

"You *know* her. She's meek to the point of agony, and so easily intimidated. It took a year for her to gather the nerve to hold your gaze for more than a few seconds at a time, remember? She twitches at every little noise."

Zane kept his silence.

"Well," she continued, a little desperate, "you've certainly never heard any mention of her when you're—gone, have you? Her name or—even just something about an English girl?"

"No," he answered, cool. "Not so far."

Lia stared at him for a moment, then drew up her knees and dropped her head into her palms. He was the last person in the world she should question about the *sanf inimicus*, the human enemies determined to destroy her kind.

He'd only become one of them because of her. Because she'd begged.

All her life, Lia'd had this unquiet Gift. Dreaming the future, hearing the future, dreading the future. No one else in the tribe suffered it. No one else in the tribe had railed against what was to come as much as she. She was not just smoke, not just dragon, but a sort of tribal Cassandra as well, barred from home with no one but the man beside her now to comfort her.

As a child she'd dreamed of a different threat to her kin, and as an adult she'd done what she had to do to defeat it. For a long while, for years after she first was married, Lia rested comfortably in the knowledge that she had done what she could to save her kind. Yes, she'd given up her family, but she'd gained true love, and in her mind, it was a fair trade. She did not dream in Zane's embrace. She just slept. And it was . . . heavenly.

That, of course, began to change.

They'd been living in the beach house in the Antilles when the dreams began to filter back. Strange dreams, always sightless, a confusion of voices and times and places. She could make no sense of them; they were as jumbled and nonsensical as those she'd had as a very young girl. Sometimes all she heard were screams. She would wake up cold and sweating, and it would take hours to get warm again. Even submerging herself in the beryl-blue waters of the Caribbean didn't help.

Single, repeated threads eventually came clear: Honor Carlisle.

The *sanf inimicus*.

A prince of the Zaharen.

A war between the tribes.

They were all entangled somehow, destinies woven together, and even though she'd applied the most potent weapon she had to the knot—her husband, her clever and criminal husband—she still had not managed to unravel all the strands.

Lia spoke against her knees. "Don't you like her, even a bit?"

"I don't like or dislike her."

Her head raised, golden hair slipping soft along her arms.

"She's fine," Zane sighed. "She's a girl. She's *drákon*. She reminds me a very little of you, but only when she's angry."

She looked at him more fully.

"Because her eyes go to fire and her cheeks color," he said innocently. "That's all. That's when she looks like what she really is."

"A beast," she muttered.

"Magic," he countered, flat. "And apparently a dangerous magic, at that. If the Alpha of your tribe thinks it a fine idea to drug her and execute her—I'm sorry. I can't afford to like her. If she does you harm, I can't falter. I can't let *like* impede me."

He knew a score of ways to kill, she understood that. He had come to her from the shadows of London, and shadows still were his trade. He slipped into locked rooms in perfect silence; he observed kings and commoners without a word, a shrewd slight smile, fingers quick and marvelous both over her body and around a knife. He was a magician, a trick of the light, vapor in the way that none of her kind would ever comprehend: human slyness and cunning and un-apologetic devotion. Should he grasp for certain that their adopted daughter would do his wife harm, Lia knew he'd end Honor's life without hesitation.

With all her heart, she tried to counter that anyway.

"So, then . . . you won't love her."

He sighed once more and sat up, rumpling the crisp Italian sheets, shoving a pillow behind his back. "Listen. Besides chocolate, I love two things in this world. Me, and you. That's quite enough."

Despite herself, she let out a rueful huff, not quite a laugh.

His arm shifted. His index finger began to trace a swirl along her thigh.

She glanced at him from under her lashes. "Which of us do you love more?"

"Well," he said seriously, watching his finger, "I *am* the prettier of we two."

"True," she agreed, just as serious.

She lay back, found the stubbled line of his jaw with her hand, an invitation that he answered by following her down. His braid became a rope, heavy and warm against her chest. Her fingers opened. She brought his mouth to hers.

She didn't want his words any longer. He wouldn't promise her anything, nor would he lie. So Lia would make no false promises, either.

But at least they had this bed, and this night. That was enough for now.

Lady Lia liked needlework. I wasn't certain why; to be honest, she wasn't very good at it. Certainly she wasn't as good as my old mother, whose embroidery had decorated Plum House with exceptional taste: cushions and samplers and even quilts, every seam perfection, every stitch utterly precise.

Joséphine Carlisle would have said, in her clipped, freezing way, that Lia's efforts revealed a mind that wandered, and I'm sure that was true. Very seldom were there even two stitches in a row of the same length. She would run out of one color of thread and pick out another at random, creating swans that were half white, half green. Windmills on ponds reflecting pink and silver skies. A round moon of yellow and puce; farmhouses casting red shadows, lettering shaded every color of the rainbow.

I watched her stab the needle into the hooped fabric on a night after Zane had left us once again, about a sennight after our conversation on the steps of the great cathedral. Neither he nor Lia would ever discuss where he went when he was gone from us. His absences stretched from weeks to months, with no set pattern that I had yet discerned.

Lia and I were seated together in the drawing room, where the walls were papered in oyster silk and the curtains were snowy damask and the light from the sconces reflected best. She was embroidering. I was pretending to read. It was far more interesting to daydream about Sandu, but Lady Amalia kept distracting me.

She seemed pale. Even for one of us, I mean. Her hair had been pinned up that morning *à l'Antoinette* but she kept pushing a hand through it, and now it had worked its way mostly loose. She was wan and fetching and lovely. Strands of honeyed blond fell in perfect waves along her perfect face. As she drew the thread long—vivid orange, I noticed, for a pillow cover of a rabbit in a winter meadow—she could have been an etching from a book depicting the ideal notion of English femininity.

"*Shit.*" She dropped the needle and held up a finger, scowling at the fresh bead of blood welling at the tip. "*Verdammt! Merde.*" She cupped her hand to her lips and sucked at the blood; after a second, her gaze angled briefly to mine. "I beg your pardon. I did not mean to swear."

"Yes, you did." I placed my book upon my lap. "Why do you sew?"

"Because it is better than rum or opium."

I definitely had no response to that. After a moment she stood, tossing the hoop and cloth to the settee behind her. She crossed to the window and stared out at the street below, still sucking on her finger.

Carrer del Bisbe was popular among the *aristòcrates* and traffic was fairly steady at this hour, all those fine nobles traveling here and there, eager for their evening festivities. Carriages careened past our little palace with horses ever squealing in dismay. Other animals didn't like the scent of us, even from behind stone walls.

"You're sad without him," I said.

She inclined her head very slightly, still staring out.

"You deserve better," I blurted. "You deserve—a husband who will stay with you. Who won't stray."

Her voice came composed from over her shoulder. "I think I have exactly the husband I deserve. He's no stray." She examined her wounded finger, slowly closing her hand into a fist. "He's giving up a great deal for me, more than you could guess. The least I can do is be patient."

I was so sick of secrets. I was so tired of all the deceptions. My temper broke.

"I wouldn't have to guess, if you would only tell me. I'm not a child, you know. Not any longer."

"No," she agreed, still composed. "You're not." Amalia turned around at last. "Come up to the roof with me."

"The roof? Why?"

Her eyes were very bright. "Because I want you to. That's all."

We occupied the upper stories of the palace. Like most of the other structures around us, the roof of it was composed of baked terra-cotta tiles, layered one atop another in an elaborate, dizzying pattern. They were very old and some of them were missing, and standing on them was a slippery proposition at best. But Lia climbed out of the window of our garret without hesitation, as if she'd done it a hundred times before.

Of course, she probably had.

I followed more gingerly. The slope beyond the sash was very pitched.

A set of bells in a nearby cathedral began to peal, followed at once by a host of others across the tip-top of the city. It was eleven o'clock, and the sky was a hazy deep dark, and the splinter moon was veiled behind a wall of sea mist rolling in from the water. I smelled salt—always salt—and fish and burning oil from the street lamps. Wet wood from the docked ships, their massive bales of flax and cotton. Unwashed cattle. Sand.

Eleven at night back home would have found most of the shire tucked into their beds, but sleepy, sparkly Barcelona was just awakening. A soirée was taking place somewhere down the street; a quartet of strings lent a formal, musical counterpoint to the last dying echo of the bells.

"It's not very like Darkfrith, is it?" Lia murmured, standing easily in the middle of the slope, a slender figure in a dim blue *chemise à la reine*, her hair and skirts swaying with the wind.

"No."

"I like that. I appreciate that about it."

I picked my way over to her. I also wore a chemise dress—no awkward hoops or fat polonaise; she made certain we kept up with the Parisian fashions, even all the way out here—and had on slippers instead of heels, but it was still a long, daunting distance down to the street below. I could feel the grinding of the tiles with my every step.

"Here, *filla*. Take my hand."

Filla meant *daughter*. When she'd first started calling me that after we'd moved here, it felt strange, a concept as foreign as the word itself. Over the years I'd become accustomed to it, though. I'd never told her so, but secretly it pleased me. I was pleased to be a Catalan daughter.

I found her hand without looking up, unwilling to tear my gaze from my feet. Her fingers clasped mine, warm, certain. She held me steady until I was near enough that my own skirts slapped against hers.

"Look," said my second mother, very soft. "Look up, Honor."

I had thought the night veiled. But I saw now that

the sea mist was just an illusion of the horizon, something to cloud the eyes of all the Others on the streets below. Above us was a well of pure, sharp black, with stars that burned silver like just-minted pieces of eight flung to the heavens.

I made a sound, something wordless. Lia's hand remained firm around mine.

"Have you ever wondered what it's like to Turn?" I felt her glance to me. "Smoke, and then dragon?"

Of course I had. Every girl of the shire wondered . . . at least, every girl I'd ever known. Of all the Gifts that blessed us, it was the Turn that most defined who we were. Nearly all of the menfolk still had that Gift, but for us—for the females born to the tribe—it remained nothing more than an impassioned wish, one that ultimately faded as we grew older. Fifteen or sixteen was the usual age for the Gifts to emerge. Perhaps as old as eighteen. Male or female, by the time you were twenty, if the Turn had not come, it never would.

Once upon a time, the village schoolmaster used to tell us, every *drákon*, no matter their sex, was Gifted. Everyone knew the joys of scales and vapor; everyone flew. But Darkfrith was so safe and green, and we settled there so comfortably. Time began to change us. Perhaps it grew easier *not* to Turn, to grow more lazy in our human skins. Or perhaps we were just cursed. No one really knew why, but in the past two hundred years or so only four females of Darkfrith had managed the Turn.

One of them was standing beside me now, waiting for my response.

Just like everyone else, I'd wanted that Gift. I'd wanted it very, very badly.

"I've heard it hurts," I said, trying to sound indifferent.

"Yes. I'd heard that, as well."

I curled my toes in my slippers. "Does it?"

"Perhaps at first. I'm not really the best person to ask that. When it first happened to me, the circumstances were slightly . . . extraordinary. But there's no pain now. Now, when it happens, it's like . . . I melt. In the most fantastic way, I melt and become nearly nothing. A nothing so light, so thin, I'm swept up and up. The stars serenade me. The moon smiles. With a single breath I become material again, but I'm aloft. I have wings. I soar. It's simply the most . . ."

She faded off, staring skyward. Silver light painted her profile.

"Why are you telling me this?" I asked, pained.

Her eyes closed; her lips smiled. "Because I want you to understand it. I want you to feel it too. Even without the Gift of the Turn, you are a dragon, Honor. It is your blood. Perhaps you'll never *Turn* to dragon, but the animal lives in your heart anyway. It is everything ferocious and strong inside you. It's what lets you hear the same music I hear, from the stones and metals. It's what hones our sense of smell, of taste and color. It's what makes us a tribe, even separated as we are. It's what makes us so beautiful."

"I'm not beautiful." I pulled my hand free. "Nor ferocious. Nor strong."

"Oh, my dear." She leaned in, pressed a quick kiss to my cheek. "One day you're going to look into a mirror and see someone you won't even recognize. I do hope I'm there for that. Just to catch the expression on your face."

"You're about to Turn," I said. "Right here. Aren't you?"

Her smile returned.

"But it's bright out," I protested, instantly nervous. "All those stars. And there are Others. Right there, just down there! Packs of them. What if they look up?"

"They will see a pretty young woman alone on a rooftop, watching the heavens. This is Spain. I'm sure they'll think you're terribly romantic."

"But I'm not! And you can't!"

"Watch," she said. "Remember. Everything I do is connected to you, and you to me. I'll be the dragon in the sky, and you'll be the dragon on the roof. Either way, we're both . . ."

She did it, she went to smoke, still smiling at me, dissolving into wisps. Her gown fell in a slow, sideways drift—and then the wind took it, flipping it about, a gentle blue ripple floating down to the street.

I watched the smoke. I watched it rise and rise until I couldn't see it any longer. I rubbed my eyes and when I searched again, I saw the dragon high above me, whipping her way from star to star.

CHAPTER FIVE

The Castle of *Zaharen Yce*, Carpathian Alps
Early Autumn, 1788

The prince sat back in his chair, frowning, stroking the stiff paper folds of the letter in his hand. The single page was stained and somewhat weathered, but no more so than might be expected of a missive sent halfway across the Continent. Stamps gummed with glue, crimson wax seal, a wide smudge near the bottom redolent of coffee and dirt. With a tilt of his fingers he was able to glimpse the watermark imprinted in the center, faint by the slanted sunlight that cut through his library window, but still one he recognized very well.

A scrolled D. The suggestion of a winged beast entwined around the curve.

It was the crest of Darkfrith. Of England.

Yet the letter had been posted from Spain.

The ink from her quill was deeply blue, nearly purple. He'd already memorized the few English words penned there so carefully.

Dear Prince Sandu of the Zaharen,

No doubt this letter will come as something of a surprise
to you. We have not yet formally met, although I've seen
you a few times before.

I will not trouble you long. I wanted only to say I look forward, very much, to seeing you again soon.

Yours humbly,
Mlle. Honor Carlisle
(of the English *drákon*)

That was what had been written, and it was what
anyone else in the world who was not him would read.
But it wasn't what the letter actually said. Because
whether or not Sandu left the paper on the polished
gleam of his desk or let it fall to rest on his thigh, the
true message inscribed there burned between those
purple-blue letters, brighter than the sinking sun. The
true message shone clear, no matter what angle he
tried: *I love you. I will always love you. I'm going to
be with you again. I will discover a way.*

He raked a hand through his hair, sighing, then
placed the letter back upon his desk. He reached now
for the other one, the one he'd hidden in the back secret drawer that no one else knew about, folded small
and much more worn.

Alexandru smoothed out the page, bending over
the thin, spidery writing that had always been his sister Maricara's distinctive hand. It was the last com-
munication he'd received from her, over four years
past.

A.,

Ill news. English restless, eager for you/clan/invasion. Putting them off long as I can. Langford's younger brother recovered after *Sanf Inimicus* kidnapping. Returned to the shire with strange news of an Englishwoman who is also a young girl: Honor Carlisle. She is *Drákon* and *Sanf Inimicus*. Know her? He said she knows *you*.

Idea that you are aligning with the *Sanf* sending the English into a frenzy, no matter how I placate.

What are you about?

—M.

❦

What, indeed?

Although Maricara was no longer one of his tribe, she'd always communicated with him in the language of the mountains. Every missive *she'd* sent had been stamped from England.

He missed her sometimes still. He missed her sharp-edged clarity. She had decided to wed the Darkfrith Alpha, Kimber Langford, for love or just love of rule, Sandu never knew. She had been leader here for a while, a pseudo-Alpha herself; her loyalties tended to vacillate with the whistling of the wind. Yet she was his blood, his last living family member. It could not be an easy thing, he supposed, to realize your husband planned a war against your brother.

For unfathomable riches, which the Zaharen no longer had.

For miraculous power, which the Zaharen no longer had.

For glory—which, Sandu had to admit, was the one thing that still thrived up here in the thin, frost-riven air of his home. The glory of the *drákon* past. The potential glory of enslaving any *drákon* present.

Four years ago he'd answered his sister's letter with a single, pointed sentence: *My oath that I do not know her.*

But now . . . by the heavens, he was very much afraid that he did.

The English *drákon* were allies once, or he thought they had been. It wasn't so very long ago that he'd hunted the *sanf inimicus* with one of their own in Paris, helped free the very Langford brother Mari mentioned from a certain death by the *sanf*. He'd been sixteen then, feverish with adolescent passions and the need to prove himself. He'd believed in those weeks abroad he'd forged a bond between the tribes; now he knew better.

The English were never interested in alliances. They desired one thing only, and that was control.

He'd helped rescue the English lordling, departed Paris warm with the knowledge that he'd made friends, saved a life, made a difference.

He'd truly known nothing about this Honor Carlisle. He'd known nothing of what had come after he himself had left France, save his sister's wedding, which he was wise enough not to attend.

Prince Alexandru had instead sent Maricara and her mate a pear tree and a cloisonné box of diamonds he'd pried from the walls of the castle in honor of their union, accompanied by a note of particularly florid wishes for their good health and long lives.

Maricara's equally florid written response expressing their gratitude had arrived a scant three months after.

Her secret missives, however, had reached the castle more sporadically than that. He presumed she'd taken the precaution of writing in Romanian just in case her new English family discovered she was smuggling him news, but Mari was the only one who might have ever guessed the truth about his unique talent. She could have just as easily written, *Sunny day, fine place, do wish you were here*, in the King's most proper English and the hidden message of her words would have shone the same: *Beware. Beware. Beware.*

Because that was what Maricara's final note to him actually said.

It was a peculiar Gift, this ability to read between lettering. In all the bound books of his kind he'd pulled from the castle libraries and cellars, in all the spoken folklore, he'd never discovered any mention of anyone else with this skill. Perhaps it had seemed too inconsequential to mention, compared to all the other amazing feats the *drákon* could commit. Perhaps it *had* surfaced once or twice in generations past, but only among the peasants—who couldn't read anyway.

So he'd had nothing and no one to guide him when it first began. He'd been just a boy, no more than eleven, and it was even thought for a time that he'd required spectacles to help him see.

They hadn't helped.

As the years passed, Sandu had come to realize that his vision blurred only when he was looking at words. Language didn't matter; ink didn't matter; paper or vellum or tapestry—none of that mattered. If he stared hard enough, if he concentrated, the blurring cleared and he could *see* the new words squeezed through the old ones. Indeed, if he studied it long enough, the old message disappeared entirely, leaving only the true one. The one perhaps the author had never meant to be read.

Oh, he'd learned reams about his people through their hidden words.

Most of it was fine. Most of it was exactly what he would expect of a tribe of bare-handed farmers and shepherds: minor disputes and jealousies, love affairs, petty thefts. They were more human than not, these scattered *drákon* of the mountains. He wondered if that was why their squabbles seemed so slight.

The royals surrounding him, however . . . they were more worrisome.

By the right of their blood, they dwelled in the Tears of Ice with their prince. They were counts and sons of counts, lords and ladies, and nearly all the males could Turn. It was through the luck of his sister, the former princess, that Sandu now ruled.

Since his maturity he'd made certain that he remained ruler by anything but luck.

He'd been graced with exceptional Gifts. Only a fool would have failed to use them.

He required his nobles to submit any request to him, no matter how inconsequential, in writing. It was how he knew Lord Oreste despised him; that

Lady Lucia's beloved son was not of her husband; that the brothers Bazna were dense but trustworthy and their cousin Count Radu of Sinaia anything but. So many secrets, just waiting to be spilled with a stroke of ink.

Until he'd been brought up to the castle at the age of seven, Alexandru knew nothing about any of these particular kin except that they were the white-wigged, glistening aristocracy of his tribe, those who neither sweated nor toiled, yet lived off the fat of the land.

Now he rather imagined he knew them better than they did themselves. He knew their hearts, at least. What they desired. What they most feared.

That was the key to power. Understanding another's true heart.

He leaned forward in his chair, pushed the two foreign-stamped letters side by side until their edges touched, until the very different words shone in their very different colors, spoke to him again in their genuine words: *I love you. Beware.*

His fingers drummed atop the pages. True hearts never lied.

∞

He'd remained in the library. He'd taken his evening meal there because it had seemed the most expedient thing to do, and because he knew it would set his supper guest more at ease. Count Radu would be smugly pleased to see Alexandru eating goulash from a tray like a common servant.

He kept most of the chamber sparsely lit, the corners all in shadow, the ceiling high above them a mask of dusk. As the twilight descended he allowed the fire in the hearth a sullen smoldering, but the thirteen beeswax candles of the candelabra just behind him burned much brighter than those last few flames. He knew the candles cast a halo about his unpowdered hair—worn long and loose, just as the old princes of the realm used to do—and effectively shaded his face and hands. His gaze. The single most telling aspect about him, in fact, would be the silver spoon in his grip.

The former Alphas stared down from their portraits on the walls, severe in their silence. Sandu kept them clustered in here, in this private domain, where he could stare back at them openly whenever he wished.

He'd never had his own painted. Probably because he never thought he'd last here as long as he had.

Radu's chair had been placed to face his prince, and so Alexandru had a very good view of him: the aquiline nose, the opaque black eyes, the deep, permanent line engraved between his eyebrows. His wig was iron gray, a plain queue, no curls. The ruffled lace along his bib glowed with the candlelight, distinct down to the last intricate knot. The count's lips kept a constant, derisive smile. Sandu sometimes wondered if it was still a willful effort for him, or if his mouth had finally frozen into its sneer.

"More wine?" he inquired, leaning forward to offer the carafe.

"No, my lord."

They were a dozen years and a universe apart. Radu was older, an animal nearly beyond his prime, and beneath his poise and his half-lidded gaze, he remained utterly hostile. Unlike Alexandru, he'd been born a courtier, and was in fact a cousin by marriage to the former prince. Had he a fraction more of the Gifts, there was no doubt he would be sitting with the light behind him in this library right now.

Praise the stars he could not Turn.

Alexandru knew the count hated him with a passion that even his letters could scarcely contain.

"A calm night," Sandu said, resting the rim of his spoon on the ceramic bowl before him. "No winds, good moonlight. I thought perhaps I'd visit your holding."

"I'd be honored, of course."

"Your sheep are well?"

The smile grew more acerbic. "So I've heard."

"Excellent."

Sandu lifted another bite of goulash, savoring the fragrance of seared beef and onions, sharp paprika. The silver spoon moaned an eldritch song against his lips.

"Are you certain you wouldn't like a bowl?" He returned the count's smile from over the spoon. "It's an old family recipe."

And it was . . . somewhat. When he'd helped his mother make it as a boy—back when his mother was still alive, on those cold, cold winter nights—there'd been onions and potatoes for the pot but no beef. Beef was an extravagance young Sandu had only ever heard about.

For an instant emotion flared behind the other man's eyes, something a step beyond smugness; beef or no, *gulyás* was the fodder of peasants. "I fear I've already supped." He gave a small nod of his head. "Noble One."

"Very well."

Sandu kept him there in the growing hush, the night beyond the windows thickening to sapphire. He allowed his gaze to rest upon the embers of the fire and devoured every bite of his meal. Radu didn't stir.

"I'd like you to draw me a map," Sandu said at last. He leaned back, touched his napkin to the corners of his mouth. "It's been so long since I've flown as far as Sinaia. I've no desire to lose my way."

"Of course," said Radu again. He rose without bowing, approached the desk and began a swift sketch with the quill and ink Sandu had already set out.

"My friend," Alexandru said, watching him, "you have your ear to the ground, so to speak. Have you heard anything new about the *sanf inimicus*? Gossip? Whispers?"

The other *drákon*'s hand never faltered. "No, my lord."

"Or of the English?"

"Nothing." Radu tossed down the quill, straightening from the map with a quick, jerky movement.

"Oh—pray don't forget to write in the names of the lakes," Sandu said mildly. "I find them immensely helpful."

∞

The map was simple but surprisingly well done. It was clear Radu had some skills, at least, beyond subterfuge; every line was certain, every image perfectly identifiable. He'd even drawn in his flocks, clusters of sheep and goats and cows scattered amid the forest meadows.

The lakes' names were scribbled in black. Lacul Rosu, Bicaz, Spatar Cantacuzino. Between each one oozed fresh red letters, bleeding through as strong and thick as all the other marks.

The red lettering said, *Serf. Usurper. I hope they eat your heart.*

∞

He was still looking at those letters when he spoke once more. Radu was gone, taking with him the odor of his stifled hate. The hallway beyond the double doors held no whiff of human or *drákon*; the maids and footmen would be belowstairs still, cleaning and chattering, preparing the castle for another day. Someone would be up for the dinner tray, but they would give him time yet. They knew not to interrupt.

There really seemed to be no reason not to acknowledge her.

"I know you're there, child." Alexandru didn't glance up from the map. "You needn't hide."

He was staring at the word *Serf*, letting it burn like fire into his vision, when he heard her exhale. He closed his eyes briefly, erasing the word, and when they opened again, she was edging forward from the shelter of the far bookcase, easing into his deliberate puddle of light.

CHAPTER SIX

I was quiet. I had been so quiet, I was a mouse, I was a mote of dust. But he'd heard me anyway. Or smelled me. Or sensed me.

I certainly sensed *him*. I sensed him across my skin, the delicious little goose-prickles he roused with the timbre of his voice. The scent of him, dark night and spice and unpolished diamonds. The way the colors of him seemed to lap up the light, deep blue soaking into his hair, gold into his skin. And those eyes, flat-clear mirror eyes, pale and empty as they captured mine from across the chamber.

I left the shadows that had shielded me. He'd addressed me directly; he was looking straight at me, it was stupid to cower, and anyway there was a part of me that no longer wanted to cower. I wanted his attention. I knew that. I was sure it was why I had come.

I can Weave away, I told myself, as my bare feet found the edge of his rug. I hugged my arms across my chest. *If I have to, I can Weave.*

I wasn't certain if it was actually true. I knew I would Weave back sooner or later, but my control was still dubious at best.

Prince Alexandru hadn't moved from his chair, his body long and lean, his legs outstretched and his feet crossed at the ankles. He wore boots, even indoors. He wore a silk shirt with pearled buttons and a waist-coat of charcoal brocade, breeches of supple soft leather. Everything about him breathed power, pleasure, luxury. Control.

I envied him that. The control. There wasn't any hint of emotion on his face; I knew my own would reveal every little fear that bit at me. It always had.

One hand lifted, bringing a finger to rub lazily against his lips. I halted, abruptly both uncomfortable and excited by that simple, sensual motion.

"Ah," he said, and allowed his hand to drop back. "You're not a child tonight, are you?"

He hadn't even glanced below my neck. I had managed to Weave not quite nude this time. I was wearing my chemise—not the dress, just the undergarment—which was nonetheless quite an accomplishment for me. It had taken me a year to manage this much. I still couldn't do anything like jewelry or hairpins. Sometimes all I ended up with were my garters.

A chemise is only muslin, however. Translucent. And the corsets somehow never made the Weave.

A single dark brow began to arch. The prince was waiting.

My mouth opened; I'd waited so long for this moment. I'd practiced my speech a hundred times to the painted walls of my room, every word premeditated, every argument clear-cut. But now, when I tried to form the words, no sound came out.

"Honor," he said. "Is that your name?"

This time I didn't even attempt to answer. My speech wiped blank. I stared at him.

His ankles uncrossed, sudden and stealthy. "Honor Carlisle. Correct?"

Oh, no—

I glanced around the room, my heart in my throat. It looked like my old father's study but larger, with glass-fronted bookcases and masculine side tables, green leather chairs stuffed with horsehair. The paintings on the walls were all gilt-framed oils of men and landscapes. There was a bronze statue of a hart by the door. The room was more grandiose than Alexandru's private quarters, antiquated somehow, tinged more of other people than of him. But we truly seemed alone.

"Are they here?" I demanded anyway. "The English *drákon*? Are they here for me?"

"No, girl. The only foreign creature here is you."

He rose from the chair, taking with him the map drawn by the other man, the dark-eyed one. He walked to the desk and opened a drawer, pulling free a smaller piece of paper, holding it out to me.

"I received your letter," Alexandru said.

"What letter?" My heart was still pounding.

His lips quirked, just barely. "The one you wrote."

He held it out, patient once more, until I came near enough to take it from his fingertips.

"I never sent this," I said, backing up again to scan it. "I never wrote this."

From the edge of my view his stance seemed to tighten, a very subtle shifting of his muscles, of the dark evening colors spilling into him. "You're not Honor Carlisle?"

"I am." I shook my head. "But I didn't . . ." *write this yet*, I almost said.

There was no question it was my handwriting. But it was so strange; I'd had no notion to send him a letter, not in all these years. I wouldn't even have known how to direct it. All I knew of *Zaharen Yce* was that it was a castle set alone amid some very bleak and cold mountains. In Transylvania. And I could hardly pop back to Darkfrith to ask anyone there to clarify matters. Lady Lia had made it exceedingly clear, ever since she'd first stolen me, that if I were to go back home, my life would be forfeited.

Forfeited. As in, given up, given away.

She would not tell me why or how. She claimed she wasn't certain. But when she spoke like that, when she spoke about her dreams, it was impossible not to feel my flesh crawl. Whatever else she hid from me, whatever other troubles we shared, the instant she'd said to me, *You will be killed there*, I believed her.

I turned Alexandru's letter over in my hands. Yes, still my writing, the imprinted wax seal of the shire—most likely from the forged stamp Lia kept in her nightstand drawer, one of her few souvenirs from childhood.

"*Senyoreta*." The prince waited until I looked back up at him, distracted, pushing a fall of hair from my eyes. "How is it, exactly, that you appear to be both a child and a full-grown maiden? That you manage to get in and out of my castle without smoke?"

I chewed my lower lip. "May I sit?"

He indicated one of the green chairs, the one directly across from him. I chose one by the hearth instead. The chemise wasn't very insulating.

"I'm not mistaken, am I?" Prince Alexandru remained standing. "You *are* that child I pulled from the river six years ago? And the young woman from the ball? From the granary and the field?"

"Yes."

Now he did take his seat, slowly, his hands relaxed upon the arms of the chair, his hair a blue-black spill caught against the cushion behind him.

I took a deep breath. "My name *is* Honor Carlisle. I'm nineteen years old. I've known you since I was a child, since I was fourteen, to be precise. That was the day I met you in the river. Oh, and, er . . . thank you. For saving me. From drowning. I don't believe I said it at the time."

He didn't take his eyes from my face. "Two weeks later we spoke in my bedchamber. Yet you were older. Like you are now."

"Yes. I was seventeen then."

That single brow began to arch once more.

"I know how it sounds," I said swiftly. "I know how it must seem to you. I'm sorry to have been avoiding you all this time, but you see, I've just recently discovered . . . I've gotten the news that we are to marry. You and I. And I thought . . . I thought it might be best if I came here to talk to you about it."

I ran out of breath. I sat there with the letter clutched in my hands and gazed back at him, feeling my face heat far warmer than the fire or the air in the room. Alexandru, however, seemed carved of pure, cool stone.

"I'm a Time Weaver." My fingers knotted harder around the paper. "That's the answer to all your questions. I'm *drákon*, and I Weave through time. No doubt I *did* write this letter to you. Or—I will. Only not yet."

"Time Weaver," he repeated, neutral.

"Yes."

"*Drákon*. And English."

"Yes, yes. I should tell you right now that I'm not certain how long I'll be able to remain—"

"Are you also a member of the *sanf inimicus*?"

Of all the responses I'd expected, I'd never anticipated this. My jaw dropped. "The—what? Are you serious? The dragon hunters? Of course not!"

Alexandru continued to regard me without expression. He only blinked once, and for a second—just a second—the mirror clarity of his gaze blazed to silver, liquid phosphorous. It was a dragon's gaze, fell and sharp, and if his voice could engender prickles, this look gave me a bone-deep chill. Then it slipped back into gray.

"Residing in Spain these days?"

"Yes. I ran away from England. Years ago. Rather, I was kidnapped."

"I wonder if I might trouble you to write that down for me," he said.

Another surprise. He seemed quite difficult to shock. "Um . . . which part?"

"Any of it. There's ink and a quill on my desk there. A sheaf of papers to the right."

I stared at him for a moment longer and he stared at me. Even in shadow, he was so savagely handsome I felt my throat parch.

I could all too easily imagine his elegant fingers stroking my skin. His lips slick against mine. Our bodies—

"Very well."

I stood and crossed to the desk, acutely aware of how I must look from behind, with my hair undone and the chemise probably revealing a great deal more of me than it hid. I found the quill, dipped, blotted, and began to scratch out a sentence on a blank sheet.

"What year is this?" I asked, without looking up.

"Seventeen eighty-eight."

I would be twenty-one in this year. Wherever I was, I was twenty-one. And apparently not yet wed. God, it seemed a lifetime away.

"Here." I thrust the paper at him. He accepted it, held it up to the light. No doubt the letters would run; I'd forgotten to sand it.

I am Honor Xavière Carlisle. I am a the sole Time Weaver of our kind. Everything I've told you is truth.

I concentrated on returning the quill to the crystal inkpot, on rubbing away the fresh smear of ebony that stained my knuckle. When I peered up at him, Sandu's expression was still stone but his cheeks had gone red.

Red. He was blushing.

"Please believe me," I said. "I wished only to find you so that we may speak frankly. We are supposed to be married. And I . . . wondered . . . if you wouldn't mind, of course . . ."

His lashes lifted. His gaze burned.

"If we didn't," I finished weakly. "If, perhaps, we could just go on as we are."

"As we *are*," he echoed.

"Yes. I'm sorry. I have no wish to offend you. But I don't wish to wed you, either. What I've seen of wedlock is—difficult. I don't think I'm suited for it. Not that you're not comely," I added hastily. "Naturally you are. I mean, look at you. You've those eyes, and those shoulders. And your lips. *Meu Déu*, your lips alone—"

"I beg your pardon, *how* old did you say you are?"

I steadied myself. "Nineteen. I'm nineteen years of age right now. In your time, however—in this year, I'm older. No doubt I'm awaiting you."

The candles in their wrought iron branches had been left aflame too long; one by one, they were flickering out. The chamber was growing dimmer and dimmer, which gave me a surge of courage.

"I've never been with anyone," I admitted. "Never even really kissed. I don't actually socialize at all. I spend a great deal of time indoors. So I don't know why I'd . . ."

"Marry?" he supplied, exquisitely calm.

"I don't desire it. Might we just have physical intimacy instead?"

I heard the air leave his chest exactly as the penultimate candle extinguished. The room, the furnishings, the prince: We were all now things of shadows, little clear but the shining stars beyond the windows.

I felt the pull coming, the swell of its tide looming over me. I was better at predicting it as I aged. I was better at holding it off, even if for mere seconds.

I spoke in a rush. "Find me now. Find me in my Natural Time. You can't tell the English, but I probably still live in Barcelona, in the *Barri*—"

I never got to say *Gótic*. I was gone again, yanked

back home to my bed two years before I'd ever hand him that sheet of paper, with only the memory of his gaze, hot and silver and pinned to mine, and of his cheeks, still ruddy in the dark.

∽◦∾

You might be wondering why I didn't just Weave right back to Sandu to finish our conversation. Certainly I tried. But a significant portion of the rules of my Gift remained a mystery to me. I had puzzled out the basics, such as that without great mental effort I would wind up nude, and in the same location. Yet the amount of time I remained in each Weave was inconstant. It might be minutes or hours or even months. And once I Wove to a certain time and place, I could never return to it precisely . . . nor to any period of time closely surrounding it. It became buffered in some way, untouchable by me.

Plus, the Weaves themselves were exhausting. As I grew older I began to develop headaches after doing them, and then minor nosebleeds. None of it ever lasted very long, but it was worrisome. Privately I wondered if this might be the beginning of the "sacrifice" for my Gift I'd mentioned to myself in that troubling fifth Letter Over Time, the same letter in which I'd informed myself I was to wed the prince. The headaches weren't exactly horrific, but they were unpleasant. The nosebleeds didn't hurt now, but who knew what they might be like in the future? I had a ghastly vision of myself gaunt and drooping in a few short years, wandering around the palace like an unfortunate wraith with a handkerchief ever pressed to my face.

Amalia and I agreed that I needed to approach my Gift with caution. That I shouldn't try to explore my limits merely for amusement.

I did not consider Alexandru an amusement. But I didn't have enough skill to Weave near to him at that age for a good while after that conversation in the castle. I knew the sensible thing to do would be to wait for him to find me, as I'd instructed him. Two years. It needn't be too terribly long.

Of course, it was.

One of the peculiarities of my kind was that, like swallows and swans, we tended to mate for life. One mate, two hearts, that's it, forever and ever. The saddest, saddest sight in the shire would be a widow who'd lost her second heart, or betimes a widower. If they were lucky, they had children to surround them and help them slip into old age. If not, well, then they had the inescapable presence of the tribe, which would never leave them alone, regardless.

But in every case, the *drákon* left behind would wither. I witnessed it with Lia, nearly every day. I didn't really know if Zane considered her his mate the way I knew she considered him hers. But watching her dwindle into slow, wistful mourning whenever he left her was misery for us both.

I did not want that for myself. The passionate excitement, yes. The ardor. But that depth of attachment that meant you were no longer whole, that your entire existence depended upon another's . . .

No, thank you. I'd be pleased enough to become Sandu's consort. I liked my heart just as it was.

Still, there *was* the promise of that passion . . .

So I tried twice more to Weave back to him. The

first time I discovered myself in a gray, gloomy hut of some sort. It had been furnished as a house, but a very rudimentary one: three rooms, a hearth built from riverstones, a chimney that clearly didn't properly draw. The room I was in contained a roughly planked table set with thick, chipped earthenware and pewter—I heard the songs—knives. Four chairs of unpolished wood. Dirt floor.

Smoke from the fire simmered against the thatched ceiling, curled sharp inside my nose. The sole window to the hut had been left open to siphon out what it could, revealing pine trees and a cobalt sky.

A woman's crooning floated from the adjacent room. I sidled over to the doorway and peeked inside.

She was seated in a rocking chair, a fine one, much finer than anything else surrounding us. She was cradling her black-haired baby in her arms, smiling and humming, and he turned his head and looked over at me.

There was no mistaking those clear silvery eyes.

The second attempt was stranger yet. I ended up back at the castle, standing outside alone in a huge, circular courtyard of crushed gravel and dead grass. An alabaster fountain cast a frozen shadow across my legs; it wasn't functioning. There wasn't even any water in it. A magnificent carved phoenix at the top was obviously meant to spit a stream from its mouth, but its wings had been broken off, and the lead pipe protruding from its beak had been bent.

I looked up at the castle. At first it appeared the same as it always had. White sparkling blocks of quartzite. Tall beveled windows. Crenulated towers, balconies, everything blinding as snowfall in the sun.

But there were no people. Not human, not *drákon*, no sounds or scents or stirring of them. Squinting up at the walls, I noticed that quite a few of the windows had been shattered. Some even had curtains tugging at their edges with the wind, their fabric faded and tattered.

Scorch marks scarred the upper frames of the upper windows. Marks from a fire.

I approached the huge double doors of the entrance, holding a hand to my eyes to shield my vision. I smelled the ruin before I saw it. The doors were of iron and oak, very ancient oak, and they had been forced apart into splinters. The bolts and hinges that had been their solid spine hung twisted from the wood. When I passed them they did not sing. They whimpered.

Zaharen Yce had been raped and gutted. I stepped around the broken glass in wonder, hardly feeling it when I cut my heel. The beautiful paintings were gone, the vases and chandeliers and marble statues were gone. The chunks of diamonds in the walls were gone. A few smashed chairs and what was left of a marqueterie firescreen tipped drunkenly on its side were all that remained of the main-floor furnishings.

Dust blanketed every inch in thick, gritty layers, undisturbed. The air was ghostly with the perfume of stale cinders and panic. Whatever had happened here had happened a long time ago.

I lifted a hand to push back a cobweb dangling from a doorway and felt the eyes of the spider high above me, diminutive life crouched back in the pitted mortar of a corner.

No one answered my calls. Outside I heard a falcon scream, but that was all.

I couldn't imagine what time this was. Where Alexandru or his people might be.

When I stepped out again into the glaring light of the courtyard, I was home, in my bedchamber. I was never able to return to that bleak, burnt castle.

I sank down to the rug on my floor. Wrapped once more in the heat of that Spanish afternoon, I'd hoped it had been just a dream. But the gash on my foot was real and deep.

He would not go to her.

The mere thought of it was absurd. He could not leave his people and his territory for any extended period of time, not even for the time it would take to fly to Spain and back.

Just to see her. Just that.

No. He'd traveled well over the years, but those had been steadier days. He'd enjoyed touring the cities of man, enjoyed their crowded opulence and astonishing innovations. He had a favorite restaurant in Bucharest, a favorite park in Potsdam. There were few sweeter small pleasures than a cup of steaming coffee in the Café Suleiman overlooking the banks of the Danube, but he'd been younger then, more convinced with the certainty of youth of his place. The threat of the English had been little more than a gnawing at the back of his thoughts.

Aye. Times had changed.

It would require days to fly to Barcelona. Taking a carriage was, of course, out of the question. Human travel barely crawled along the surface of the ground. *That* would consume weeks.

But days in flight, some of it over open waters. And then to hunt her, to find her, that river-girl who'd haunted him so long now . . .

He remembered her face from that night in the library. The dark bruised eyes holding his. The rosebud lips, never smiling. She was more lissome than she used to be, he thought; lissome yet still lush, any childish contours melted away to reveal the bones and angles of one of his own kind. A beast of beauty beneath pastel skin and copper-rose hair. He'd craved her from the moment she'd slid into the light.

Married, she'd announced, as easily as if it were already fact. It was insane.

Yet he could not wipe her face from his memory, any more than he could wipe away the true words of her note. The second one. Words describing the things he would do to her, what she wanted, what she craved of him. Positions, taste, scent. Words in English and Catalan and he barely knew what, so thick was his red haze of desire, and Sandu knew that he was doomed, because he would go to her, after all.

Amants. Lovers.

He'd see.

CHAPTER SEVEN

H.,

Tonight is the night. Be at the *Palau de la Diputació* on *Carrer de Sant Sever* at nine for the king's Revelry. Listen for the bells.

—H.

Barcelona was on fire.

Even though he arrived after sunfall, Alexandru realized from leagues away he'd have to navigate a celebration of some sort. He let the soft sea winds lift him as he studied the grid of the city below, every lane, every little passageway, it seemed, aglow with pinpoints of golden light. What appeared to be a parade was winding through the larger streets, brilliant with torches, trailing carousers in a long, bobbing tail. When the winds shifted he heard snatches of music as well, clanging bells and drumbeats striking off the hard, flat waters, soaring to heaven—sweeping through one lone black dragon first.

He was not entirely black. That was a significant

portion of his dilemma. He was also silver at his edges, with bands of amethyst and deep azure scoring his flanks in diminishing lines. Nighttime was usually a most excellent cover for him. He'd traversed half of Europe in such a way, landing in tucked-away places, emerging from alleys or parks or empty warehouses as an ordinary man. He'd not expected to have to return to earth tonight amid a festival; the silver tipping of his wings and talons would gleam like the sun in all that firelight.

He could go somewhere else. He could come back another night, when it was done.

But *she* was down there, somewhere, and he knew he wouldn't.

So Alexandru hovered awhile in silence with his satchel in his claws, eyes closed, miles above, and listened to the musicians and the merrymakers and smelled their food and sweat and torchsmoke. He let it wash up and around him until his hunger drove him downward, down, scattering a flock of wild-eyed gulls, sending an albatross into looping shrieks, past the docks . . . inland, to an elaborately Gothic stone belfry on a massive stone building, near the very heart of the chaos. It was a risk, he supposed. But then, there were no hidden spots in the city center, where he needed to be. Not tonight.

Belfries tended to be unoccupied and unilluminated. Good enough.

Sandu went to smoke, just another plume in a very smoky sky. Should any of those revelers jostling below bothered to have cast their eyes skyward, however, they might have wondered at this particular plume descending instead of rising.

Emanations of alcohol, of *cava* and ale shimmered through him with a near-physical force. Sandu doubted very much anyone was looking up.

He'd already dropped the satchel to the roof, managing to land it damned near the belfry, too. Lucky shot. After Turning back inside the stone shelter—nearly smacking his head on the bell first—it was a simple matter to crawl out and quickly retrieve it.

He descended the tightly wound wooden stairs of the belfry dressed as a gentleman, if not a prince, and stepped into a sea of perfumed, glittering chaos.

Inside the building it was somehow even more crowded than without. It was truly impressive, the decorations and furnishings far more extravagant than the plain brown façade that faced the streets would imply. In fact, it seemed to be an actual palace, with stonework carved into delicate filigree arches, and intricately inlaid walls, and vaulted ceilings so high and tall he could scarcely make out the frescoes in their curves. Chandeliers dripped with strands of cut crystal, blazing with light. What he glimpsed of the floor was pink and blue marble edged in black, geometric patterns repeated over and over.

A palace, yes, yet it was little like his own home. Underneath its thinly sophisticated veneer, *Zaharen Yce* had been built as a fortress, designed and created by creatures with claws, anchored to its harsh mountain by the will of long-dead monsters. But this lavish and sensual place had never been used for defense, it was clear. This place was purely about wealth. And there must have been plenty of it.

Crushed flower petals stained the marble. Petals rained from the fingertips of the younger children, who carried them in baskets and laughed as they tossed them into the air, at each other. Dabs of falling color clung to wigs and hooped skirts, skimmed the sheer lace veils covering the faces of the women, snared in their combs. Diamonds twinkled behind the lace, a million little rainbowed stars; the men wore pearls and powder and dark satin jackets and spilled their drinks over their cuffs. Somewhere nearby an orchestra labored against the noise, a sudden rising of strings and horns that pierced the highest rafters, overcoming even the hectic human clamor for a few bars.

It was hot and reeking and he could hardly breathe. To his left was a door that would eventually lead him outside; he could taste the fresher air wafting in, getting there was the trouble.

A woman—a girl—laughed in his ear, took his arm and looped a chain of tiny round bells about his wrist. He caught the flash of her teeth, a few whispered words, and then she was gone and a new girl was beside him, handing him roses, yellow roses, their wilted fragrance a sudden assault on his senses, and then his other wrist was captured and Alexandru received more bells, and then the next shadowed girl who moved before him handed him an orange, and as his fingers brushed hers through her gloves he felt the razor-sharp ache of his own kind, and he realized that it was she.

It was Honor.

Behind the netting of her veil, her eyes met his. Her lips curved. She took his hand and led him away.

He was taller than I recalled. He was taller than nearly every man there in the Grand Salon of the palace. If I hadn't recognized him by that tail of indigo hair pulled back with a velvet ribbon, then certainly I would have found him by the bells.

They were small, tin, strung along cheap bracelets like charms for the celebration. Rich or poor, most of the men were wearing them, laughing and gesturing with their hands in that flowing, Catalan way so that they'd chime. But only on Alexandru did the bells sing.

And they did sing, beautifully. Even the less valued metals adored us; on him the bells rose into a sound like raindrops striking a cool, alpine lake. Every note pure and sweet.

When my hand touched his, they swelled from raindrops into a storm. And then I looked into his eyes, and they ceased to matter.

I'd been to the king's residence only once before, but I'd memorized my path for tonight. Carlos himself wasn't here, but two royal cousins were on hand, puffed proud in splendid bronze uniforms to represent him, and on this evening all the people of the province clamored for entrance.

Naturally, most of them were kept out. Only the most rarefied of Spanish society was allowed to step foot in the inner sanctum of the *palau*.

The rarefied . . . and I. But I, of course, had stolen in. I was, after all, *drákon*.

I'd chosen a veil of net, because it was easier to see through than lace. It was tradition for the ladies on this night to shield their faces, just as it was tradition for us to dress as courtiers from nearly a century past, with wide fan hoops at our hips, and stomachers of embroidered satin, and short trains that swished behind us and caught beneath the soles of the unwary. I wore black, not an uncommon color for formal Spain, not even for a festive gala such as this. I'd powdered my hair and skin and liked the effect: a snow-white face with crimson lips, chocolate kohl about my eyes that made them seem darker and even more blue than they were, pink-hued locks held in place with lacquered combs.

I seldom wore jewelry, mainly because I never wished to lose it in a Weave. But tonight I'd borrowed something of Lia's, a simple choker of rose quartz drops, barely more rose than my cheeks and hair. Beneath all the noise of the gemstones surrounding us, they offered a ballad, a gentle rhythm to match the pulse in my throat.

I hadn't wanted diamonds tonight. I hadn't wanted to distract myself from any single detail of him.

He kept the orange I'd handed him but passed off the yellow roses to a maiden of about twelve, with limp curls and sallow skin and a French-beaded gown that must have cost a ransom, presenting them to her with a smile and a nod of his head.

The child watched Alexandru walk away with startled, adoring eyes.

She could have been me. It was far too easy to see myself there in her, skinny and alone, clutching sagging flowers to her chest.

We reached the palace chapel, sealed off from the rest of the *celebració* with a scrolled iron gate that fit snugly from floor to ceiling. The pair of liveried guards stationed beside it did nothing to acknowledge either me or the prince, but when we neared the guards by the lock, one turned about swiftly, fit his key into the socket, and pushed the gate open for us. It shut behind us just as quickly.

I guided the prince into the shadows. He followed with agile deliberation, the heels of his shoes hardly clipping the floor. His fingers curved warm, very warm, in mine.

There were always candles lit above the altar, I'd heard, although their radiance was muted, shaded red and gold by the colors around us. I released his hand and turned to face him, taking a long, leisurely look at him for the first time tonight. For the first time in two years.

Pale and chiseled, deep blue and ivory and an ice-clear gaze. Still a head taller than I, still a world I'd never guessed at shining from his eyes, even though at last our ages were closely matched.

"How much did that cost?" Alexandru inquired in English, his words low and amused.

We could speak nearly without sound; in closed spaces such as this, even with the cacophony beyond us, our hearing was acute.

"Less than a single topaz from your mantel," I answered, just as hushed. "And yet more than a year's salary each." I took a step back, lifted a hand to the softly glimmering room. "I thought it'd be worth it. Do you agree?"

"I do."

He turned to take in the perimeters of the chamber, making certain he remained beyond the timid glow cast from the row of candles; the bells at his wrists subsided back into rainfall.

The chapel was truly gorgeous, alive with buzzing gilt and old dark murals, tapestries of kings and saints draped along the walls. A reliquary of solid gold rested on the table before us, throbbing with song.

There was only a single way in and out. Past the iron gate the party continued its rhythm of surge and ebb, framed now by bars and the silhouettes of the guards in their old-fashioned costumes and wigs. A woman nearby stumbled into one of them and erupted into peals of laughter; the man steadied her without moving his feet.

My gaze was angled downward. Through my lashes and the netting I was admiring Sandu, the jade green hue of his velvet coat and breeches, the shape of his calves in cream stockings and the silver buckles on his shoes. He paused by a draped corner of the altar; I heard the song of the reliquary soar into bliss with the stroke of his finger, and I thought, *Oh, I know.*

"Are you shocked?" I asked, mostly to cover that song. "That I'd resort to bribery?"

"Not at all. I admire a woman of practicality. A few more minutes out there in that mess and I might have had to Turn and eaten my way out."

I glanced up at his face. He fixed me with that light, strange gaze; the corners of his lips lifted into something like a smile.

My heart began a tattooing skip. *He's here,* it beat, *finally here, here, here.*

"Ah," I managed. "Not a good idea, I'm afraid. Look up, my lord."

He did, and then I did, both of us taking in the elaborately carved arches of the wooden ceiling, the impressive round medallion centered above us that depicted a knight on his horse. The dying dragon at their feet.

"Tonight is the *Festes de la Mercè*." I lifted my veil with both hands, flipping it over my hair. "Some say it's to honor the Virgin. Others say it's for him."

"St. George," discerned the prince, his head tipped back. "Lovely."

"And the unlucky dragon, whoever it was. No doubt right now someone somewhere nearby has partaken of too much wine and brandishes a rather wicked lance. Probably several someones—they're quite fond of *Sant Jordi* here, I fear. Better tonight to be just a prince, I think."

"Yes," said Alexandru, in his untroubled tone. "No doubt."

We paused, both of us; my gaze dipped downward again. The shadows shifted, and Sandu took a step closer to me.

"And you knew to bribe the guards . . . ?"

"Because I knew you were coming tonight."

"You saw it. From the future."

"Actually, I left myself a note." I shrugged. "I tend to do that."

I watched him slowly shake his head.

"It's true," I insisted.

"I know. It must be. As mad as it is, it's the only explanation. You travel through time. Yet it's so . . ."

"Bizarre?" I offered, feeling a knot begin to clench in my stomach. "Off-putting?"

"Astonishing." He grinned at me then, a genuine grin, one I'd never seen before; it transformed him into someone I didn't know, someone young and heartbreakingly handsome. He looked me in the eyes and the knot inside me began to melt like sugar stirred into hot tea. "The most astonishing Gift *ever*. You are . . . remarkably fortunate, *Mademoiselle* Carlisle."

"Oh," I said, feeling the blood rush to my cheeks. "I'm pleased you think so. You're very kind, my lord."

"No," he said, and took another step closer to me. "I'm actually not."

I don't think he realized he'd spoken Romanian to me then. It barely registered even with me, but I'd spent the past two years disciplining myself into fluency—as fluent as one could become without an actual tutor. I'd not dared to inform Lia or Zane of my intent. No doubt I was better at reading Romanian than speaking it; his accent was unfamiliar to me, but the words were clear . . . as was his tone.

His voice had darkened. His eyes had darkened. It was a reaction I was beginning to receive more and more from human men as I aged, but coming from another of my kind, from an Alpha prince . . . my physical response ripped through me like lightning. Yearning. Excitement. Every nerve ending in my body began to jangle.

One more step—

"Do you know what's before us?" I asked in English, breaking the moment. I motioned toward the reliquary.

Sandu shook his head again, never taking his gaze from mine.

"A femur. That's what they say. His femur. One of

the most celebrated dragon-hunters of all time, reduced to bits of bone and dust, enshrined in gold and kept behind bars. I wonder what he'd think of the two of us, standing free here before him."

I was prattling and I knew it. I closed my mouth with a snap.

Alexandru lifted a hand to my face. The festival receded, the bells and stone songs and my nervousness and all the human chatter receded. I felt his fingertips skim the curve of my cheek, glance the powdered coils of my hair. An energy hit me, *his* energy, waves of swooning power floating through my veins, and it felt so splendid and so *right* I thought I might never move again.

I smelled orange and spices and him. His next words reached me soft as silk.

"Are we still to be wed, Honor Carlisle?"

"I don't know," I whispered, unable to look away. "I haven't told me."

His smile again, that subtle one. His gaze dropped to my lips.

From beyond the walls of the palace came an explosion. The crowd in the Grand Salon let out a cheer, began to press their way upstairs or down.

"Fireworks," I murmured. "For the festival."

The pair of guards looked back at us, both of them at once. Sandu gave a slight shake of his head, eased away from me.

"May I offer my escort, *senyoreta*?"

I nodded, mute, and he presented me with a formal, seamless bow that even the king would have envied.

She took him to an inner courtyard paved with limestone but dotted with living trees, each one shaped precisely, emerald oval leaves, a lingering hint of nectar still discernible from the sap beneath the bark.

Orange trees, thriving out here in this arid, perfect heat. He felt the fruit he still held in his palm, the pulpy weight of it, and let his nails dig in a little to release a spray of scent. It was better than the human perfume that clouded around him. It was second best, however, to the scent of Honor, standing still and calm less than a foot away. She was close enough that her skirts brushed his legs, and still he wanted closer.

She smelled like . . . he didn't know. Like herself, like his dreams, like sweet breezes but more sultry. Like jasmine and honey.

She wore no human cologne. The powder on her hair was scented, and the satin of her gown was scented, but he'd learned to dismiss chemical notes like those a long while ago. Her lips were rouged, and might have tasted of raspberries had he nerve enough to find out . . . perhaps he was imagining that. Perhaps it was only a wish. He enjoyed raspberries. And he enjoyed gazing at her lips, their sweet reddened pucker.

She felt his attention. With a howling-loud firework discharging into white above them, her eyes cut back to his.

Brilliance; a hot clear light that lifted her irises nearly to turquoise, that reflected off her skin in a way it never would for a human female. She looked back at him soberly, framed in curls and a dark fall of netting. Above them a shower of luminous sparks began their slow dying float back to earth.

Alexandru felt strange. He felt almost intoxicated, actually. It was disconcerting enough that he pressed his nails harder into the orange, let the juice run over his fingers. He looked away from her to break it apart into segments, and then ate one without tasting it.

Honor watched the heavens. When he offered her a wet piece of pulp from his palm, she accepted it without glancing back at him again, without even removing her gloves. She brought the piece to her lips and sucked at it thoughtfully, and the strangeness enveloping him rose to dizzying new heights.

The people around them were gasping and clapping at the show, applauding every *boom* that shuddered the air. Several of the youngest children had abandoned their baskets of petals to simply squeal in delight.

The winds from the sea were sending ash-colored smoke into streaks, blowing the white sparkling flowers in the sky into pinwheels, into comets.

"Will you come home with me?"

Her invitation was low and even. When he turned to her she was still in profile, blinking at a dazzling new blossom of fire.

He didn't know why he hesitated. There was no reason to. He'd come for this, he knew that.

Sandu frowned down at the broken fruit in his hands. He'd come just for her.

"I've a supper prepared," she said, replacing her veil. With her features completely covered once more, she faced him. He was graced with that enigmatic smile. "Only that. If you like."

He made himself nod. He dropped the remains of the orange to the limestone and presented his arm, and together they began to wend their way out of the palace of the Others.

CHAPTER EIGHT

Zaharen Yce will die like this:

It is a time of advanced weaponry. Mankind has mastered the technical intricacies of shooting metal balls through soft flesh at high speeds: bullets replace musketballs; cannonballs replace arrows. Sabers and bayonets are still satisfyingly lethal at close range. Horses are still used in most battlefields.

But there won't be saber fighting within the castle. And there are no horses willing to ascend the mountain. Even the mighty birds of prey avoid the winds that rush along the white-crystaled slopes on this day.

It begins after breakfast. In the morning salon, servants are clearing the main table and sideboards, stacking china platters in their arms, retrieving silver salvers, the Belgian coffee service of etched gold. The air is still redolent of sausages and buttered crumpets and eggs. One of the younger footmen bobbles a cup but retrieves it midair, right before it would have shattered upon the floor. It earns him a stern look from the steward but a quick hidden smile from an even younger maid, which warms the footman from head to toe.

They are childhood sweethearts. He plans to wed her. He's already consulted her father and the Alpha of his tribe, both of whom have given their consent.

By now the sky burns that hard, lapis blue visible only from the most exalted places on earth. There are no clouds. There is only the teasing scent of spring, elusive, because it's March, and even though the true thaw won't come for another two months, green shoots have begun to break the crusted snow along the riverbanks. The dense layers of beech and pine comprising the forests seem less skeletal. A day before a single brown bear was seen loping through them in a panic, the first bear to venture close to the castle in years.

The enemy advances from the south. They chose this direction with great deliberation. South is disingenuous; south is not their home. However, south is more mountains—curving, distant peaks not so high as that of *Zaharen Yce*, but high enough.

It is the Alpha, fittingly, who senses them first. He's on his way up the main grand staircase, which is of marble. His fingers trail the banister, which abruptly feels different to him somehow; it's of gold-plated brass. Both the metals sting his hand.

He stops. He looks around, the hair on his scalp and arms prickling. The nearest window faces east, which shows him nothing amiss. He swivels about and bounds down the remaining stairs and Turns to smoke at the last step, leaving behind in the foyer his breeches and shoes and the imported silk shirt he favors.

He does not take the time to Turn human again to command open the main doors of the castle. He barrels through a south-facing window, shattering the glass, something smoke is not supposed to be able to do.

In the music room his wife finds her feet, lifting her toddler in her arms. She rushes to her own window, where beyond the eaves the sun begins to steal through, and observes the Alpha transforming from smoke to dragon, an ebony thread with wings flashing silver against the blue.

He is a lone speck. She watches as other threads begin to join him from below, but they are slow, all of them so slow, and the Alpha is far ahead.

There are not many Zaharen with the Gift of the Turn. Nearly everyone feels the sudden wild tug of their leader, but only seventy-eight of them are able to drop their bread or hoes or shepherd's crooks and take flight to follow.

They meet at the shining edge of the horizon. They meet a force of over five hundred.

There are no bullets. There are no bayonets. But there are teeth and talons, and blood begins to rain from the sky and stain the snow below. One meadow in particular appears abloom with scarlet flowers.

Later on, the peasants will refer to this meadow as the place of *trandafiri moartea*. The roses of death. It will be considered profane.

Dragons may perish in any of their three forms. Very few of the Zaharen are smoke when they are killed; most of them fall to the ground in pieces. They fall without noise. Dragons have no vocal cords.

There is a hamlet nearby. It is walled, like most of the alpine settlements. The people inside it never cry out, never weep. They hide in root bins and cellars. They burrow into mounds of turnips or potatoes and shield the bodies of their children with their own and flinch against the steady, ominous shuddering of the earth.

Their Alpha dies out there.

He was a particular target. His body is severed at the neck from behind. It lands heavily against an edging of trees, the wings ripped apart by bare branches.

The initial conflict lasts twelve minutes. In another eight minutes, the first of the invaders reach the castle.

There are a handful of Zaharen dragons awaiting them there. Older males, or the very young. Their blood splatters the castle walls, more red on white.

The wife of the Alpha is no longer in the music room. She has retreated to the dungeon with her child and a few servants and has armed herself with the best of human technology: a repeating rifle, a pistol, and a very sharp cutlass. She is adept with them all.

Of all the dragons of the mountains, she alone could escape unharmed. But she alone is the reason the invaders have come. And she will not leave her toddler.

The invaders find her at once. Her scent is distinctive, as is the scent of her power.

She slays three *drákon* in rapid succession but the fourth one reaches her, swipes out a claw and snags her in the arm, the one holding her child.

She screams. The child drops. She's dragged to the ground and just as the dragon leans down to close its jaws upon her head, she vanishes, still screaming.

The year is 1791, two years before France will enter its final, convulsive death throes and devour its monarchy.

Honor is twenty-four. Alexandru was twenty-six. Their daughter was nearly two.

CHAPTER NINE

She lived, apparently, in the halls of an empty cathedral.

It *was* a cathedral, or had been once, but it wasn't truly empty. After the press of people in the palace, jammed in the streets, it was a shock to discover a building such as this, with open passageways of colorful ceramic tile, and chipped pillars of onyx, and towering stained glass windows, many broken, covered from the outside with boards. Alexandru smelled no rodents, no pigeons or even insects, only the residue of all of them, and the heavier, more fragrant whiff of rain, perhaps a few hours away.

But there were humans dwelling in the shadows. Young ones, a few very old, all of them shrouded in blankets or shawls, all of them watching in silence as he and Honor crossed the floors. A child of about seven had cracked open a side door for them at Honor's single sharp rap; that child trailed them still.

Male. Grubby. Brown-eyed, garbed in cotton and wool with an incongruously new leather belt stiff around his waist. Sandu sensed no metal upon him but for the buckle, so if the boy was armed, it wouldn't be with a gun or blade.

Honor had exchanged a few muted words with one of the older Others before melting into the shadows herself. He heard her pause a few paces in, felt the weight of her gaze as she turned about. She'd smiled back at him and tipped her head toward the dark, an invitation to follow.

"It's safe," she said. "I promise."

So he was following.

The cloistered air carried a dull, cool tang. In fact, it was much cooler in here than it had been outside, certainly far more so than the overstuffed palace. He moved through its gloom listening hard: the hushed singing limestone, the rumbling onyx, a few brighter notes of garnets and granite thrown in.

Angels in the windows regarded them with flat glass eyes. Every now and again they passed a single-flamed lamp set within an alcove, and then the colored panels would flare and shimmer in time with his footfalls.

Honor made no attempt to touch him again. She seemed perfectly at ease with the child behind them as they glided deeper, and then higher, into the bowels of the building. With her hair covered, her figure draped in elaborate ebony, she blended too well with the shadows; he followed her by the sound of her gown, the skirts brushing the floor, a cadenced bare hiss of satin over tile.

At the end of a corridor the boy suddenly darted ahead. He rushed to a pair of closed wooden doors and pushed them open with both hands, revealing a slender rectangle of light, a glow that deepened and expanded until it was a pair of blown-glass candelabras on a table, a gleam of blue and violet against the night.

It was a private chamber, even more splendid than the halls, with settees and chairs and rugs and that long, glossy table laden with food.

Honor began to strip off her gloves. She waved a hand at the boy, who dipped a bow and shot Sandu a look from the bottom of it, then retreated as far as a corner, settling on a stool.

"I purchased it a few years ago," she said, and for a peculiar instant he thought she was speaking of the child; serfdom was a very recent memory in his land. But then she glanced at him from over her shoulder, freeing herself of the veil, and Sandu realized she meant the cathedral, this echoing and glass-shining place.

"You reside here?" he asked.

"Sometimes."

The table was set with china and silver, platters of cold meats and olives and cheeses, a carafe of chilled red wine gathering dew along its curves. Sliced bread lay in a fan upon a platter, surrounding a bowl slick with oil and spices. He realized that he was hungry—it had been a long while since he had eaten anything but the orange and he was starving, actually—and when Honor took a seat at the head of the table he was already only a step behind her, in time to hold her chair, to glimpse the movement of her fingers against the burled wood arms.

"An interesting home," he said. "Very . . . Gothic."

"Romanesque, actually." She reached for the wine, began to pour into the goblets nearby. "It's the devil to heat, if you'll forgive the saying. At least it's temperate here most of the year."

"Who are those people?"

She positioned a drink before him. Secure in his corner, the boy produced a fiddle and bow. "Just people. People who needed a place. Strays, rather like me."

"They're not your servants?"

"Not in the traditional sense. They're Roma, their own unique tribe. Grandparents and parents and grandchildren, everyone interconnected. They stay here betimes, I stay here betimes. They bring me things when I need them. It suits us all."

He'd spent too many years holding court; the compliment came easily, without thought. "You have a generous heart."

Her head tilted as she looked back at him, neither agreement nor disagreement, only that rich blue gaze, unsettling. Her skin glowed pearl against the stark bodice of her gown, the ice-pink teardrops of her necklace.

Alexandru glanced away. He unwound the bells from his wrists, set them gently upon the table, as the Gypsy boy began to play.

Slow notes, almost a lullaby. The boy was surprisingly good.

"Do they know about you? About . . . what you are?"

"I don't know," she answered, frank. "I imagine not. Certainly not the Weaving part, and as for the rest . . ." She lifted her hands, palms out. "They have no reason to suspect I'm more than what I seem. I look just the same as everyone else."

Hardly.

He nearly said it aloud—she could not be so ignorant of her own person as to be serious—but this time something in her gaze stopped him. Alexandru said instead, "Yet otherwise, when you're not here, and not, ah, Weaving . . ."

"Otherwise I am the obedient daughter of Lia and Zane Langford. Yes, you know that name. We rent a set of apartments here in the city."

He sat back in his chair. "I didn't realize—you are their child?"

"Lia says so." The doors opened again; a pair of adolescent girls slipped inside bearing ladles and spoons. They moved to the food without speaking.

"They're my second family. My first was back in Darkfrith. If you'll recall, I mentioned this before. In fact," Honor lifted a hand again and one of the girls pulled a sheet of paper from her apron, handed it to her with a curtsy, "I took the liberty of writing down some of the more salient facts. Since you seem to enjoy that."

Sandu accepted it, skimming the words.

> *Stolen as a girl*
> *My Life in Danger from the English*
> *Saved by Zane and Lia*
> *But Trapped in Barcelona*
> *Drawn to you*
> *Don't know why*
> *Sorry*

And gleaming between all that, her secret message: *You Make Me Unafraid*

He refolded the sheet, studying her, the face of perfect lines, the hair coiled in tinted powder, the intense eyes painted dark, sophisticated. She was, by her own admission, two years older than the last time they'd met, and the changes were subtle but there. Yet he found that he could still see that little girl in her, that girl he'd first met, who'd had no paint or powder or even poise. He could see that same burning concentration behind her gaze, passion and stubbornness and tremulous courage.

It was the strangest sensation, like he was looking at a rice-paper image traced over another. Old. New. And yet they were both the truth.

The song from the fiddle began a crescendo. Honor flicked her gaze toward the boy. He caught her whispered "*suaument*," and the melody softened instantly back into its lullaby.

Alexandru pinched a hand to the bridge of his nose. He was becoming light-headed again. That had to be the reason for his lack of mental balance around her.

"Are you unwell?"

He shook his head, tried the wine. Cinnamon and tannins, a welcome rush of flavor. He took another swallow, then replaced it carefully by the chains of bells.

"I must confess, Mistress Carlisle . . . I've never known anyone like you."

"I know," she said.

Far and away, the first of the thunder began to rumble across the Mediterranean.

His hostess was running a finger over the crystal rim of her goblet, lightly, around and around. "I feel that . . . for the sake of utter honesty between us, I should tell you that, technically, you purchased this cathedral for me."

"Did I?"

"Yes. And thank you."

He began on the bread. "What a generous fellow I am. When did I do that?"

She ducked her chin and smiled. "As I said, a few years back. I have no income of my own, you see. Had I remained in Darkfrith, I would have been considered something of an heiress. But here, I'm as penniless as young Adiran over there with his begging songs. Zane and Lia feed me and clothe me. You provided my shelter."

He paused, watching that smile, small and not quite abashed but *knowing*, a slight curve that spoke plainly of mischief.

"You have," she said, after a moment, "a great many gemstones embedded in your castle. Uncut diamonds, right there in the mortar. Every room."

"Ah."

The last of the Zaharen wealth. The last glimmering, corporeal link to their heritage, the overflowing riches of those first few dragons.

"I've taken only the slightest of them. You've not even missed them, have you?"

"No. Not yet."

Her smile erased. "I apologize. I wish I could say I wasn't raised to steal, but truthfully, nearly every aspect of my adult life has been shaded with thievery. It feels rather natural to me now. And it seemed to me, that if, in the future, I'm the mistress of your castle, or even just a consort, it couldn't *really* be considered *stealing . . .*"

Alexandru pressed his fingers back against his nose.

"Sorry," she said again.

More thunder. The notes of the fiddle, rising and falling. The room felt heated now, the scent of food and *her* surrounding him, flooding him, erasing all thoughts of practicality and caution, promising pure magic in return.

"I'm enjoying the wine," he said, when he could speak again.

"It's from the Roma," she responded gravely.

Jasmine and honey, her smoky voice, her luminous skin. He wanted her so badly he thought his blood would boil dry.

Sandu dropped his hand.

"Do you realize what it would mean, were we to wed? To be involved at all? The trouble it would cause?"

She tipped her head again, impassive.

"We are at war," he said. "Perhaps you don't know that. It seems impossible that you wouldn't, but it's so. It's a silent war, one without blood, but very real nonetheless. Your tribe is determined to oust me, to take what is mine. For years they've been stalking us, sending spies, attempting to feel their way around my grasp on my kin. I think perhaps the only thing holding them back now is my sister—her last, lingering loyalty to me—but she can't keep them out forever. I know our ways. I know what I'd do, were I the English Alpha. I would have sent an army a full five years ago, and done what I could to win. War is pitiless, and war is cold, and I guarantee you someday your tribe will strike. We've done what we can to prepare, but I don't need *you* to be their excuse."

She regarded him without moving. "The English are no longer my tribe, Sandu."

"I don't believe they view matters quite the same way. You disappeared from their shire, you claim they want you dead. Do you even know why?"

Her lips flattened. She shook her head.

"Because they think you are *sanf*. That you are a member of the *sanf inimicus*."

The fiddle song died. Honor leaned forward, biting off her words. "That marks the second time you've accused me of that. I don't appreciate it."

"I don't accuse. I repeat to you what I was told."

"It is a lie."

"It doesn't matter. Lie or not, it's what they accept as truth."

She shoved back from the table. "Then someone is lying to *them*! The *sanf* are an atrocity! I've never had anything to do with them."

Yet.

It lingered in the air over the fading echo of her voice, that single unspoken syllable, sinking heavy between them.

One of the serving girls inched forward, placed a hand on Honor's arm. Slowly she resumed her seat, a well of satin puffed around her. Her face shone even paler than before.

"I would never," she vowed softly, her beautiful eyes vehement. "Never."

Alexandru lowered his own, finding her sheet of paper on his lap, their ardent sideways sentences.

"*Da,*" he murmured, without lifting his own gaze. "Gentle One. I believe you."

❧

He left her at the door to his chamber. Rather, she left him. It was, after all, her cathedral, not his, no matter how she'd managed the payment. She'd taken a lamp from one of the alcoves and guided him here, to this small square room with a faded mural of what appeared to be apostles and cherubs, and a bed with feather ticking, and a basin of water on a stand.

There was no scent of her within. It wasn't her bed, and the disappointment that jagged through him at that realization was tempered only slightly by strained, prudent relief.

He hardly knew her, or even what to think of her. If nothing else she was a gentlewoman, and the gentleman in him—*serf,* sneered a malevolent voice from the black corners of his mind—would respect that, no matter how bright her skin or smoldering her gaze.

She *would* mean war. He knew it down to the marrow of his bones. Taking her, claiming her, would unquestionably shatter the frigid, watchful stalemate he and the English had managed these past few years. *Sanf inimicus* or just a stolen child: They'd never abide his mating to her.

"Good evening," Honor Carlisle had said to him, her hand on the door.

"Good evening," Sandu had replied, a bow to her curtsy.

She'd left trailed by that Gypsy boy, who was the

only one throwing glances over his shoulder as they faded into the gloom.

Outside, the autumn storm drew nearer, promising wet and wind.

Tomorrow Alexandru would return to the belfry, fetch the satchel he'd left there, and go.

CHAPTER TEN

Across the city, across the man-built grimy peaks and turns of the many rooftops that made up this particular quarter of Barcelona, above all the other noises begat from the *Festes de la Mercè*, Lia heard the music.

She was standing at the balcony off their bedroom, modest enough in her wrap of flowing silk that was pale as peaches, as the first light that would spill over the long blue horizon of the Caribbean and break into opals across the waves. She kept her hands fixed to the iron railing before her, because it hurt a little—iron always did—and that kept her grounded to earth. That kept her from Turning.

But the music would not cease.

Like the roofs, it was also made by man. A fiddle, she thought. Perhaps a viol.

She did not know why it struck her so coldly on this warm night. She did not know why she felt a chill as the melody pulsed around her, tantalized her, repelled her. It was a song she'd not heard before, she was sure of that much. Yet it spoke to her as if they were old familiar friends.

I'm here. You tried to stop me. But I'm here. It has begun.

Perhaps it was just because of the festival. Perhaps she was oversensitive to this particular night, to the parties and drunken carousing. The smoke in the air.

One year, their second autumn here, she and Honor had ventured out to become swallowed by the *Festes*. It had been a first for them both; for all her years away from the deliberate isolation of the shire, Lia'd never grown comfortable in truly large crowds of Others. There was something about them that whetted her animal instinct, some subtle, tingling, disquieting thing: beyond the smell of them, beyond their bodily noises and emissions, their garish loud ways . . .

Shoulder to shoulder with them, unable to see her way clear, Lia felt ensnared. And ensnared was a dangerous feeling indeed for a barely leashed dragon.

But the festival swarmed the streets with its own siren call, and Honor had stood here—right here, just beside her—on the balcony, watching, inhaling the smells, and whispered only, "All that laughter. What must it be like?"

So they'd abandoned the balcony, dressed up in crisp Spanish lace and shawls and descended their tall, locked-away palace down to the crooked streets.

It had been every bit as noisy and stinking as Lia'd feared. Beneath the veil her eyes were running from the smoke, and her ears were throbbing from the drums and bells and people shouting, and Honor's smile was so wide and delighted that when she flashed it toward Lia, the extravagant, *drákon* beauty that only just waited beneath the surface of her youth shone more brightly than all the torches.

They'd remained out all night. They'd danced with strangers, dined upon warm fruit and sweetmeats, shared wine. At the tail end of the celebration they were seated together alone upon the damp brink of a beach, shoes off, their veils discarded into long twists of lace snakes that rolled with the breeze against the sand.

An abandoned bonfire had mumbled down into a pile of embers upwind; the air smacked of charred laurel and brine.

Lia's coiffure had begun to weigh too heavy upon her head. She was working on removing her pins, collecting them carefully to her lap, when Honor spoke.

"Why did you save me from the shire?"

She glanced over with her hands still up in her hair; Honor only gazed fixedly at the sea. She sat curved with her arms wrapped around her knees, her shawl a tender bunching of cashmere against her chin and cheek.

Amalia lowered her hands, the last pin between her fingers. There were so many things she could have said.

Because the dreams told me to.

Because you were innocent, and did not deserve to die.

Because parents should always protect their children, even drákon *parents.*

Because I was heartsick for a family. And so were you.

"Because we're kin" is what Lia finally answered.

"You're not my mother."

Under the inexorable slap of water to sand it wasn't an accusation, only a softly stated fact . . . but oh, it stung.

She kept her face to the breeze. "Do you remember the wild dogrose that would grow in Darkfrith? How it'd wrap along the hedges and creep into the rye, and come back every year, even when the farmers pulled it out?"

From the edge of her eye, she saw Honor hesitate, then give a nod.

"Love is like that. It grows in thorny fields as well as fertile ones. It's inexplicable, and undeniable. There was a hole in my life, and a premature ending for yours. So fate gave me my dreams, and you a longer ending. A *much* longer one, I hope. We were chosen for each other. We were meant to be."

"You . . . love me?"

"Yes. You're my daughter now. You're of my heart."

Honor had said nothing else, only hunched down deeper into the sand.

It was a sennight later, long after the last of the smoke had cleared from the air, that Lia had discovered the note shoved under her pillow, written in an unmistakable girlish hand.

Thank you. I will love you too.

She was not *Mama* or *Mother* or even *Mare*. Honor had never once called Lia by anything but her given name. But she had penned that note.

The nightsong from the distant fiddle paused, started again. A clot of men on the street below had staggered to a halt beneath her to sing off-key, their torches casting a diabolic glow straight up to where she stood.

The silence of the apartments behind Amalia beckoned. She released the railing, turned back to her room and to her empty bed.

∽≈∾

When I was twenty-one, what I knew of the *sanf inimicus* would fill barely a thimble. Our ancestral folklore was rife with stories of humans hunting us; even human history boasted tales of brave men slaughtering dragons, or of dim-witted women being stolen by them. We knew we were unwelcome in the world of the Others, of course we knew. It was the reason we pretended to *be* them. It was the reason we spent our lives, generation after generation, incognito.

But I don't think we English *drákon* had a specific name for the hunters. I don't think any one of our stories ever called them by that name.

Still, they did exist.

They had been conceived in the Carpathians ages ago, just as we had been. Confirmation of them had only just surfaced in the shire right before Zane had taken me away, and that was the last I'd even thought of them until Alexandru's first accusation to me, there in the library of *Zaharen Yce*.

Yet my initial introduction to the *sanf inimicus* actually came by way of Joséphine and Gervase.

My father was a trusted advisor to our Alpha, probably because, like the Alpha, he was obsessed with ensuring the tribe's silver fortunes. There was a lot of it to ensure.

Whenever he was home, Gervase reeked of silver. I

don't believe he spent much time deep within the mines themselves, but he worked surrounded with all forms of the ore. As a girl I used to imagine that the crude metal had permeated the crevices of his body and hardened around all his inner organs. He would bawl, spit, and sweat silver.

Like the rest of us, he knew his place in the tribal hierarchy. He was both smart and obedient; he would never challenge for a higher status. Why bother? He already had Plum House and the Alpha's ear, and a position all but the council members would envy.

Whilst I, the runt of the litter, had evolved into a very skilled eavesdropper.

So when the whispers about the human dragon hunters began, I opened my ears. I learned that the Darkfrith Council had secretly sent out ambassadors to the Zaharen *drákon*, sent three strong young *drákon* men to the wild crescent of the Carpathians to seek out our hidden cousins—one, two, three.

The *sanf inimicus* had tracked and killed two of them nearly at once.

Not merely killed.

"They took their hearts," my father told my mother, his voice so strained with rage I barely heard it through the keyhole of their bedroom door. "Their *hearts*, Jo. Ripped them beating right out of their chests, like godforsaken *wolves*."

My mother made a stifled sound.

"Aye, their hearts and all their papers, their wallets and horses—the bastards took everything. Left only their tribal signets, so we'd know. So we'd know they knew about *us*."

Joséphine's response sounded far more composed. "Will they come here?"

I don't know why my father lied to my mother; I wouldn't have. She was very good at detecting lies, at least with me. Perhaps the smell of so much silver dulled her senses.

"No," he said. "No, pet. We're far too protected for that."

It occurred to me later, much later, that he'd been disingenuous about the wolves as well. Tearing out the hearts of their prey sounded much more like something a dragon would do.

∽∾

I lay in my bed in my cathedral that night, thinking about what Prince Alexandru had said. About how my old tribe believed I was *sanf* somehow. That I would betray them in the most despicable manner possible.

I had not been happy in my life in Darkfrith, but joining the *sanf inimicus* would mean striking out at everything I was, not just my kin but my heritage. It was unthinkable.

Free from the restrictions of the shire, I'd learned to embrace what dragon traits I had. I *liked* the slow, budding ferocity that had trickled—and then gradually rushed—through my blood as I had grown older. I liked hearing stones and metals, and being fleet, and being strong. I liked the looks men sent me now. That my complexion had finally gone to alabaster. That my hair no longer resembled reddish straw. I'd never possess Lia's cream-and-honey beauty, but I had my own kind of allure, something a bit more untamed. Or so I hoped.

I liked Weaving. I liked being able to escape the confines of ordinary time and place, even if only temporarily. The only thing I actively disliked still were the aftereffects from it, the shooting pains that would inevitably wrack me from my head to the tips of my fingers. The bloody noses that would leave me dizzy.

None of that was the fault of the shire, though. Was it?

Besides, I couldn't imagine why a group of humans who desired to hunt and kill dragons would *accept* a dragon in their ranks. It made no sense to me.

However . . .

Against my will, my thoughts returned to the letter I'd written to myself so far ahead, that fifth Letter Over Time. Its tone of understated discontent, which vexed me more than I liked to admit. Twenty-three years from now I seemed morose, confused, yet determined to change something I'd done. I'd spent a long time now trying to guess what that might be. Surely if it were joining the *sanf inimicus*—I'd never, never do that, but if I *did*—I would have told me. Something like that, something so spectacularly important, no matter how confused I was, I would have mentioned it.

Dear Honor, please do not become evil and hunt down your own kind.

Ridiculous.

I sighed and adjusted my nightrail so that my shins were uncovered. Even though it was September, the darkness felt too warm and I had already pushed off my covers. After dinner I'd taken the trouble of washing the powder out of my hair, which cooled me slightly, but it was very long and took forever to dry. I'd spread it out around me like a sunburst along the pillows, away from my body.

The old cathedral was long and skinny and yawning open in the middle, but lined with smaller, private chapels both abovestairs and below. I'd claimed an upstairs one that must have once been devoted to some high church official; it was more spacious than the others, more elaborate, with carved, figured stone and rounded windows I'd already torn the boards from. I kept them cracked whenever I could, to allow the outside scents in. It was open and interesting and another aspect of my life that I liked, that I had this clandestine place, essentially all my own.

The Roma bedded down all over, scattered about the rooms or in the central atrium as it suited them. I never instructed them on where to sleep or eat or congregate. They dwelled here and I dwelled here; we were like ghosts haunting the same ancient home, brushing sleeves when we needed to, otherwise drifting through our own private worlds.

Once upon a time the cathedral had been named after a local saint, but I had unofficially renamed it *La Casa de Cors Secrets*. The House of Secret Hearts. I didn't think Zane or Lia knew about it. I'd never told them, and they were well used to me vanishing without word for hours at a time.

I'd come here whenever I needed an escape from the careful formality of the palace apartments. From Lia's sidelong, worried looks, or Zane's more blatantly watchful ones.

A terrible new notion struck me: Did Zane and Lia realize what the tribe thought of me, that I was *sanf*? As far as I knew, we were all three still in hiding from the English, but perhaps I was wrong. Perhaps they'd covertly resumed contact with Lia's family. Or maybe Lia's Future Dreams told her something, that I was tainted, not to be trusted.

It would explain those looks. It would explain—

No. It wouldn't be true, and for one very simple reason: Zane would have killed me already. I knew without a sliver of doubt he would destroy any threat to his wife, and that certainly included the *sanf inimicus*.

I brought my hands up to my face, closing my eyes in relief. I was never more unreservedly, profoundly grateful that my human father had turned out to be a ruthless son of a bitch.

Someone had made a horrible mistake, that was all. I wasn't evil. I was never going to be evil.

Beyond my windows a late storm was brewing, but it wasn't raining or even humid. Dry thunder grumbled through the floors and walls, and occasionally lightning flickered close enough to reveal the outlines of the room in pitch and ice-blue, the posts of my bed, the canopy curtains, the commode and armoire.

Young Adiran was bold and brash and not yet asleep. Between the thunder a floating string of melodies from his fiddle ricocheted up and up from the atrium. I wondered if he were playing so loudly on purpose now, to provoke either me or the prince. More likely the prince, I decided. His chamber was much closer than mine.

I'd placed Alexandru in one of the chapels that ringed the floor below. Obviously, we were not sleeping together. It had been clear from the moment I invited him across the threshold of the door he wouldn't consider it. A part of me was glad for it, but another part of me—that *drákon* part—burned red inside me. Hungry.

I wish I could say I was shocked at myself. I was not. I was becoming more and more accustomed to the dark, silky beat that thrummed through my blood now. It was nothing of the porcelain-faced, human-shaped female who wore gowns and drank wine in tiny sips and crossed her legs at the ankles to be polite. It was animal. And as much as it still sometimes scared me, out of every mysterious force that shaded my adult life, I liked it best of all.

Not evil, just animal. The most normal thing in the world for someone like me, a woman with a dragon trapped in her heart.

When the lightning flashed again, Alexandru was standing in the doorway of my room.

It was like a street magician's surprise—or more probably, something I myself would do. He was not there, he was.

I sat up, tugging my nightrail back down to my feet.

We gazed at each other for a long moment. He was barely perceptible against the paler limestone, mostly phantom color, shape and heat, although the *heat* part was almost certainly my imagination.

"Did you wish to fly?"

His voice was so soft, tailed by another growl of thunder and one of Adiran's more forceful refrains.

I tipped my head, puzzled. Was it a test of some sort?

"Of course," I said.

"I meant," he cleared his throat. "With me."

"Oh." I sat up straighter. "Yes. Of course again."

"Now?" he inquired, when I made no move to leave the bed.

"There's a storm."

"We'll go above it."

"Will I be able to breathe?" I asked doubtfully.

I saw his sudden smile. "I don't know. You'll have to tell me when we get there."

The most envied girls in the shire were the sweethearts of the boys who could already Turn. I was old enough by the time I'd left that I, too, seethed with that envy, though the idea of any of those radiant, glimmering boys throwing me even a second glance was laughable. Still, I had a tender heart. I dreamed. And I sighed with the other unmatched maidens over the girls who could soar to the clouds with their loves, girls who kicked off their buckled heels and tucked up their skirts and climbed astride the backs of slender young dragons, their hair dancing out behind them as they'd take off.

We grounded things lived through their adventures, we simmered and ached as they described what it was like.

Utterly smashing.
I never stopped laughing.
He turned loops! He was upside down!
We tore through a rainbow. Did you see?

I maneuvered out of the bed, shoving my damp hair over my shoulders so that it licked at the small of my back.

Sandu's smile was gone. "You're very fair," he said from his position by the door, now sounding severe. "But you know that."

"So are you," I said.

"Do you require a change of clothing?"

"No. You've already seen me wearing less."

He looked away from me, around the room.

"Is there an access to the roof?"

"Through the bell tower."

"Very well."

He turned around and left without me. I wondered that he knew where to go until I realized that he probably always knew, in a general way, where the highest entry of any building would be. Anyone Gifted with flight or smoke would have ducked through countless bell towers, figured their way around every sort of architectural quirk to get to and from attics and roofs. And sure enough, he led the way without hesitation to the small timbered door that opened to the tower without pausing once, not even to see if I followed.

He knew that I would. He would hear my heartbeat, if nothing else.

I heard *his*.

The door had a rusted bolt but was otherwise unlocked; there was no real reason to secure it. The only other dragon in the country was Lia, and if she wanted to come in, she'd probably have the good manners to knock at the main doors first.

I felt the gathering attention of the Roma downstairs. I heard the fiddle begin to taper into silence.

Sandu's hand was an elegant shape against the wood. He released the bolt and pulled at the latch, and the tower door cracked open without a squeak.

CHAPTER ELEVEN

Thin, gray residue of saltpeter from the fireshow sifted down around us like the rain that would not come. I actually enjoyed the scent of it, even though it smarted my throat. The festival was officially over and the fireworks had ended hours past. A few bonfires still burned on the beaches, and pockets of people still staggered along the streets, but most of the city was now abed. Sea winds spun about us, stirring the litter below and that fine, lingering saltpeter above. I caught my blowing hair with one hand and scrubbed the other across my eyes, clearing them to the dark and the shadow that was Sandu right in front of me.

The bell had been removed from the tower, who knew when. We had space to stand and face each other, near enough that this time I knew I wasn't imagining his aromatic heat. The odd thing was he seemed no longer fragrant with night but with day, with blue skies and hot sunny fields that enveloped me in sweetness, welcome as the summer dawn.

"I've never done this before," I whispered.

No one could hear us, I was sure, but it seemed appropriate to whisper anyway.

"Neither have I," responded the prince, also in a whisper. "Well, not like this, in any case."

"Like this?"

"For pleasure."

"Oh." I felt that heat between us mount; it might have been my blush.

"In emergencies, of course, we . . . my people, we double up, we fly how we must. And there are courting couples. It's not forbidden for them to explore how best they . . . fit together."

"Oh," I said again.

He looked away from me. "But I never have," he finished, more brisk.

I found his hand in the dusk. "I'm glad, then," I said. "First time for both of us. Don't drop me, please."

"No. I won't."

His eyes glanced back to mine. The winds lifted the fall of his hair, blew it behind him and then forward again, so that the ends tickled my cheeks.

I inhaled once more. In that moment I breathed both saltpeter and him, and together they were delicious.

He was gazing at my lips. His heart rate had increased; his eyes were half-lidded and pooling into dragon silver, shining beneath his lashes.

I was ready. I knew I was. I leaned into him, so very slight, an unspoken permission with my fingers around his and his scent drowning me in sunlight.

Nothing else happened. Alexandru was a statue.

I leaned farther, so close now my exhalation brushed his chin, the column of his neck, and his lashes drifted closed. Yet his brow wrinkled into a frown; he looked like he was in pain, and it was so painful for me to see that, to think, *Oh, he hurts*, that I leaned the rest of the way in and up and touched my lips to his.

I'd thought about this moment over and over as the years had passed. I'd thought about it practically from my very first memory of him, when I finally realized where I'd gone on my first Weave, who he'd been. I'd imagined him hard and cold and I'd imagined him warm and tender, as a jet-black dragon and as an ivory-pale man but I'd never, *never* dreamed his mouth would be so—soft. So lovely and soft and firm, better than satin, or the salty caress of the living sea.

I'd written *married* to myself and imagined that too, but nothing had prepared me for this. For Alexandru's awakening, his sudden shift in stance that brought our chests together, his free hand rising to cup the back of my neck through the mass of my damp hair, the fingers joined to mine now a tight grip that hurt. I wasn't kissing him any longer. He was kissing me, bending me back in his ferocity, and it was as if all the air had been sucked from my lungs. I could not breathe from rapture.

I felt his tongue, my bound hand released as he pulled me closer by the waist, and through the cotton of my nightrail he was solidly male, a fine shirt and those velvet breeches and his heartbeat racing, just like mine.

I brought my own hands up to frame his face. The planes of his cheeks, the scrape of whiskers just emerging from his last shave. I'd never touched a man's face before. I'd never known skin that could be both coarse and smooth together, provocative. I thought, dizzily, *I never knew that there were so many things I've never known*.

Sandu pulled back, releasing a breath almost like an explosion. His fingers curved into me hard again; when he opened his eyes they were fully incandescent, bright as stars.

"Climb out to me," he said roughly, and Turned to smoke. I was left holding empty air. All his fine clothing collapsed into a pile.

I shivered with the unexpected lack of warmth, then swung about, trying to discover where he'd gone. There—there on my right, a blur of roiling vapor above the roof, gossamer gray that expanded and thickened into shape. The smoke curled away to reveal the animal left behind, a creature so very black that all I saw of him was the dull glisten of the street lamps off his scales, and the faint, angled outline of metallic silver that defined his wings and talons.

And those eyes, brilliant, slanting back to find mine.

I hitched up my gown and clambered over the rim of the tower railing, my feet cautious upon the tiles, my toes digging in. He awaited me, massive and beautiful, poised with a delicate balance right at the edge. As I inched nearer he held out a wing to me, just as he had so long ago in that glacial river. This time, though, I grabbed it, grateful for the support. I finished the rest of the way to him with quick, careful steps, the boned curve of silver-and-ebony arching to surround me like a cloak.

I did what I had seen all those other girls do. I took up the folds of my nightrail once more, used my other hand to twine my fingers though the ruff of his mane, and hefted myself atop him.

If I'd thought him heated as a man, he was ten times warmer as a beast. His scales cut hard as diamonds against the bare flesh of my inner thighs. Prince Alexandru held absolutely still as I shimmied into place, scooting forward until I could hook both legs above the joints of his wings, my calves gripping his ribs just under.

He turned his head and looked back at me, a long, assessing look. I adjusted my gown once more and then gave him a grin—I couldn't help it. I was here and he was here and I thought I could already taste the storm clouds above us. Excitement bubbled through me. I squeezed my thighs harder around him and his head jerked forward. I just had time to wrap my other hand in his mane as he launched from the roof.

It was almost as thrilling as the kiss.

~∞~

He tried to fly smoothly. He tried not to jostle her, to soar slowly and evenly into the pitch of sky above the city haze. But ascension required wing movement; it was impossible not to buck. She would be strong—she was *drákon*, so of course she would be strong—and he felt the tug of her weight through her hands, the pressure of her legs hugging him, somehow both arousingly muscular and troublingly frail.

Anyone riding his back would feel slight, he told himself. She had a good grip. She would not loosen it.

The dry air below them changed rapidly into humidity, and then to the first of the clouds. Sandu pierced through them without hesitation. The cove of the storm amassed miles away yet; the vapor around them now was merely damp and chilly. He felt no threat of electric charge.

Water beaded his muzzle, caught in his lashes; the air finally tasted clean, nothing of mankind. Yet he remembered, belatedly, Honor's concern about breathing. With a jet of warmer air supporting him in a glide, Alexandru glanced back at her.

She shone with moisture, her skin agleam against the purpled mist, her hair still bright as a beacon, even after all these years. The sheath of cloth molding to her figure had gone transparent. Her eyes were closed, and she was smiling.

He tipped gently to the right, following the airstream, then climbed higher, breaking free of the cloud.

Starlight, moonlight, a cloudscape below them like cottony thistles blown about, peaceful and silent. He stretched his wings fully then, willing to drift, to let the shifting winds move him.

Daybreak wasn't far off. He felt that as clearly as he did the winds, a subtle quickening in his blood, dampened now, but it would begin to peak. He'd been aloft to witness the rising sun more times than he could remember, but he'd always been home in his mountains then.

A dragon descending to land at *Zaharen Yce* was nothing extraordinary at all. A dragon descending over the tame skies of Barcelona would cause a frenzy. People fleeing, animals rampaging, the press; even in this seaport town, far from the heart of Europe, there would be press.

He considered it. Decided they had time yet.

The clouds below slowly changed their aspect, growing thicker and more ragged. In the not too far distance lightning forked, sparking light in distinct segments, transforming what would appear to be a smooth bump of violet into boils of darker violence.

Sandu angled right again.

He'd been keeping his ears ticked back toward Honor, listening to the sound of her respiration, alert to any change. So he heard the difference in her before she moved: a suspension of breath, a soft rushed release. She came forward, crawling to do it, fist over fist through his mane. He felt her face press against his neck and—God, he was sure of it—her lips against his scales. She kissed him, nuzzled him, then crept even more forward with her legs tight around him, the hot center of her almost burning, and said, very throaty, "Higher."

He must be mad. He must be delusional, because all he could think was how he didn't want her to move back, how if anything he wanted to feel those legs go tighter still, that space between them pressed hard against him, the incredible hot burn of her sex. So he cocked his wings and caught the next jet that blasted by, a sudden wild lifting that shot them fifty feet in seconds, if he had to guess.

Honor laughed. She screamed and laughed and he bared his teeth at her exhilaration; if he could have laughed with her, he would have. She kissed him again, still laughing, rubbing her face to him, and when the next whoosh of storm-scented air pushed against his belly he rode it. She screamed and he rode it, and it registered on him only a second too late that she was screaming from below him now.

She'd lost her grip.

He was a prince and a peasant and a leader of dark fairy-tale fiends; at the age of sixteen he'd taken the life of the first formal challenger to his rule, and by nineteen he'd killed three. Whatever terrible, trembling edge of fear still dwelled within him had been long ago pressed flat by his greater will to win.

Alexandru did not panic at the loss of the dragon-girl on his back. Instead, with a cool and calculated calm, he arrowed after her.

Wings folded, neck stretched, his eyes gone to slits. He heard her now, even though she'd stopped screaming. He heard her nightgown snapping and tearing around her, the length of her hair making a noise like tremendous static, like the lightning behind them. Her arms were stretched up toward him, her fingers splayed. Her mouth was open, a silent cry.

She flipped about and the nightgown ripped free. It whipped past him and just missed entangling with his legs, but Sandu had no time for that, he was gaining on her, he was sleek and made for velocity, and she was small and tumbling. He was going to catch her. He was *going*—

The sea was a white-peaked, infinite floor, rushing closer with stomach-clenching speed. If she hit it, it was going to be like stone. It would smash her apart. There would be no recovery, no second chances. So he was . . . *not* . . . going . . . to miss—

He snared her with his right front claws, the abrupt change in his equilibrium wrenching him sideways, reeling them into a loop before he could recover. The sea became a smear of gunmetal and foam, the tang of bitter salt filled his mouth and nose, choking, but then he was in control again, flinging them both higher to the safety of the open air.

Alexandru wasn't actually certain which part of her he'd caught, only that he *had* caught her, and her hands were clutching at his leg, and her hair now streamed up and around his chest. After he stabilized he peered down at her, hoping he'd not pierced her with a talon.

He had her at the waist. Naked Honor was half-wrapped around his foreleg, her cheek and torso hard against him.

And she was laughing.

⬿⤬⬿

They returned to her roof. There seemed to be no better location to land besides the flat fields plowed in rectangles beyond the city, but landing out there would mean having to figure a way for them both to get back to the Gothic Quarter somehow at dawn, without clothing or coin or anything else. He considered leaving her there, returning as smoke to the cathedral and then hiring a carriage back to her—if he could locate a carriage; if he could secure one without horrifying the horses or chickens or sheep or any of the other myriad of cattle being transported along the streets—but by the time the sky was beginning to bleed scarlet at the horizon, Honor Carlisle was already pointing downward toward her bell tower, tugging at his leg.

There truly was not room to safely alight. Dangling a live female at the same time made things rather worse. Still, he forced a gradual descent, his wings beating frantic, rushing grit from the tiles and he thought, *hummingbird, hummingbird*, as he managed nearly a hover until her feet found purchase.

The second she dropped to her knees, he went to smoke. The relief was stupendous.

He Turned back to man as she watched, still standing on the sloped tiles. He Turned below her, for her safety, then took her hand and guided her back to the bell tower. She seemed unperturbed by the loss of her nightgown. When he gave her his shirt, she accepted it with a nod but didn't put it on.

Sandu discovered his arms and legs curiously weak. Electric snaps were shooting outward from his spine to his rib cage, both painful and not; even his skin seemed foreign to him, too tight, as if he'd shifted back into the wrong shape. When he looked at Honor all of these sensations intensified, and the notion that he was no longer himself, that he had changed into something new and unpleasantly alien, anchored into his thoughts.

Aside from the drag of her weight, he hadn't been able to feel her at all in his claws, not her skin or her heat. He might have grievously injured her and not known it. He might have actually cut her in two. A dragon's claws were beyond sharp, they were harder than steel and meant to slay, to gouge both flesh and solid rock. It was a goddamned miracle he *hadn't* hurt her, but she didn't even seem bruised.

The bleed of sky beyond the rooftops became flame, and the stars singing above him began, one by one, to disappear into a rising sheer blue.

He noticed his breeches on the tower floor and

turned his back to her to put them on. He sincerely hoped she'd at least have the sense to hold the damned shirt up to her chest when he turned back around.

She'd shrugged it on. The sleeves reached past her fingertips and the hem down past her thighs. Only she hadn't tied it, merely held the panels closed with one fist, wrinkling the ruffles. Her hair stirred in long, spiraling locks down her breasts to her waist. Her legs were long and muscled, just exactly as they'd felt.

"I apologize." His voice sounded so calm; another strange miracle.

"For what?"

He couldn't help the mirthless laugh. "Are you jesting?"

"No."

She appeared genuinely puzzled, small and female with her hair blowing about and her lips pursed, as if she hadn't nearly ended up in pieces not ten minutes back.

"I *dropped* you," he said carefully. "You *fell*. You might have died."

The purse of her lips became a blinding smile. "No, but you caught me again."

"Honor—"

"And you didn't truly drop me, you know. It was my fault. I had my arms out, to better feel the wind."

He felt that snapping in his spine ratchet higher. "You did what?"

"Had my arms out. Like this." She lifted them straight from her sides, her fingers brushing one of the limestone columns of the tower, and his shirt rippled apart like some gentle, tormenting dream. "It was the nearest I'll ever get to flight. I wanted it to be real. I wanted to hold the wind."

"The wind," he repeated, feeling dazed.

"Yes." Her smile widened as her hair danced around them, coppery-pink strands to blend with the sky. She pushed them back from her cheeks with both hands. "Oh, Sandu. It was *utterly smashing.*"

He looked away. He decided to lean against his own pillar, his bare back to the stone, and let the steady, peaceful music of the limestone sink into him as he examined the sunrise.

All the sunrises of his life, all the same, with rich colors and a slow staining of the heavens, against mountains or plains or against the buildings of man, clouded or clear, winter or summer, every one of them he'd spent alone or with the others of his kind on some official business or another. Every one of them.

Except this one.

Except with her.

"You weren't afraid?" he asked, low.

"No."

He felt himself shake his head. "You should have been."

Her answer came serene. "I knew you would catch me."

Sandu shoved off the pillar. "That's just damned stupid. I might not have. Easily! Do you have any idea how hard it is to fly like that? To sustain that sort of control?"

"No," she said.

He brought a hand up to cover his eyes. A distant part of him was aware that it was trembling.

"*Hard,*" he said.

A donkey pulling a cart below them let out a snuffle. Its plodding steps reverberated sharp up the vertical walls.

Honor moved to stand before him. She didn't try to touch him; he felt the ends of his shirt brushing his stomach.

"I think you're right," she said. "I think I should have been afraid. I'm not sure why I wasn't. Why I'm not now. It's something to do with you, I imagine. Something about you. I don't know." She gave a hushed laugh. "I've been afraid my whole life. Just not with you."

"Stupid," he sneered again.

"Perhaps."

He wished she'd move back. If he dropped his hand and opened his eyes she'd be right there, more perfect than the sunrise, and he would have to manage that. He'd have to have the will not to kiss her, not to shove the shirt back over her shoulders and let it slither down her arms to the floor.

"It's unbearable, isn't it?" she asked after a moment in a different tone, very cool.

Sandu spoke through his teeth. "Yes."

"It doesn't have to be."

He opened his eyes and looked at her, her fresh and dewy beauty. He thought of war, of dragons that were living blades in flight, of the vulnerabilities of the hamlets, the crops that would scorch, the children who would perish. He thought of the castle he'd sunk his heart into, the years of struggle and defiance, of proving to himself and everyone else that he was more than just a farm boy chosen by his royal sister to rule. That he was worthy to command his species, their history, and the gemstones that hummed and preened at his touch.

He thought of the hot spurt of liquid that had covered his face when he'd torn out the throat of the first Zaharen *drákon* to challenge him. How it had tasted in his mouth like rust and lush, demented victory.

How, in that red and dangerous aftermath, all he'd wanted was *more*.

"I have an idea," Honor said, her eyes shadowed and endless. "I've been saving the Weaves, saving my Gift, so to speak. I can't Weave to any unique time and location more than once, and I can't go there at all if I'm already there—if the future or the past me is physically anywhere nearby. But I've been thinking. I'm going to Weave ahead, just a few years. I've tried it before, but I wasn't skilled enough to pinpoint the time. I believe I can do it now. And since I'm planning it now, to go there then, I'll be able to do it, d'you see?"

"What?" he managed again.

"I'm going ahead, Sandu. I'm going to slip into our future for a moment, just to see. I've been waiting and waiting. If I'm not there with you—if it's not meant to be—I'll come back and tell you. Then we'll know."

He felt a surge of alarm. "Honor, I don't think—"

She stepped back at last, haloed in magenta and russet and flaming blue, unsmiling. "Wait for me. I'll see you soon."

Then she was gone, and he was left to squint at the first dart of sun stabbing under the clouds.

CHAPTER TWELVE

I was in a forest. It was a summer forest, by the feel of it. Ferns and wildflowers whispered in blankets around the shaggy trunks. The dirt I stood upon was soft, coffee-black, and when I rocked back on my heels to look upward it sank with me, loamy.

Conifers reached high above, perfuming the air; when a delicate breeze swept through they didn't even shiver, although the tiny vermilion and orange wildflowers nodded all around.

I heard crickets far off, and even farther the strumming of a guitar, the player picking through the notes with relaxed fluidity.

It felt like twilight, although it was difficult to truly tell. The trees were so thick and tall they blocked most of the sky. The air was faintly green and pleasantly dim, and from deep beneath the soles of my feet rose the treble lilt of silver, still trapped in veins inside the rocky deep earth.

Was this Darkfrith? Had I Woven to the wrong place? It was familiar, no doubt, but were the pines this massive back in England? I wasn't certain. Perhaps it was a part of the woods I'd not been to before.

The shire had forbidden areas, places even I had not ventured to. Was I in one of those?

The breeze returned, laden with resin, and when it died I heard something new: a tinkle of crystal, like chimes. Lots of it.

I walked toward that sound.

There was no path but it was easy to pick my way through the undergrowth. I tried to make as little noise as possible but there was no disguising the scent of the flowers I couldn't help but crush. The truth was, this place didn't feel like Darkfrith *or* the land around *Zaharen Yce*. It felt olden, darkly ancient. I sensed no animals nearby but there was *life* everywhere, as if the trees themselves were breathing, watching me.

The crystal-chime sound began to ebb. I paused, glancing around me, my fingers tying closed Sandu's shirt, which thankfully had made the Weave with me.

Something flashed ahead, to my right. It vanished against a haze of deeper green, then came again—a wink of light, small as a forest fairy.

It actually *was* crystal, a cut-crystal pendant like a lustre from a chandelier, strung with thread and suspended from a lofty tree branch, half lost behind a fan of needles. I walked to stand beneath it, gazing up at it as it spun and sparked in lazy mystery.

The guitar playing rose behind me, but I still felt compelled to go forward, away from it, toward the denser darkness of the trees. A few feet in I spied a new crystal—no, two of them together—hung near enough that they might ring, if another breeze would come. A few more steps, wildflowers gilding my legs with pollen, and there were more pendants, high and lower down, some so low I could reach up and stroke their pointed tips, creating my own cascade of sound. The woods before me were draped with them now, crystal lustres tinkling and swaying, a hundred fairy winks guiding me on.

It was like a dream, this forest, so fantastic and inexplicable and yet still teasingly familiar. I glided through it like a dreamwalker, like I could walk and walk and never tire.

But that's not what happened.

I didn't really come upon the clearing as much as it came upon me. I had been hiking enthralled, unheeding of much beyond the pendants and the flowers and the aroma of shadowed, balmy woods. It seemed that when I blinked, it was there: a meadow of plush grasses and more wildflowers, a sky above that showed it *was* twilight, just the beginning of it, and a stream at the other green edge that burbled and purled.

In my dream, Alexandru stood by the stream.

I halted in place, still beneath the canopy of trees. I trusted my eyes but I trusted my senses more, so I inhaled deep and sought the scent of him and yes, there he was, his wonderful perfume of night and day. There was a blanket spread on the grass between us, food and wine upon it, and I smelled that too, but more than anything there was him. Raven-blue hair, broad shoulders, lean. A silk shirt similar to the one I wore, but burgundy instead of white, and with a cravat, no waistcoat, leather boots and doeskin breeches.

He turned around. He found me at once, and his lips turned up into a smile.

"Réz," he said. "You *did* come."

I stepped forward, glancing around us. There didn't seem to be anyone else nearby. The prince only stood in place as the lustres threw sparkles at the corners of my vision.

"*Perdoni,*" he murmured, and shook his head. "I'd forgotten how you looked in that shirt."

"I beg your pardon," I said, enmeshed in that dreamlike calm. "Are you addressing me?"

"I am." He came toward me, circling around the blanket. I noticed vaguely that his hair was even longer now, down past his chest, but he still didn't bother to tie it back. "We changed your name when you first came, to throw off the English."

"To Rehzz?" I asked, trying out the sound.

He had reached me, stopped just before me, still smiling. "It's from the language of the mountains. It means something like 'red-haired.'"

"Really?" I said, disgruntled. "That's the best you could do?"

Alexandru laughed. Truly laughed, a deep and lovely sound that sent those prickles along my skin and unlocked something fragile in my chest, something carefully unfolding.

He found my hand, curled his fingers around mine. "You liked it at the time. At least, you told me you did."

"I'm not a very good liar," I said. "So if you believed me, I'm sure I meant it."

The crystals let loose another round of rippling chimes; his smile began to fade. Through the dusk, through the gloaming, he looked at me with a clear gray intensity that seemed more than ever animal, even though he was fully in his human form.

And he was older. Not much, but I could tell. The lines around his mouth were slightly deeper, his cheeks a bit more hollowed. His skin looked darker too, although at the moment it was hard to be certain. I thought he might have a hint of a tan, because there were faint, faint, paler lines around the corners of his eyes, as if he kept his face to the sun.

But, oh—he was still the most handsome *drákon* I'd ever seen. Still with those sensual lips, and lashes so thick and long that when he dropped his gaze, they masked the gray entirely.

"Well," I said, or tried to, but my voice came out more as a croak. I tried again, stronger. "I suppose then I made it here after all. That's why I came. To, um, ensure that we're supposed to . . . be . . ." I wet my lips. "This *is* where we live? The Carpathians? We're a couple?"

"We are," the prince said.

"And . . . where am I now? The me in this time?"

"Away. So that you could come."

"Did we wed?" I asked, and the prince glanced up again with a very dry half-smile.

Well, hell.

"Not yet, but a fortnight ago," he said, "you at last agreed to be my wife." His smile grew more wry at my silence; he pinned me with that mist-pale gaze. "It's been over a year of me asking, Réz. Every morning. Every night. You're a most stubborn woman. But it happens that I'm a most persistent man."

"Oh," I said. "I see. Fine. I'll just . . . I'll be . . ."

I ran out of words. It was rather ludicrous. He was

the same Alexandru, the same person. But with his hand covering mine, my confusion of thoughts seemed blown to the wind. I could only feel.

And I felt—panicky. Like my skin had been rubbed raw and every second I remained with him flayed me deeper, a pain that was both exquisite and agonizing at once.

He was *older*. He was so *composed*. We were going to *wed*. And despite that sardonic, knowing smile, he looked at me like I was one of the succulent little fishes that used to swim by him, back in those days when he lounged on his throne in that cold, cold Great Room of his castle.

Those days that might be right now, I realized.

"Don't go yet," he said easily, and drew my hand through the crook of his arm, forcing me to step by his side. "I've brought a supper. All your favorites."

Most of the dishes were. Shallots in almond sauce, roasted pork sausage. Minced olives and capers as tapenade, torn bread for dipping. Fresh cheese drizzled with honey, cubed melon, *coca* cake. Even paella, yellow with saffron. But there were other provisions there I'd never seen or smelled before. As I settled upon the blanket, tucking my legs beneath me, I leaned over to take a closer look at the nearest one: a ceramic bowl holding a red stew of some sort, with shredded meat and a pungent, peppery spice I could not name.

"That one is *my* favorite," said the prince, sitting beside me. "*Tochitura*. It should be served hot, but we do what we can alfresco. Will you have some?"

"No, thank you," I said, which prompted another smile.

"You never have, you know."

"I'm sure it's delightful," I hedged.

He tipped his head in acknowledgment. "An acquired taste, perhaps."

Alexandru began to serve me. I followed the movement of his hands, his deft purchase on the knives, the shape of his fingers against the blanket and the ghostly curves of the platters and plates. The light above us was fading rapidly, but there was already a moon, lovely and full, rising above the conifers.

"I brought a lantern," he said, setting my plate before me. "If you'd like."

"No. This is nice."

"I agree."

He eased back to the blanket, lifted his wineglass toward me and waited until I lifted mine.

"To fate," he said.

I had no ready response to that. The rims of our glasses made a *ting* like the crystal lustres.

"Alexandru."

"Réz."

I hesitated. "*Am* I *sanf*?"

"No," he said instantly. "Never believe it."

I sighed in relief. The wine tasted much sweeter after that.

∞

He knew what would come next. She'd told him, after all, all that time ago, and then reminded him again before she'd left. And although Sandu had never yet had reason to doubt Réz on any of her so-called predictions—or more plainly, her tellings of what was to be—he found himself slightly flummoxed at this one.

It wasn't Réz with him now, but Honor. All the fine and resplendent months he'd spent with Réz simply did not exist for this young woman, and would not for a while to come. Yet she had Réz's face, and Réz's voice, and those blue-bruised eyes that never changed, that had belonged to both Réz and Honor, even scrawny little river-soaked Honor, all the while.

So he knew it was she. He knew her scent and her flavor and the way her lashes would drift closed as he kissed her. How her hands would feel upon him. The shape of her palms, the tension of her fingers and nails. The pretty noises she would make.

Prince Alexandru looked away from Honor Carlisle. He poured himself another glass of wine and gazed up at the shining white moon, which also never changed.

∞

I thought it was that the air was thinner up here, way up in these unsullied mountains of Eastern Europe. It must be why the moon seemed so extraordinarily bright, why it was becoming increasingly more difficult for me to taste the meal or fill my lungs with any measure of satisfaction.

I thought the supper well prepared. I thought the wine refreshing.

I thought.

But the truth was, I ate and drank because I couldn't force my mind to consider what else there was to do here in this isolated place, with the blanket and grasses and the languid night—and because Sandu was doing the same.

He ate with care from his selection of dishes, one or two bites of each, leaving most of it untouched. He tried a few grains of my paella and made a face, which wrung a laugh from me.

"It's the saffron," I said, holding a spoonful of rice up to my nose, inhaling with appreciation. "Another acquired taste."

"An English dish?"

"No. Not at all."

In fact, glancing around the blanket, I realized that nothing there was English fare. It had been so long since I'd had a true English meal, I barely recalled what they had been like. I barely recalled what *I* had been like, a young English maiden in my corsets and frilled lace caps. She was a child from another life.

"Crumpets," I said.

"Excuse me?"

"I liked crumpets. I remember that. Toasted crumpets with jam and melted butter to fill all the little holes. We've not found them in Spain. I haven't had crumpets since I was a girl."

"There are crumpets back at *Zaharen Yce*," said Alexandru seriously.

"Truly?"

"The chef prepares them just for you."

The unfolding thing in my chest opened wider, a trapped dragon waking, stretching under his gaze.

He flicked a stray lock of hair from his cheek with a frown. "I'm sorry. I should have brought some."

"No," I said, and moved to place my hand over his. "This was perfect."

A soft, soft silence descended between us.

I realized I had changed something then. With that one impulsive, straightforward touch, I had changed entirely the energy flowing from me to him, and him to me. And all at once, everything made sense. I knew exactly why I had come.

And so did he.

Alexandru's hand turned under mine. His fingers spread, interlocking with my own. I stared down at this, our simple union, and noticed for the first time that his hands were darker too, also of the sun. My own were as pale as the moon.

He brought our joined fingers up to his lips, his breath a bare wisp across my knuckles, the lingering caress of his kiss.

Desire bloomed inside me, luscious as honey. The air grew hot, the thin drift of silk I wore grew abrasive against my flesh, and when Sandu slanted his gaze back up to mine from over our hands I leaned into him, just as I had done mere hours or maybe years before, only this time he was no statue in response. He leaned down to me and took my mouth with his.

He tasted of the sweet light wine and, more faintly, of the pepper of his stew, but instead of being pungent now it was utterly delicious, flavored with him. His hair draped my face and his, heavy strands that clung to my cheeks and neck and collarbone.

I thought, *It's the same*, and, *No, it's not*, but it hardly mattered, because whatever else it was, this kiss lit through me like the white blazing moonlight, and I was aflame.

His hands came up to my shoulders. I felt him

through the fine weave of the shirt, and he was being so gentle, so careful, even as I was gasping and his lips traced a path from the corner of mine to my jaw, beneath my ear. I felt his mouth open and his teeth press lightly against the artery in my throat; he pushed me back like that to lie flat against the ground, Alpha even here.

I surrendered. Grass on one side of me, the combed woolen blanket on the other. My hair was pinned beneath us, and his still fell across my face, slipped between the high open collar of the shirt in a sensation caught between a tickle and something much more gratifying.

He lay above me. He was half on me, half off, his weight on his elbow. His leg skimmed possessively over both of mine, leather and muscle, the pressure of his arousal along my thigh, and then his knee went between mine. My legs slid open, and he made a sound like a growl in his throat.

His hand found the curve of my hip, rode it upward, crumpling the shirt. The grass felt tender and the wool felt coarse against my newly bared skin, but best of all was his palm, his clever fingers, exploring the curves and valleys of my body, stroking the underside of my breasts. Finding a nipple, tugging at it, pinching, until my back made an arch and I had to turn my flushed face away from his.

His mouth replaced his fingers. He suckled me there through the silk, his teeth and tongue far more torturous than his fingers. I felt the fire of his sucking, the white moon fire, lance my body all the way down to the new yielding wetness between my legs.

My mother must have done this, my father. Lia and

Zane, certainly. But no one had ever explained to me what it would be like, this coupling between male and female. I had only guessed and daydreamed, fueled by romantic ballads and books, and the way Zane stared at his wife, as if no one else in the world could be real.

This was real. This was Sandu rising up to strip off his shirt and cravat. Returning to me, his hand moving downward as his mouth made that fire, his fingers tracing the flat of my belly, combing through the patch of curls beneath, a place no man had ever touched, that even I had hardly touched, but he found the bright hot center of me and stroked me there, and I could not stop the cry that rose from my chest.

His head lifted. He watched me with his silver beast eyes, his hand moving up and down and up again, his fingers like demons, demolishing all the astonished words I might have used to protest—sparking the demon in me, aching for him. Opening my legs wider and twining my fingers in his hair.

No, not a demon. The dragon in me.

"Touch me," he rasped. He lowered his lips to mine, not a kiss, a nip, a bite, pulling back just enough to form his words. "Touch me, Réz. You know how."

I didn't, though. Maybe she did, this creature I was to become, but all I knew was that his pelvis was moving against me in a rhythm that throbbed in my veins. The thing inside me, the new and awakening beast, whispered, *there; he wants you there*, and shifted the back of my hand to the taut pressure at his breeches, exploring the outline of him through the supple doeskin. The way he stilled and then pushed harder against me.

you have power, whispered the beast. *he is the alpha but you have power over him. show him that you do.*

His breeches were buttoned up on two sides, a style I did not know, but my fingers found the way of it.

One button at a time, forever and ever as his lips ravaged me, as his fingers slowly pressed their way inside me, another place no one else had ever touched.

your boots, commanded the dragon and I together aloud, and he pulled away from me abruptly, bent over and shucked them off.

I admired the flexing curve of his back. The sheen of muscle across his arms, how his tendons pulled, the hard hands firm over brown leather.

your breeches, we said, and he yanked them off as well, peeling the doeskin down his legs, pulling free his stockings and garters until he was as nude as he had once been at that bell tower in Spain. When I had not been able to look away from him against the new dawn clouds, but he'd never noticed because he'd not met my eyes. Shy, beautiful prince.

He met them now. He held them steady to mine as I found him and cupped him, shocked at my own boldness, but the Réz-dragon purred *yes, yes,* and so I kept going, learning the shape of him, so hot and firm. His skin there was softer than anything I'd ever felt. I curled my fingers and dragged my nails up along his length, to the full head atop, the most satiny skin of all.

His eyes closed; his mouth tightened. He pushed into me again, a forced caress, but I wanted so much more.

"Please," I begged, no bold dragon to me now, just raw pleading.

"Love," Alexandru said, and came atop me.

I was aware of the aroma of flowers and grasses and sweat. Of the pollen that had smudged between us, musky gold, mingled with the scent of our desire. The tight pull of the shirt, caught beneath my breasts. The crystal pendants flashed with moonfire now, a field of them beyond his shoulders, slight fallen stars littering the forest break.

He pushed that satin head into me, stretching the place where his fingers had been. And it hurt—but the dragon smothered that, chanted, *yes, yes*, again and *slow, deeper, slow,* and I did not think we had spoken out loud until he obeyed, and I was able to crush my fingers into his arms and gaze up, alarmed, at his face.

"This is how it is," my prince whispered above me, his eyes locked on mine. "This is how we are."

He moved. It was a gentle rocking at first, a short stroke, and it hurt too. But beyond the hurt was something else, something Réz instinctively understood.

Hunger. Curling deep hunger, with the promise of a great rushing tide pressing closer.

He moved and he moved. I lifted my legs up to cradle him, a vermilion streak of flower upon my right thigh, smelling the grass and the moon and Alexandru, who captured my face with his hands as he worked deeper and deeper, plunging into me, as he ground me to the earth and began to break me apart.

It hurt, it didn't. It made me into the white fire, it lit me up and dissolved my bones. I was pure ache and pleasure and that wave that wanted to come, that was coaxed closer by his body thrusting into mine.

I tipped my head back and could not close my eyes. When my climax crested over me, when I came with white-wringing cries, I saw only black Sandu and the moon, and the bright silver flame of his gaze as he pumped his seed into me, shuddering and moaning a sound like my new name.

~∞~

good, whispered the dragon named Réz. We lay with our arms wrapped around the prince, our legs at his waist, still stretching and yielding with his slowing respiration. *that was good.*

CHAPTER THIRTEEN

Despite the many myths that abound regarding these two mortal enemies, the truth is that the dragons existed in peace before the dragon-hunters decided to shatter them.

Dragons drew their first breaths into raw lungs ages before mankind thought to mine the iron from the earth, to forge it into steel and shape it into barbs that might—might—stab through a glossy *drákon* scale.

Before spears, before swords or crossbows were the serpents of the skies, magnificent in their lives, solitary in their deaths.

But humankind does not well abide magnificence above it, and so the *sanf inimicus* came into being.

A loose collection of human clans at first, slowly they gathered forces, recruited more, refined their skills. The *sanf* shone most brightly in what we now call the Dark Ages, when men in chain mail took pride in wounding or destroying all things lovely and mysterious. All things of magic and stars.

It was the *drákon*, in fact, who granted them the title

sanf inimicus: the soft enemy, villains without scales. It was meant as both a warning and an insult . . . but the humans seized it as a compliment instead.

They were the declared enemy of the dragons. *They* had caused actual suffering among the beasts, and it gratified them mightily to be so noticed.

Their wars swelled and lessened and swelled anew; the human weapons did reap their toll. Remorseless *sanf* chased the *drákon* over continents, over the seas, yet small as their numbers became, the dragons retained their unbending majesty. They would not surrender.

Surrender, no. But *hide*, on the other hand . . . hide to safeguard their offspring, to ensure their future, to disguise themselves as their very foes . . .

For a long while, for time stretching into centuries, the *sanf* discovered there were no more dragons to easily hunt. Men who had bathed in the blood of the dying monsters were themselves dying out, until their stories became worn, thin and distant, and their lessons washed over the fresh ears of human youth with barely a ripple of meaning.

Eventually, the very notion of knights and dragons invoked little more than daydreams among the Others. Fairy tales, silly parables, nothing more.

So matters stood for lifetimes. Until one day there came a creature who decided to change all that.

Who decided to reignite the wars between monster and man, because the wrong side—the creature's own-blooded side—had survived, and so had won.

And thus, in the mad, latter days of eighteenth-century France, the *sanf inimicus* were reborn.

CHAPTER FOURTEEN

I had fallen asleep. I hadn't noticed when, or even dreamed. I had blinked, that's all, but when my eyes opened it was daylight, not night, and the prince lay behind me instead of above. I was on my left side, curled up, and he was spooned to my back, his upper arm a pillow for my head, and the blanket that had been spread beneath the food was now covering us both.

A blade of grass was brushing my nose. I think that's what woke me. I lifted my hand to wipe it away but it sprang right back. I mashed my hand over it to keep it flat.

Daylight. A warm, masculine body curved into mine, and his other arm slung across my waist. I blinked again, and this time everything stayed the same. Sandu behind me. Sunlight above. The grass at eye level such an opulent and vivid green it didn't seem real, like such a wet, heavy color could not even exist except in fevered imagination.

The stream at the other edge of the meadow kept up its steady babble. In any other place in the world, except one, there would be birdsong rising from the woods to celebrate the day. Not here, though. Not with the two of us nestled here.

"*Jó reggelt,*" rumbled a deep voice behind me.

"*Bon matí,*" I replied, and eased my way upright to sitting. I lifted a hand to my heart—the dragon there awake too, for now content—examining the surrounding forest, the misty beams of eastern light slanting through. "*Is* it morning?"

"Yes."

I looked down at the badly creased shirt covering me, that bed of meadow grass with its unreal saturation of green.

I had been intimate with Sandu. I had had carnal knowledge of the prince of the Zaharen. Out here, in the open, without even birds to sing over the dried smears of blood on my inner thighs.

The silver below us, though—that sang. And the crystal lustres too, spinning brighter than ever from their boughs.

I waited for the usual blush to heat me; I could never seem to control it. But slowly I began to realize that I wasn't embarrassed or ashamed. Far from it. I felt . . . liberated.

Sandu traced a finger down the length of my spine. He lay otherwise unmoving, only watching me when I turned my head to glance down at him.

He *was* more tan, not just his face but his body as well. It made his eyes paler, his gaze even more mirror-clear. His hair fanned out from under one bare shoulder, a rich smoky shadow across the green.

"When are we to wed?" I asked.

"December. You hoped to give your parents time to come."

I looked around at the fragrant summer meadow. "Lia and Zane don't live a season away."

"No. The other ones."

"What, the *English* ones?"

"Aye. You thought it might be something of a peace offering, to invite them here. Things have—changed for us, Réz. I've promised not to tell you how. But we both thought your parents back in Darkfrith might have cause to celebrate our union. You've gone there now in a Weave, to see them."

"But—how could I—"

"Believe me, *I* wanted to send a letter. But you're good at your Gift, despite the consequences. You were certain you could manage to be there just a few days ahead or behind today, and you gave me your word you'd go directly to Gervase and Joséphine, and see no one else in your tribe. In and out. It was so important to you. You swore you'd stay safe." He sat up, examining the slanted light. "And now, love . . . there's not much time left."

"What do you mean?"

But as soon as I uttered the words, I knew what he'd meant. I felt the slow gathering pull of the Weave that wanted to come.

I looked at him with wider eyes.

"Thank you," he said. "Thank you for coming to me. Thank you for staying."

"Sandu—"

"No, Honor. Listen now. These are the things you must remember. Yesterday was the eighteenth of August, in the year 1790. This meadow is called Sanctuary. You named it." He rolled to his feet in a quick, graceful movement, found his breeches crushing some wildflowers nearby. He dug into one of the pockets. "Take these with you."

I stared down at the rings he placed into my open palm. Two of them, gold, unadorned. Just like wedding bands. A folded slip of paper beneath them.

"I can't," I said, and tried to give it all back. "I can't Weave with metal, not even paper, I think."

He rebuffed me gently. "You can, actually. I know that you can, because you already did." He broke into a grin. "Notice how I said that so well? No fumbling at all, no tripping up on the past and present. I'm getting better at this. You can take the rings and the note, Réz, because you already *did* take them."

The tide of my Weave was a vast, airless vacuum reaching for me. It would suck me in.

Alexandru crouched down to kiss my forehead, his fingers splayed in the tangled mass of curls that clung to my cheeks.

"Give the note to me when you return," he murmured. "You can read it if you like, but it's for me. The rings are for us both."

"I—"

"Good-bye, river-girl."

And I was gone.

❧

He waited for her. He waited all that morning, as the sunrise faded into gloom, and the storm clouds puffed and receded, and then switched direction again to begin a swift, more menacing rolling in from the sea. He left her bell tower only once, to return belowstairs searching for food; Alexandru was ravenous still, most likely from all the days of constant flight—not to mention last night. He went back to the room where they had supped but the table had been cleared, down to the last speck. The chamber stretching before him was stained with colored glass and decidedly lacking in food.

When a girl slipped in behind him he turned to face her, very much aware of his missing shirt and stockings and shoes, finding her watching him with her back square against the wall.

Pansy-purple skirts, a cinched bodice, a bulky cloth napkin folded up in her hands. She had to be about fifteen or sixteen, with dark eyes like the fiddle-boy, artfully arranged ringlets of powdered hair . . . yet she looked like nothing so much as one of the peasants from his own mountains, a child of the sun and fields.

Perhaps it was only her frock. His people wore bright colors, too.

They regarded each other in silence. Then the Roma maiden thrust out her hands, offering him the contents of the napkin: a handful of pistachios, a crusty heel of bread and a chunk of hard cheese scented of marigolds, still in its rind.

Sandu nodded his thanks. Carrying the bundle with him, he climbed back up to the bell tower.

The promised rain of last night swept closer. He followed it as he ate, the slate-gray diagonal smear that bridged the sky and sea, pushing winds ahead of it, churning up the dead leaves in the gutters along the streets, plucking a host of golden-orange ones from the city trees.

He deliberated going to smoke to fetch his satchel before it hit. He had more garments there, a shaving kit, dried fruit, his boots. The temperature was dipping lower and while he didn't mind yet, it was going to be a true autumn storm, and he'd rather be garbed for it than not. He could get dressed at the palace, find a way to steal out past the guards, and walk back here again.

But what if she came while he was gone? What if she thought he'd left too, for home, and attempted to follow?

Now that he considered it, would she even return here, to this little tower she'd Woven from? He'd seen her leave him on a handful of occasions, but he'd never once seen her return to her place of origination, her—what has she called it? Her Natural Time. It was possible she'd Weave back to some new site entirely. She'd never said how that part of it worked.

Sandu scowled at the floor, eyeing the pistachio shells he'd dropped in a pile, the crumbling lime mortar laid in lines between the pavers.

No. He'd wait here. She'd come back here. He didn't know how he knew that, but he did.

He perched a hip along the balustrade and watched the storm devour the curve of the horizon, all prospect of the sea and sky erasing into blank gray.

It looked, to his eye, just exactly like an impending obliteration.

❧

The Weave sucked me back. I stood immobile for a moment to adjust to it; the first seconds were always the most disorienting.

I was in my bell tower, with the wind gusting. I was looking inland, at the long, low roof of the row of shops next door: a watchmaker, a haberdasher, a mercer. A clutch of women stood in front of one of the windows below, chattering brightly in Spanish about a hat one of them had bought, the quality of its plumes.

I whirled about. Alexandru was there, sooty clouds looming beyond him. He had balanced atop the railing with one foot up, his back against a pillar; his head had slumped forward and his eyes were closed. That's all I had time to take in before the headache hit me.

I went to my knees. Through the vicious pain I saw my blood splattering the floor, great big circles of red that splashed back up to fleck my legs.

I don't know if I made any sound. I couldn't hear.

But the world tilted suddenly, a nauseating slur of color and light. I glimpsed the clouds again, the inner bowl of the tower ceiling. The cracked wooden beam that had once supported a bell.

My body clenched, another bout of agony ripping through me. My breasts felt warm and wet, warmer than the rest of me, and I realized it was because the blood from my nose now ran down my front.

I was held. I was being carried. More awful shifting light—my head limp against a cool, firm surface. Sandu's chest.

I didn't hear his heartbeat but I felt it. It pounded through him and into me, its rhythm carving into me like a path, a deep steady drumbeat that led to merciful darkness.

I followed it so that I wouldn't have to feel the pain a moment longer.

∽◌∽

There was blood everywhere. It soaked the shirt she wore, and her hair, and his stomach and breeches, slipping slick between them. It was an appalling amount, and at first he thought she'd been shot or stabbed, but a frantic quick search of her body showed him no wounds.

It was all a nosebleed. But by the stars, he'd never seen a person lose so much blood from such a thing.

Sandu kicked open the door at the base of the stairs; the hinges failed and the wormy wood crumbled apart. He ducked through the threshold with her, dribbling a trail of crimson through the fresh dust.

Before he'd gone more than ten feet, the Roma emerged from their unknown places to surround him, to touch her sleeves and face, to prattle in their staccato, unknown language and try to pull her from him.

He ignored them, walking more briskly. He made his way to her chamber and laid her carefully atop her bed.

"*Aigua,*" he commanded, but they were already there with basins and towels.

The bleeding slowed a few minutes later, then stopped, although Honor didn't wake. Her body was boneless as a doll's as he lifted her and removed the shirt, mopped the blood from her chest and stomach, careful, so careful with the towel around her face.

From the corner of his eye he spotted the boy pretending to be invisible by the armoire, thin and avid. When he noticed Sandu's impending snarl, he ducked swiftly back into the hall.

The women found a chemise for Honor, snapped

fresh sheets beneath her while rinsing out her hair, for all the world like they'd done this countless times before. One of them had lifted Honor's arm, was rubbing a damp cloth up and down it to clean the last of the blood when she made a surprised exclamation.

Honor's hands had fisted with her faint. It was more than a faint, he imagined, it was nearer to a seizure, but now her fingers relaxed enough to show that she was holding something.

It was made of gold. He heard the metal, didn't see it, until the Roma scowled at it closely and then held it out to Sandu.

A pair of golden rings. A crumpled piece of paper with writing, speckled red on one side.

He didn't know the rings, but he knew that handwriting anywhere.

She'd been to see him, after all.

Alexandru blew a breath through his teeth, his gaze drawn back to the bone-white mask of her face. Lips of lavender ice.

What the hell had he done to her?

◦≫∘≪◦

Worth it.

Two words circling me, repeating themselves, and I didn't know what they meant but there they were, blooming and circling, persistent in the dark empty stage of my mind.

Worth it.

What was? I wondered groggily. Had I purchased something? Done something? I couldn't quite recall.

But I was cold. I realized that. So cold I wanted to shiver, but for some reason could not. A whisper began to reach me beyond those words, which were fading now in any case, distant, like they no longer mattered. The whisper grew louder, became a rushing patter of water striking rock and . . . glass? Rainfall. On walls. On windows.

I opened my eyes. Everything was gray. Even the man seated beside me.

"That," said this younger, somewhat harder-looking version of Prince Alexandru, "was bloody frightening. Forgive the pun."

I was in my own bed at the cathedral, and the rain was stinging down hard. Sandu had taken a chair from the corner and pulled it close by. He was wearing Roma clothing and looked extremely fine in it, a tight shirt and wool breeches and a kerchief tied around his neck. In both posture and demeanor he presented a portrait of a rogue at his leisure: eased back in my paisley-striped chair with one leg crossed casually over the other, his hands folded over his stomach. But for the paleness of his skin and the truly inhuman beauty of his face, he might indeed have been one of the Gypsies, those lanky, freeborn men made of sinew and laughter and dark polished glances.

When Sandu turned his head to regard me more directly, however, his expression was far from laughing. It was frozen and fierce.

I lifted a hand to my face, my fingers finding my cheek, my lips and nose, all still there.

"Was it very bad?" I asked, unsurprised at how hoarse I sounded.

"Very," he said. "Ridiculously bad. I had no idea

someone so small could bleed so copiously. I've seen stuck boars bleed less. Are you *vampir*, perhaps?"

My lips twisted into something I hoped resembled a smile. "Not quite. I've turned out to be a fiend of a different sort."

"Honor," he said, and paused. He seemed to be searching for words. "Did I . . . do that to you? In the future?"

"What? The nosebleed? No, my prince. That's what happens every time."

"Great God," he said faintly.

"Although this one did seem rather worse than normal." I touched my face again; all the pain was really gone. "It didn't used to be so extreme, but as I've aged—do you mind? There are blankets in that chest over there. I can't seem to get warm."

"As you've aged," he prompted, moving at once with his lithe grace to the Spanish chest. It was pushed beneath one of the windows, and the gray light fell softly pearled across his hair and the breadth of his shoulders.

"The . . . physical consequences of the Weaves have grown noticeably more severe. It's one of the reasons why I try to save them up. When the Gift first took me, I could flit here and there without even a suggestion of a headache. But now . . ." I had to clench my teeth to stop them from chattering. A shiver wracked me, my body finally waking to the fact of the chilled room and the wet September air.

"Yes, now," Sandu said curtly, shaking out a fleece blanket above me, letting it float down to my body. He tucked in the corners with brisk efficiency, as impartial as a nurse to an ailing child.

I watched him through my lashes. By moonlight and rainlight, the same man, the same lips and eyebrows and tone of voice. The same hands that pushed a fold of fleece beneath my shoulder now, just last night stroking me to heaven, to vibrant, ecstatic life.

Last night. Months ahead.

I'd long since become accustomed to thinking of time as being malleable, and all of us within it as unfixed as toy boats bobbing in the sea. But it was disconcerting, even for me, to know that one day, a year from now, this frozen and savagely handsome male was going to meet me in a forest meadow and feed me paella and kiss me until I melted.

"The rings," I exclaimed, remembering. "Oh—did they make it? The rings and your note?"

"Yes," he said. I shivered again, and he folded one of my hands in both of his, looking restlessly back toward the door. "There's no hearth in here. I want to get a brazier. I think I saw one below."

"No, I'll be better soon. I heal quickly, I promise. What did the note say?"

He gazed down at our hands, that odd, frozen aspect of him intensifying. "Would you like to see it?" he asked slowly.

"Yes. You said I could, in fact. In the future."

He'd kept it in a shirt pocket. The paper had obviously been crushed and then smoothed flat; it resembled a battered leaf. He turned my hand over in his—*last night, his palms to mine, our fingers interlocked*—and laid the note against my fingers.

I raised it close to my face. Without candles or lamps, the chapel was very dim.

A single sentence, and some unsettling blots of

what could only be my blood. But my eyes went straight to that bold, slanted line: *True hearts never lie.*

A surge of heat took me, nothing at all to do with the blanket.

"What the devil is that supposed to mean?"

I was annoyed. I'd been expecting something along the lines of *You Are Destined to Love Her*, or *She Is the One*, something grand and romantic. Not this, this enigmatic and frustratingly impersonal remark.

"Shall I tell you what it actually says?" asked the prince quietly, reclaiming my hand.

"Ah! Is it a code, then? Yes. Do tell me."

"It's not a code, Honor."

"Then . . . ?"

"Listen, river-girl. Clearly you don't know everything about me yet. I'll tell you what it says, and you will tell me what occurred when you left me this morning. When you went ahead in time. Have we a deal?"

I had learned during my brief night with Future Alexandru. Every second, every movement and sensation had seared into my memory. So when I brought our joined hands up to brush my mouth, it was deliberate.

Without taking my eyes from his, I kissed his fingers, one by one, and watched his gaze begin to silver.

"I like it when you call me that," I murmured. "Deal."

CHAPTER FIFTEEN

The hell of Versailles, Zane judged, wasn't just that Lia wasn't there with him to laugh and gasp at this feverish fantasia of a royal abode—although, all things considered, that was probably the worst of it. But the other hell, the constant, day-to-day ordinary hell that nipped at his heels here like a mangy, friendless dog was simply the food.

All the lovely, lovely food.

The residence of the king and queen of France seemed to be the center of the universe of flaky, buttery, savory, sauce-dripping *grande cuisine*.

The fact that he was meeting the leader of a sadistically murderous gang at one of the most bedazzling locations on earth did not make the grounds any less spectacular, or the absinthe in his glass less heady with licorice, or the *pâté de foie gras* on the plate set before him less enticingly creamy.

Murderers, as Zane knew very well, enjoyed a fine meal just the same as kings.

Certainly Versailles was a most elegant place to meet a killer, just as it was a most elegant prison for all the preening lords and ladies forced to dwell here. None of them looked too terribly miserable about it, despite the heat of the day and the fact that they were all seated outside in the Grand Garden awaiting the leisure of His Majesty, who was, naturally, late returning from yet another hunt. No one could dine before Louis, not even the queen, whom Zane had heard whispered was sequestered at her make-believe peasant village anyway, playing at being a shepherdess.

The notion of it gave him no little secret amusement. Marie Antoinette shedding her diamonds and satin to mingle with sheep, and Zane the thief donning the same to mingle with her courtiers.

None of whom, at the moment, were allowed to eat or even walk away from the banquet table because the king. *Would*. Arrive.

So the thirty-two roasted suckling pigs remained uncarved. The forty mauve-and-white iced cakes with their garlands of sugar roses and violets gleamed pristine. All the cheese platters were sweating. Seven of the fifty-five asparagus-and-truffle salads that he could see were beginning to attract flies, but royal pages in turbans had been stationed over them, fanning the insects away as best they could with giant ostrich feathers.

There was nothing to be done, however, about the ice sculptures. The one nearest Zane resembled a thinning, listing heart more than the pair of swans it had been an hour past.

He imagined that somewhere back in the kitchens of the palace was a gaggle of chefs near to weeping with fury.

It was a blinding autumn day, one of those days that had been so rare back in dear old London-town, with a sky like crisp blue linen, white clouds that never amounted to more than a few coy wisps. A company of acrobats was tumbling on the grass before the vast stretch of the table, the gilded horses of the Fountain of Apollo shining so brightly behind them the gold seemed to melt into the water.

At least alcohol was being poured. The trapped nobles surrounding him seemed content enough with that. And surely at least some of them realized how much safer they were here, at this feast they were not yet permitted to touch, than anywhere else in France these days.

Zane, who had been placed near the western end of it all, was pretending to be just as content.

He was very good at pretending.

It was doubtful anyone but the murderer would have noticed how he never truly relaxed in his seat, how his eyes never ceased to take in his surroundings. How he'd refused wine entirely, or how the absinthe he'd accepted in its stead remained practically untouched.

As far as the lumbering machinery of Versailles was concerned, the closed-lipped gentleman in the second-to-last chair was a visiting Hungarian *vicomte*, wealthy enough to dine at the table of the king, unknown enough to be seated nowhere near his fat royal arse.

It suited him well. He'd been stewing here two months already, establishing his persona. Anticipating this day.

The *marquise* to Zane's right had spilled her claret twice so far. She was giggling about it, red-cheeked, the stuffed canaries decorating her enormous wig trembling in an alarming fashion. The dandy on her other side kept up a constant patter of droll wit, which made the lady laugh harder, which forced the birds to quake more. She hardly seemed to notice how the fellow was running an envious finger up and down the strand of rubies resting upon her ample bosom.

They were top-notch, Zane had to admit. Under other circumstances, he'd give the dandy a run for it, and win.

But the chair to Zane's left, the very last chair of the king's majestic table, remained empty, and that was what occupied most of his thoughts.

He was very much looking forward to discovering who would fill it.

This morning, the sixty-sixth morning of awakening in the cramped little cell he'd been assigned at Versailles, had at last delivered to him what he'd been trawling for. A discreet note slipped under his doorway, anonymous, informing the *vicomte* that He Whom He Most Desired to Greet would be awaiting the *vicomte*'s pleasure at the king's Garden Luncheon this afternoon. And to kindly wear the new lemon-satin garments the *vicomte* had commissioned in Paris three months past.

Merci beaucoup.

Zane was not astonished that they knew about the new clothes. He was not astonished by much in general, or by the *sanf inimicus* in particular. He'd spent too many years learning their ways, and he had, after all, gone to some rather extreme lengths to be noticed.

So he was wearing the lemon-satin rig. He did not

mind the wig of expensive human hair that curled down to his shoulders, although it itched. He didn't mind the rouge on his cheeks and lips, or the kohl he'd applied with a practiced hand around his eyes—in fact, he rather liked the kohl. It sent his amber irises to yellow; he fancied it made him look a bit more exotically unhinged, just the sort of chap who would arrange a meeting like the one that was—surely—about to begin.

He didn't mind the heavy damask coat and waist-coat embroidered with so much silver thread he positively glittered, or the high Italian heels that pinched his feet, or the ridiculously ornamental grip of the rapier slung to his hip, which of course he'd made certain was as lethal as a plain one.

He didn't even mind the waiting.

He minded the damned food.

All his years he'd been starving. He'd been born into starvation, he'd nursed from its teat, and the constant, dull ache in his stomach was such an eternal companion to him now it was more friend than not. It reminded him that no matter what else, he was alive, when so many others he'd bumped shoulders with were not.

Aye, hunger was good. Hunger kept him keen.

He ignored the *foie gras* with a mixture of envy and disdain, and sipped instead the sugary green absinthe, which he despised so it never got him drunk.

The empty chair at his side remained that way, its tapestry cushions showing every knot and tuft of silk under the unrelenting sun.

He'd previously observed the head of the *sanf inim-icus* only once. It had been in Lyons, years past, and

the fellow had been hooded and cloaked and surrounded by his minions. He'd been leaving a tavern,
stepping up into a carriage before heading off to God
knew where next. He'd never noticed Zane. Yet just
that single encounter had been enough to chill Zane's
blood.

He was not a superstitious man. He could not afford to be. But he would've sworn there was an air of
what he could only describe as *malevolence* about
that hooded figure, even without seeing his face.

Zane toyed with the stem of his absinthe glass,
watching the acrobats through slitted eyes.

It had taken him years to reach this table, this moment. The *sanf* weren't a group known precisely for
either their cohesion or their sense of trust. He'd been
a loyal crony, had wormed his way in and in with absolute patience, and every time he wished to slam his
fist through the face of one of these unwashed French-
men who thought they knew the secret heart of dragons, who thought they were so extraordinary because
they *believed* in the myth, they *believed* they'd been
chosen by God or the devil or some ruddy peasant
out in the provinces casting runes and mumbling
over chicken guts—every time he reached that point
of smiling and unleashing his fury and blowing it all
to hell, Zane thought of Amalia.

Of She Who Always Expected Him Home Again,
however far he roamed.

Amalia, who was actual myth transformed. Who
could soar and scrape the heavens with *wings* and
who still could have been the better Helen, commanding armies to the fore with just her jaw-
dropping, staggering beauty.

And who had used her quiet magic to peer past the famished child who still rattled inside Zane and seen something else, something Zane himself had never even guessed was there: a man who could love.

She loved him.

All the world could be scorched and ashed. Lia Langford loved him.

She had no armies, his enchanted wife. She had him.

He sat in this chair, in this garden, awaiting the one who wanted her dead, because of that.

A pair of footmen approached from behind. He did not stiffen at their arrival, only managed a casual, upward glance at the closest one, his right hand not on the hilt of the rapier but instead the hidden dirk at his waist.

"Pardonnez-moi, monsieur." The footman was pulling back the empty chair, shifting again to guide closer the person Zane had not yet seen, the person who shuffled slowly forward between both men.

It was a woman. An old woman, at that. He felt a harsh burn of disappointment, also skillfully hidden, as she eased with her wide, quilted skirts into the chair. The footmen were angling her carefully nearer the table; Zane glimpsed a withered forearm poking out from a pink-embroidered sleeve, frail, spotted hands gripping the wooden arms for support.

The servants backed away, bowing. The woman lifted a hand to ensure her wig had not slipped awry, then turned her head and smiled at Zane.

His body went to ice. With a peculiar sense of inner shrinkage, of horror, he was aware that for the first time in his adult life he couldn't move at all, not even to save himself.

"Hello, Father," the old woman said.

Every guest of the king's feast had a personal attendant to serve them, with a beverage maid for every three and a carver for every seven. But damned Jérôme had taken ill not ten minutes past; no doubt he'd been nipping from the cognac cart again. He'd fallen unconscious and was snoring behind the statue of Aphrodite in the labyrinth nearby.

"Fucking asshole," grumbled monsieur le maître d'hôtel, eyeing Dimitri balefully, as if it were somehow his fault. "There's no help of it, boy. You'll have to serve both Madame and the Hungarian vicomte until we can get someone else in his livery."

"Yes, sir."

From their hidden vantage point behind the hedges, they viewed together the unlikely couple, who faced each other without speaking. The sparkling fountain beyond them forced tears to Dimitri's eyes.

"God grant His Majesty comes soon," muttered the maître d'hôtel. "That Hungarian looks greener than Jérôme."

One word engulfed him. One word, the only one that now mattered.

Lia.

Oh God, and he'd left her alone with this creature, left her alone in Spain with her, the younger her—

"You'll be thinking of Mother, I expect," said the

woman, nodding. She leaned back in the chair and crooked a finger for the attendant, who bobbed forward in an instant. *"Un verre de vin blanc."*

"Oui, madame."

She glanced back at Zane. The same eyes, dragon-blue, in a face so fine and wrinkled he might have walked past her a hundred times and not noticed the truth.

Honor. Honor in this elderly thing before him, a shadow of Honor's unnatural splendor still apparent in the cheekbones, in the lips.

Honor Carlisle, that skinny blasted snip of a *drákon* child, that girl Lia had dreamed about and fished from the shire to save—she *was sanf*—she was the sodding *head* of the *snake*—and no sodding wonder the tribe wanted her dead and he'd left them *alone*—

Zane shoved back from the table. He stood and the inebriated *marquise* ceased her tittering, and the footmen behind him surged forward, murmuring concern.

"Please," the elderly woman said, staring straight ahead. "I could Weave to Barcelona in an instant and kill her. You must realize that."

He glared down at her, frantic, his jaw clenched so tight he was unable to speak.

"I won't," she said gently, and sent him a sidelong look. "And I'll tell you why I won't. But first, I'd very much appreciate your help with a riddle. Do sit," she added, when Zane didn't move, not even when the king's men had resettled his chair, urging him back to the table.

"Don't you want to hear my mystery, *Vicomte*? It's to your advantage, I promise you that."

Everyone was staring. And she could leave in a blink of an eye anyway, he knew that.

Zane resumed his seat.

"I want you to know," said Honor quietly, in her unfamiliar, elderly voice, "that I never despised you, or your wife. Even now, I can appreciate the risks you both took to save my life. So understand that what I say next is not motivated by any sort of intimate passion. I want you to help me to find a way to destroy the English *drákon*. All of them, save your wife."

He couldn't help it; a huffing choke of laughter escaped him. "You must be mad."

She gazed at him flatly. A serving maid in powder and an apron and gray-frizzed wig brought the wine, then slipped back into the shadows of the box hedges behind them. Zane waited until she was gone.

"You *are* mad," he said. "I wouldn't, even if I could. Which I can't."

"If you don't, I will execute Amalia. Without delay."

"Honor—"

"No," the woman interrupted. "I'm Réz now. Pray call me that."

He paused to breathe, to truly take her in. He'd seen all manner of wickedness before. It had been the meat and bread of his entire life, really, starting from his very first memories, that cutpurse gang of urchins who'd plied him with gin and taught him to sob on demand; Dirty Clem, the picklock who'd fed and tutored him and then stabbed him near to death. The streets of London held iniquity aplenty for a child with no protection but his own wits. Zane could full tell when a bloke was confident enough to play at being vicious and when he was cold enough to be sincere.

Réz, with her stylish tall wig draped with feathers and pearls, her embroidered gown of salmon-pink with curling mint leaves, her withered shoulders and her straight blue gaze . . . Réz was sincere.

"Why?" he asked, blunt.

"Because." She tasted the wine.

"That's a bloody big venture, just for 'because.' "

She shrugged.

"Why don't you have your hired hacks do it?" he demanded, reckless. "All those poor bastards who think they're doing God's work, ripping out the hearts of your kind. *Sanf inimicus*," he sneered. "Did you make that up or just dead steal it from history?"

Réz spread open her fan, peering down the table. "Wherever do you suppose Louis is? Probably diddling about with his horse. I do wish he'd hurry, don't you? I'm quite famished."

A great wave of emotion swept over him then: hatred, mingled with nauseated desperation. Zane made himself very still until it passed. He picked up his absinthe, set it down again. The light from the fountain flashed and flashed in his head.

The old woman sighed, tapping the lace fan against her mouth. "All right. I had a plan like that, if you must know, not too long ago. It didn't work out. A great many of my hired hacks, as you say, perished underground, all thanks to a single dragon. Imagine it—one dragon, forty-five hand-picked assassins destroyed. Such a pity. It's taken longer than I thought to rebuild their ranks. I find I grow impatient. I find that . . . time is short."

He closed his eyes against the light.

"You are the only living being who knows the shire of Darkfrith as well as any *drákon*. I daresay you know it better than I. Plus, you have all those useful years of surviving as a criminal. I can't Weave back there undetected. I can't even walk to its borders. I'm ninety-one years old, *Vicomte*. I don't desire to walk. That makes you the ideal candidate for my proposition."

He shook his head. "How long have you been planning this?"

She sighed again, a quavering sound. "Questions regarding time are always so tricky. Allow me merely to say, since I was a much younger woman. Since long before I realized it was *you* who has been stalking me these past few years, the wild-eyed Englishman everyone spoke of, who already knew about dragons, who could control them with his magical spells." Now she laughed; he heard the young girl in it, the girl he knew. "You used your ring, didn't you? You used those fragments of *Draumr* you once used upon me. But now your ring is gone. Yes, I took it. Are you surprised? It was never meant to belong to an Other, you know. I promise you I've made good use of it."

"Bloody hell, Réz. If you have *Draumr*, why not just use it to have them destroy themselves? Set them to fighting?"

"I do wonder if you're attempting to be devious or are merely that ignorant. Surely you realize that the chips from the ring work most effectively on one dragon at a time, perchance two. Had I the whole stone, unbroken, perhaps it would be feasible to take on the entire tribe. But as things are . . . no. Believe me, I've considered it."

"Go back in time. Steal it before it's broken."

"I've tried. Apparently as a whole it's untouchable. A few things are. The Weaves won't take me to it."

Zane twisted in his seat to address her squarely. The curls of his wig slid heavily along his shoulders. "I can't kill them all. It's not possible."

"No. You mean that you *won't*. I confess myself disappointed. I really rather thought you loved your wife."

Blood rushed to his cheeks; he struggled to keep his voice in check. "Damn you. I can't kill them because there's no clear way about it! They're fortified in there, they've an array of defenses. There've got to be close to a thousand—at least!—who can Turn, and that's just the males! *Think* about it. And in any case, there's—"

"What?"

Rue, he'd nearly said. Rue, amazing Rue. The one who'd begun this whole wretched, remarkable game that amounted to his newfound life. Rue, who had saved him from those London gutters as a lad, and taken him in, and eventually had had the grace to give birth to the woman he would wed.

"Langford," Zane said. "The marquess. He's a wily old bugger, believe you me, even if he has given over the title of Alpha to his eldest son. I've dealt with that son of a bitch since I was a child."

"Ah," said Réz softly. "Ah, yes. You have in mind the marchioness, of course. Rue Langford. I'd heard you loved her. And not just as the mother of your wife."

"Shut up," Zane snarled.

"It's not really my concern. The Marquess and Marchioness of Langford abandoned the shire years ago."

"That's a lie."

"It's not. I swear. What have I to gain with a lie? You'll go there, you'll find out for yourself anyway. I suppose you truly *haven't* been in touch with any of the English, or you'd know. They left, oh, around eight years ago. In your time."

To say that he was staggered would have been a pitiful underestimation. Rue leaving the shire, fleeing with her husband, that by-the-book stickler of a leader with all his rules—

"Off in search of their youngest daughter," continued Réz evenly. "Who, apparently, they've never found. So all that's left in Darkfrith are those you *don't* love. Those you've hidden Lia from, who would harm her still if they could." She spread her palms, reasonable. "They're the ones I want."

One of the smaller acrobats ended a flip just in front of them, a boy in tight clothing and a sweaty, panting face. Réz and the rubied *marquise* offered a smattering of applause.

"Envision it," she said under her breath. "No more hiding, no more threats. Just you and she, free to live as you wish, where you wish. You have my word that I'll leave you both alone forever. But I need your help first, Father. I need your cunning, and your knowledge of the shire."

He picked up the absinthe, drained the glass in one shot. "I'm not a lunatic."

"I am," she said, simple. "I didn't choose this path, but here I am on it. Consequences of my Gift, consequences of my very birth. And I'll tell you something else, something I think you already know: Love is a demon that destroys your soul. It eats and eats inside you, it hollows you out, and you'll do anything to keep feeding it. That's all I'm doing."

"Hon—Réz. I've no notion what you're talking about."

"Don't you?" she said, smiling her old lady's smile.

From the other end of the garden came a flicker of silver and blue: royal bunting on poles, followed by a blare of trumpets. Louis had arrived.

Everyone at the table began to stir, but Zane never looked away from Honor's face.

"You *do* love," she whispered, nodding. "And if you wish her to live, you'll do as I request. The one thing I ever understood about you, Zane, was that you would be ruthless in the protection of your heart. Your heart is Lia. I merely expect," her smile grew wider, wrinkled, old and young, "you to be ruthless. It's what you're best at, after all."

She leaned over, gave his sleeve a motherly pat.

"I'm glad you wore the lemon satin. I've always admired you in yellow."

CHAPTER SIXTEEN

"Imagine," said Prince Alexandru, "that you were born a rather ordinary child. Ordinary for your kind and place, I should say. And you grow up living as any other child around you would. Mostly happy, sometimes not. Muddy, clean, fed. You don't live in a castle but you have a room with your own real bed, not a pallet, and parents who care for you as they can. But then one day, without warning at all, something extraordinary happens to you, something you did not anticipate in any possible way, but it befalls you anyhow."

"Ha," I said, from my place in my bed, covered in blankets and propped up upon pillows. The rainlight was thick as soup, but he'd found one of the Venetian glass candelabras from the dining chamber and had lit every candle; the single brazier in the cathedral, as I had already known, listed dangerously sideways, as it was missing a leg.

He'd placed the candelabra atop the commode. Light danced up the chiseled stone wall above it, smoothed thin by the time it reached the window; the glass branches had been shaped into snakes and flowers, glimmers of violet and sapphire blue.

I'd hung a long mirror on the opposite wall, which caught the reflection of the flat windowpanes. With the proper tilt of my head I could view an infinity of colored snakes and Sandus, each one tinier than the last.

He'd released my hand to go fetch the candelabra, and since he'd been back, even after pulling the chair up close to my bed again, he had not reclaimed it.

I kept both hands folded on my lap. The blankets were drawn up to my shoulders. It was still cold.

"What was this extraordinary thing?" I asked.

"Two things," he said, holding up two fingers. "One, you're seven years of age, and your older sister comes to you in the dead of night and proclaims that you're the new Alpha of your tribe, because the old prince is dead."

"Your . . . sister?"

"She was the bride of the former Alpha. Technically, even after his death, she had no power to rule, but she held on to it anyway. She passed that on to me."

"The hut," I said, understanding. "You were born in a hut, not a castle. I saw it."

"Did you?"

"Not the, er, process itself. I saw you as a baby. I'd been trying to Weave back to you after our conversation in your library, but I ended up there instead. You were with your mother."

Alexandru glanced downward and then back up, regarded me broodingly.

"I was only there a minute," I said, and paused. "She looked happy."

"Yes." He sighed, leaning back. "So now you are

the new prince, and you do live in a castle. And for a while you have guidance, you have family who are there with you to aid you, and despite all the folk of your tribe who stare at you and judge you and find you lacking, you feel . . . as if it might work. As if it might indeed be destiny. When the Turn comes to you at fourteen, you're beyond relieved. It means your position is just a little, a *little*, more secure. But one by one your family either succumbs to death or departs your realm, and you end up alone."

"How old were you then?" I wondered.

"Fifteen."

I'd been taken from my parents at nearly the same age. I remembered how that felt, to be young and solitary, a stranger amid strangers. Even with all the excitement filling my days, the cacophony of astonishing new places and things, there remained that seed of fear—of rejection, suffering, pain—lodged in my heart that never withered.

I didn't wait for Sandu to take my hand again. I reached for his.

"I'm sorry."

"No, don't be. I don't tell you this to gain pity. I'm telling you so you'll understand. Two great things happened to me. Two." His lips made that dry smile. "Would you care to guess the other?"

Me, I wanted to say, and bit my tongue.

"It might have been you," he agreed, reading my face, and his smile softened. "But I wasn't counting Honor Carlisle. Not for this tale. The second unexpected event that came upon me was a new Gift, one I'd never heard of anyone else having before, not human or *drákon*."

"Really?" I pushed myself up higher on the pillows. "What?"

He picked up the battered note I'd brought back from the meadow, which had been resting upon my legs.

"I Read," he said.

"Well, so do I, honestly, but—"

"No, Honor. I can Read, the way you can Weave. An utterly unique dragon trait. I Read the true lettering behind any words. I Read the true intent of the scribe behind the ink. Fresh words, invisible to everyone else."

One of the Roma below us in the atrium had begun to practice a song on his guitar. Someone else joined in with the harmony. I realized without an ounce of surprise it was the same tune I'd heard drifting through the dark green crystal forest.

"You Read true hearts," I guessed, and the prince inclined his head in acknowledgment.

"Then—you must know mine. You had me write out all those things. That was why, wasn't it?"

"That, and I wanted to see if one of us belonged in an asylum. It seemed like it might actually be me."

I shook my head.

"Think," he said. "A comely maiden, a dragon-maiden, magically appearing and disappearing throughout the hours of my life. No name, no fixed age, just a face and blue eyes and not even smoke to reveal her. What might *you* have thought, were you me?"

"That I would have damned well asked her to write me out something sooner."

He laughed, his face sharp as a hawk's in the gold-

and-gray light. "You're wiser than I, no doubt, *sen-yoreta*. I cannot be surprised at that."

I flicked the edge of the note he held between his fingers. "Did you write this? What does it truly say?"

"I did write it. And it says . . ." His lips curved in an expression that might have been cynicism or might have been doubt, or a mixture of both. "Between the words, it says, *She belongs to you. Claim her. The ending no longer matters.*"

We stared at each other as the song below us lifted into its rippling chorus.

"That . . ." I rubbed my palms along my thighs. "Is that good?"

"I don't know. I was hoping you might be so gracious as to consent to tell me."

The Gypsies broke off their playing. Their voices reached my chamber in echoing spurts and laughter, a good-natured argument punctuated with plucked notes.

The infinite Alexandrus in the mirror all leaned closer to the woman in the bed; every endless fall of black hair a sift of dark along their shoulders.

"What happened next, Honor? Now the story returns to you. What happens in our future, the one you just touched?"

There seemed no better answer than the truth.

"I live with you," I said candidly. "At *Zaharen Yce*. We're a couple, engaged. And when I found you, we made love. It didn't feel like the end."

"I—I took advantage of you? Just now, in the future?"

"No, my prince," I replied. "I would say there was no advantage. We were on near equal footing, although you had the comfort of already knowing the outcome. And it was lovely, that outcome. I'm not sorry in the least," I finished, taking in his affronted air. "I'd do it again if I could."

He stood and pushed a hand through his hair. He paced to the mirror but didn't look into it, staring down instead at his hands, at the note he still held.

"You kissed me," I said, unmoving, watching him, "and you held me and you made me feel like I was cherished. Like I was adored. I'd never known that depth of kindness or attention. You're the most astonishing being I've ever encountered. I wish only that you could have been there. *You*, Sandu of right now. Because the person you're going to be, Alexandru of the Zaharen . . . there was no shame. I'm your mate. You knew it, and you were brave enough then to claim me, despite all my flaws. I've never in my life felt so safe."

His fingers crushed the note as if it were afire.

"I did that?"

"You did. And thank you. Thank you yet again."

"Perhaps I only fooled you. Perhaps I made you feel the way I thought you needed to feel to . . . give me what I wanted." He glanced up, and through the mirrored glass his eyes held mine. "I'm not a kind man, Honor. Never believe it. There's no real place for that in my world. A kind man would have been slain as soon as he'd been left vulnerable at *Zaharen Yce*. An Alpha, however—an Alpha manipulates every situation to win. That's what I do. I've grown extremely skilled at it. Perhaps it's even a Gift."

"Do you suppose you've won?" I inquired, curious.

He dropped his gaze; a corner of his mouth curved. "Apparently."

"I'd say we both have."

With a sudden rousing *"hep!"* of encouragement, the men below took up the song again. It echoed the rain now, threaded back and forth through the pattern of the storm.

"There's something else I must tell you," I said. "Some other time I Wove to accidentally, that you need to know."

"Yes?"

"I think it was the future. It must have been. But I don't know how far ahead I went. I was trying to find you again, and I was there at your castle, but it was empty. No one lived there. I think there had been an attack. Things were broken. Everyone was gone."

"*Zaharen Yce* has been attacked by man before," the prince said. "In the past."

"I don't believe this was the past, or the work of men. Even the diamonds were gone."

He closed his eyes and tipped his face to the ceiling. *The ending no longer matters.*

"I cannot," he began, in a flat, tense voice, and then paused. "I cannot let my reign lead to the end of us. Of my kin. Even if I loved you. Even if you loved me, forever and all time, I cannot let that come to be. It *does* matter."

I sat up; all my wooziness was gone. I swung my legs to the edge of the bed and pushed free of the covers. The floor was a shock of hard cold against my feet, but it was all right. I drew up behind him and wrapped my arms loosely about his waist, resting my cheek against his back.

"I'll tell you what I think," I said. "No—what I believe. I believe that endings can be changed. I believe that time can be twisted like wire, and reshaped. And I refuse to believe the man I met years from now would put his own pleasure above duty, yet still he wished to wed me. We can control our ending. Maybe we've already begun it—every change we make now, everything we do, spreading in ripples out to our futures. We know what the English want, and what they believe. We work to defuse them. And maybe the Prince Alexandru I met in that meadow in the months ahead of us knows all this too, which is why he wrote to you what he did. I tried to Weave back to the empty castle, and I never could. So maybe that future has already been erased."

I felt his hands skim the backs of mine. "That—was one of the most self-serving arguments I've ever heard. There must be something wrong with me. I found it exceedingly seductive."

"If you found *that* seductive, why don't you turn around? I'll teach you how you taught me to kiss."

His head dipped; silent laughter shook his body. "Which me?" he inquired after a moment, husky.

"Both," I answered, and freed my hands to step in front of him.

She was chilly, still made of ice, his time traveler. She'd been washed and dried and he smelled no blood about her any longer, but she looked so blanched, her hair a messy tangle down her back, it seemed impossible she'd be up on her feet already. If he touched her directly he had the uneasy notion he'd shatter her, a thousand little shards of white-and-copper Honor at his feet.

But her arms about him had felt strong. Her grasp seemed certain.

He started with her hair, his fingers finding one of those warmer-looking locks. Yet even that was cool, he discovered, with a texture that was not quite silky soft, but more interesting than that, because it curled like a spring unwound around his finger. He let his hand open into her hair, feeling the coils slide between all his fingers—and then the sudden difference in the surface of her shift, muslin, paper-thin. A narrow strip of lace framed her bare skin from her shoulder to the scoop of the neckline. It was the color of browned sugar, almost hidden behind the shimmer of her hair.

"Have you seen my home in the winter?" Sandu heard himself ask, unreasonably fascinated by that contrast of sugar and copper-rose.

"Yes," Honor said.

"There's a moment at sunrise. It only comes with the December snow. There's this moment when the sun is nearly there, but not, and the light is lifting behind the peaks, and right before the sun breaks through, the whole world is washed in color. *This* color." He lifted his hand and let her curls slip free between their bodies, drifting back to her chest. He shook his head, bemused. "I never thought to see it anywhere else on earth."

"We're getting married in December next year," she said gravely. "That's what you told me."

"Did I?" He felt that slow, sinking intoxication gliding through him again, that feeling that none of this could be real; she looked at him without coyness, without teasing, only that sharp, fragile beauty that defined her, the elusive impression of *ice* still surrounding her.

He wanted to make love to her. He *would* make love to her, blackguard that he was, he already *had*—

Sandu shook his head again, fishing for a lucid thought. "You said you had no desire to wed."

Honor considered it, her brow puckered, her gravity undiminished. "I must suppose I'm going to change my mind."

"We'd wear crowns in December," he said, and let his fingertips touch the top of her head, lightly, hardly there. "Crowns of holly. That's our tradition for weddings. Every season, a crown of greens. Gentians for spring. Peonies for summer. Wheat for fall. But for winter we wear the leaves and berries of the snow."

"What else?" She placed her cool hands against his chest.

"Hot wine." He eased into her slightly, wanting to feel her resistance, the pressure of her palms, and as if her mind knew his, she obliged him, pushing back gently, less a rejection than a testing of the space between them. "Spiced with cloves and cinnamon, heated in a cauldron, because there'll be so many of us. Music. An orchestra, with dragons in livery to play. We'd be in a round chamber as big as a ballroom, with soaring windows on every side, the mountains purple and white everywhere you look. Painted stars above us, painted beasts, all of them silver against darkest blue."

The rain shifted outside, blowing harder and then

not, and the candle flames bowed low in unison before steadying. Honor took a step closer to him.

"And it will be snowing," she said. "Softly, nothing fierce. Enough just to rim the windows. I remember snow like that. So downy and thick that when you stepped out into it, it was like you were muffled in a great white blanket."

He closed his eyes, seeing it as if he were there, so clear: the Convergence Room draped in gold and ivory, the snow building against the blackened solder of the northern panes, because the winter winds always blew from the north. His people there, standing, witnessing. Honor's hands clasped in his.

"We'll dance all night," she said, another step to him. "We'll dance after the snow stops, and the sun begins to rise. Then you can show me your color."

Her last few words had been a murmur against his chest. He bent his head, brushed his lips to those December curls. She *was* real. He knew that. She felt real, and she tasted real, and going forward with her into this future she'd created for them would mean a reality he could hardly yet fathom.

She was going to love him. That was the other hidden message behind his future note. He was reminding himself of her first letter, and that whatever else this was, it was love.

He'd had so precious little of it in his life. He'd had his parents' distant kindness and his sister's determined guidance; to Sandu love had been a kinship of blood and common purpose, and he had turned to it enough to recognize its comfort, but what he felt with Honor Carlisle was not comforting.

It was arousing. It was to acknowledge a deep, dark

splinter of vulnerability, somehow wedged in his soul. It was to become too easily entranced with the play of light over her soft skin, all kinds of light. To fight his constant compulsion for her touch. To dream of her eyes and lips during hard, restless nights.

To hunger.

His instincts howled at him to bind her to him now, to claim her in truth. If she was ice then by God she would melt; what came after that, he did not know, but it seemed to loom beautiful and wild at the brimming edge of his imagination, just beyond reach.

When Alexandru spoke again, it was barely a whisper.

"Are you certain this is what you want?"

"My prince. This is what I've crossed time itself for. Over and over, for you." She lifted her head, her face all in shadow, ghost and ice and dark winter eyes. "For you."

He kissed her. It wasn't like before, in the tower, when he'd tried to be soft about it and instead had been helplessly aflame. He wasn't attempting softness any longer; he *was* the flame, and when her arms encircled his shoulders he only pulled her closer, thawing her body with his heat.

He felt her lips part, and that fed the scorching in his blood. She returned his kiss with an ardor that was anything but cool.

Because the winter still has the sun, he thought dizzily. A flush of color, and light brighter than diamonds across the snow.

He was beyond combing through his thoughts for sense; she was the snow and the sun, the ice and the flame. He was weight atop her in the bed, the dragon only just holding on to his skin; the man who buried his face against her neck to find her flavor there, that pulse in her throat that excited him in the blackest way, deep in his groin. He kissed her, he licked a path up to her ear and inhaled her again, and all the while his hands were finding the shape of her, the smooth, firm chill of her arms, the dip of her waist. The shift crumpled in his grip, the paper-cloth tugged higher and higher until he rolled off her to remove it completely.

She didn't rise to help. She only arched her back into a pretty bow and stretched her arms hard, and when it caught against her hair she collapsed down again, smiling.

He thought she might be smiling. Everything was shadowed, like a veil across his eyes, a sheen of desire and animal lust. She fisted a hand in his hair and pulled him down to her. Her kiss was a bite, and Sandu knew then that the smile had been more a baring of her teeth, a distinctly feminine dare.

For an instant her eyes flashed cobalt in the dark, her own dragon rising.

He didn't wait to disrobe. He yanked at the waist of the foreign breeches they'd given him, freed himself of the wool. She took his weight again with her legs spread and he came upon her in his borrowed shirt and shoes and that unclothed part of him, rigid and searching, a rapid thrust deep into her center, and Honor accepted his dominion with a hiss in her throat.

He pushed his tongue past her lips the way he pushed into her below. He felt the buildup like a Turn scarcely restrained, bone-deep and clawing into him.

He thought he should stop or slow but the dragon had control, and the dragon wanted *more* of her, pressed harder into her, exalted in her silken wet heat—and yes, she was hot at last, hotter than he, in that place of their joining, and it felt so—*good*—she was life and good and burned him up—

Sandu moaned, his mouth to hers, her breasts crushed against his shirt, her nipples hard as pebbles. She dug her nails into his back and lifted her legs to cross her ankles at his waist. He went even deeper then, lost all sense of air with it, but incredibly he managed to do it again, and again, shoving into her with such force the bed shook.

"Amant," she whispered, and arched her back again with a breathless cry. Her climax wrung through him; he dragged his lips from hers and let it consume every inch of him, and while she still shuddered and trembled beneath him he came too, an explosion of pleasure so powerful he had to turn his face away, to gasp for air or perish in this terrible, rolling dark bliss.

Honor closed her teeth on his bared throat. Her nails never unclenched from his back.

❧

We sat together outside on a blanket on the roof. The rain was done and the tiles were already releasing their tiny curls of steam as they dried. The storm had cleansed everything, all the sand and dust and dirt of the town washed away, leaving only what shone fresh and new.

I was a part of that. I was fresh and new.

Above us burned that black well of stars I'd first

ever seen with Lia. They tinseled Sandu's hair, cast the shadows of the rooftops and spires surrounding us in edged relief.

"I've been thinking . . ." said the prince, easing back to rest on his elbows beside me.

"Yes?"

"If you return with me to *Zaharen Yce*, we might disguise you a bit. If that's all right with you."

"What did you have in mind?"

"Nothing elaborate. We'd have to maintain whatever it was for your entire time there, so simple is always better. I thought, perhaps, merely a different name."

I looked at him. Smiled.

He sent me a sideways smile back. "How about . . . Réz? It's a good girl's name. Elegant. Strong."

"I like it," I said, and leaned over to kiss him again.

CHAPTER SEVENTEEN

I've met someone. A man. A drákon, *I mean.*

Oh?

A prince, actually. I . . . he's . . . he's really quite wonderful. In fact, I love him. So much.

Another cup, my dear?

What? No. No, thank you. Did you hear me, Papa? I've found my mate. It's Alexandru of the Zaharen. We're engaged.

Ah.

I live in his castle . . . we have a little . . .

Yes.

. . . you'll be so . . . pleased . . . she's—

—Lia would toss in her sleep, frowning—

Tell us the truth, Honor. Tell me. Are you involved somehow with the sanf inimicus?

. . . mmm . . .

Honor! Tell me!

—Her heart rate would increase. Behind her closed lids, her pupils would begin to dilate—

I'm sorry. It will be swift. But it's best if you go now.

—Her blood would be changing, chemical changes.

The magic in her, the animal, would be heating every cell. Her fingers would clench her sheets—

No, no, I don't want this. I've changed my mind, I don't agree to this! Let go of me—he's here! My lord! My lord, I beg you! What happened? Tell me what happened! Tell me what you did to my—

Nothing happened, Joséphine. Before I could touch her, she Wove away. Even in her sleep, *she Wove away.*

God help us.

No, Gervase. We won't wait for God.

—Lia would open her eyes, gasping, and lose control—

❧

Her dreams had begun to twist out of shape.

Perhaps it wouldn't have been so troublesome had she not been sleeping alone for so long. Zane had been gone for three months, eighteen days, eleven hours. None of the clocks in the apartments were ever wound precisely and so none would ever chime in unison; she didn't know how many minutes to add to her tally.

Zane had been gone too long. But it always felt like that.

It seemed to her that she managed to muddle through her days well enough. She had a household to run, however unusual it might be. She had servants and shopping and even lent her hand in the kitchen from time to time, although this tended to silently enrage Mateo, the cook. When she'd had enough fuming, sidelong glances and burned soup with supper, she retreated back to her own domain.

Plaster and gilt. Gemstones and silk. A missing husband, and a daughter whose growing absences were no less worrisome.

In her darker, grimmer moments Lia would ponder the notion that she wasn't entirely sure what she was about, what *any* of them were about. She'd set her little family on this path because the dreams told her she would. She'd had Zane steal Honor because the dreams revealed Honor was stolen by Zane. She'd moved them all to Barcelona because in the dreams they were in Barcelona. She'd even put her husband at risk because the dreams had him with the *sanf*, and those were the worst dreams of all. Thank God they were short; she'd never once had to suffer through more than a few minutes of Zane immersed in his own very dark moments, surrounded by those who plotted to eliminate her kind. Becoming one of them.

And he was good at it. Naturally he was, the infamous Shadow of Mayfair, a man still with a bounty of over four hundred pounds on his head back in London—she checked the foreign periodicals at the circulating library, which were refreshed every other month—a man like that was going to be very, very convincingly wicked.

A few spoken exchanges. No sight, of course, in the dreams. The words were enough.

—like this, see? You hold the knife the other way, they're going to have time to Turn.

Yes, I see.

It's the small ones you need to worry most about. The females. Remove the head, or remove the heart. It's a lot of blood if you—

Whenever Lia awoke from one of these dreams, these particularly nasty glimpses into that Other World she'd sent him to, she would have to leave her bed, and sometimes her room. And sometimes the apartments entirely.

More than once she'd discovered she'd Turned to smoke the second her eyes had opened. She'd be halfway to the moon, a wisp of almost nothing material, before she felt safe enough to Turn again.

Up there in the sky, she was protected. Nothing was going to harm her there. The city below was a smeary fretwork of light, and no man or bullet or arrow could fly as high as she. Even the dreams couldn't chase her if she ventured high enough; they died without the thick miasma of the earth to support them.

At least, that's what she wanted to believe.

On especially bad nights she'd fly far, far over the sea. She'd imagine what it would be like if she kept going. If she just didn't turn back. If she managed to hug the curve of the globe she might one day end up back in the Antilles, and if she landed there, he might be there too, waiting for her. He might be standing on the white sand crescent beach that had backed against their home, with coconut trees shading the roof, and the enormous turtles that swam, undisturbed, in the warm shallows close to shore.

Every year, sea turtles were born on the beach. They would hatch and crawl toward the water as quickly as they could, and there would be Zane, that dread wicked Shadow, guarding them from the stray dogs that wanted to come, or the gulls, his island trousers rolled up and sand sprinkling his calves and his hands out as he coaxed them forward, as if by his voice he could herd them more quickly to the safety of the waves. And then Lia would walk out in her bare feet past the deck, and all the little baby turtles would scramble faster.

If she just kept flying, she might see that again.

But that was not where her future lay. Not yet.

Zane was in France. She knew that because he'd taken great pains to keep her informed of where he might be next, and what he might accomplish. They were both excited about the fact that he'd finally broken through to the upper echelon of the *sanf inimicus*, that he'd finally been invited to hover in the orbit of their leader.

Their excitement had, naturally, taken different courses. Zane had delivered the news over tea, his voice an unaffected murmur, his eyes a feral gleam in the cool civility of the Blue Parlor of their palace suites, which had been done up in aquamarine and azure, and had the turquoise rug from Morocco spread at an angle across the civilized floor.

They'd made love on that rug, back in the beach house. Too many times to count, she'd been on her back on that rug, or he on his, perspiration and kisses and slippery limbs and laughter. She'd stared at it as he told her, found the swirl in the corner that always reminded her of a rose, though it wasn't, and kept her gaze there as he talked.

Because when his eyes shone like that, yellow and fierce, it shook her to the core. It reminded her of all that he was and was not: human, not *drákon*. The entire sum of her soul, and just a man. Who, despite the force of her ferocious, monstrous love for him, was never going to have an armor of scales or the elusive trick of smoke.

Who was in mortal danger because of her.

Stupid, selfish Lia.

She'd sent him straight into the mouth of the beast. And he had only sipped his tea and smiled at her when she lifted her stricken eyes to his. He'd leaned over the tea table and kissed her quickly, before she could voice any of the useless protests that were ready to come.

She had begged him to join the *sanf inimicus*. And now she was begging him to get out. She'd never wanted him so close to their center.

He wouldn't do it. All this time invested, all this hatred, and he would no sooner leave now than he would leave Lia forever, because her cause had become his, just as everything in their married lives had done.

He could find the leader, he told her. He could get close. And then ... he could do what he'd been known to do back in the days before they'd wed. Mad King George's hair-raising bounty wasn't entirely without cause.

But he'd been gone now for three months, eighteen days ... twelve hours. And she didn't like to sleep without him.

Her dreams were twisting. New endings, shorter interludes, more often snippets than entire scenes. They were losing their cohesion as well. Or at least her understanding of their cohesion.

Yet Darkfrith was a corpse, over and over.

Different causes. Fire. Desertion. Ambush. Poisoned wells. They all amounted to the same deathly conclusion, including the new one she'd had tonight. The one that wrapped around her in slow creeping horror. The one that had felt so, *so* real.

An old man talking, his accent thick and coarse. A girl, better bred. The smell of grass overwhelming again, of rocks and dirt. The buzzing drone of a horsefly or a wasp.

Lia'd actually felt the heat of the sun beating down on her head as they spoke.

Watch it, luv. You don't never want to go in there. I wasn't.

The girl was quick, defensive. She sounded young enough to feel guilty at her trespass, old enough to be sly.

Yeah? 'Cause it looked to me like you was just about to scale that fence. Can't you read th'sign, girlie?

What sign?

That one there. The one wot says 'Danger, Influenza' in them big red letters. You blind?

A silence. Then the girl spoke more slowly. *Is that what happened to them? Influenza?*

Aye. Every single one of 'em, dead as a doornail. Whole village wiped out. Manor house too, buggering marquesses and earls. The man spat, very clearly. *Cursed place.*

But . . . that was long ago. Wasn't it? Years past.

Aye. Years and years. Funny thing about curses. About 'ow people don't forget.

Surely . . . after all this time . . .

Nah. You listen to me, now. Darkfrith's a dead man's

land. Never a reason in the world to climb that fence, you 'ear? Not unless you got a taste for an early grave. Go on, then. Get 'ome to your mum.

Her voice turned surly. *I haven't got a mum.*

The man spat again. *Bugger you, then—just buggering go.*

❧

Amalia gazed up into the darkness of her bedroom. She did not Turn to smoke. She stared very hard at where she knew the decorative cornice lining the upper length of the wall at the foot of her bed would be, although it was nearly impossible to see, just a suggestion of molded acorns and vines and birds highlighted by the street lamps shining beyond the balcony doors.

She didn't know the old man in this dream. But the girl . . . the girl had sounded almost exactly as Honor had once. Fourteen- or fifteen-year-old Honor, or perhaps a little younger, although Lia had never heard a younger Honor's voice. Only the cadence was different, the vowels a tad more drawn. It lent the girl a refined, brooding tone, one Lia remembered well from her brief stint in finishing school: The very most blue-blooded girls spoke in such a way, those gimlet-eyed, drawling girls born of coroneted dukes and princes and earls. Had Lia spent more time in human society, she herself might have spoken the same way.

This female was not Honor. But who the devil else could it have been?

Amalia sat up. She slipped from the bed, found her wrap and walked silently to her daughter's chamber.

When they'd first arrived, the rooms that were to

become Honor's had been decorated in a theme that Lia had privately named Bloody Awful Red. The walls were red, the rugs were red. The chairs and divan and bed covers, all red. The only relief came from glimpses of the waxed linden floor, and the muddy yellow accents that might have once been more goldenrod, but now resembled dried mustard.

She'd allowed Honor to choose the new décor. She'd guided her new adolescent daughter away from the more lurid bright purple she'd seemed initially to favor, and Honor—so biddable then!—had instead decided upon walls of pale, cool lavender, with accents of apple green and seafoam and pearl, and real gilt applied along all the edging, because they could afford it. And because petite, timid Honor had held Lia's hand and confided softly that it sang her to sleep like a harp.

Not tonight though, apparently. Lia stood at the threshold of the doorway and knew that adult Honor wasn't sleeping in her bed now, harp-gilt or no.

It was the second night in a row she'd been missing. It was senseless to fret over a Time Weaver's unexpected absences; she'd long ago learned that. Honor was here and then she wasn't, and that was simply the nature of who she was. Who she'd turned out to be. She'd be back here again when she was here again.

When she was sixteen, she'd vanished for an entire ten and a half months. Months. Lia *had* fretted then; she'd wept and worried, and even Zane had developed a habit of pacing through her bedroom twice a day, checking.

When she'd Woven home again, she claimed she had no memory of where she'd been, or when. She seemed sincerely astonished that it was winter now instead of spring, and what had happened to summer? And why did her gowns no longer fit? Or her stockings or slippers?

She'd never vanished for so long again, and she'd never gotten those memories of her sixteenth year back. Or so she'd said.

Lia'd never had real cause to doubt her daughter's word . . . but perhaps there was a sliver of the Shadow in her, after all. They'd been married long enough to grow saturated in each other's ways, even the secret ones. She loved him for his light and his dark.

And the dark Shadow inside Lia whispered, *She's not away right now. She's in hiding.*

Hiding from what?

As if it were a just-right cue in a play, a faint, thin scratching came from the direction of the front door, the sound of a single fingernail being drawn slowly down the wood, so very small and furtive Lia knew none of the servants would hear it.

None of them were meant to. It was a sound designed specifically for Lia, for her dragon hearing.

She worked the series of locks without needing to see them, her fingers knowing the proper twists and turns. They were oiled every month; she made sure of that. They produced only the barest of clicks.

She cracked open the door, acknowledged the figure standing there in the unlit hall with a nod of her head, then shut it again.

∽∽∽

He waited for her on the park bench, just where he always did. Day or night, rain or sun, they met in the same place, on this bench, underneath this cypress tree. The path that led to the bench was gravel and not very popular; there was a greenhouse farther down the way containing koi in pools and giant tropical flowers, but it had a cobbled lane fronting it and that was the way most people took.

It was a wooden bench, and the slats were still moist from the rain of before, but it wasn't so bad. He was a child used to discomfort, and used to dismissing it. Up until the Girl had invited them all into her *gorjo* church, he had never guessed what it had been like to have a fixed roof over his head. They had wagons, his clan, and they moved about at will. But for some reason the elders had decided the discarded church would become their new center, and the boy Adiran was no longer lulled to sleep by the sway of his pallet, or the clopping of horses' hooves, constant in his ears.

He had a real mattress now, though, and the rain never leaked through the tiles to tap him on the head the way it would before in the wagon. Those things were pleasant.

Adiran unsheathed his knife and began to clean his nails, alert to the night sounds of the park while he waited. There were bugs and rats scurrying about, and the three-bowled fountain nearby making its muted *splish-splish-splash* as the water dribbled over the edges of its basins. A pair of toads were grunting in the underbrush. There were larger sorts of rats hanging about as well, human rats, but he knew how to avoid them. They lingered in the densest of the shadows, men looking for women, men looking for other men . . . or boys.

Adiran was especially skilled at avoiding those.

It was a large enough park that most of that sort lingered at the other end, closer to the back gates, and anyway there were plenty of places to hide, so he never truly worried. Yet when he first heard the footsteps coming down the path he tensed instinctively, ready to bolt.

But they were *her* footsteps. He'd trained himself to recognize her gait, more subtle than a cat's. In fact, he'd spent a good many hours in private trying to imitate it, with moderate success. If he could learn to move as silently as the Lady did, who managed it bound up in her *gorjo* skirts and baubles, who knew where barefoot, unadorned Adiran might go? It was a good trick, especially for a woman. He admired all good tricks.

Behind the cat-tread sound of the Lady came a new one, also stealthy, but far louder than hers. He shifted forward on the bench, searching the shadows. There she was, a female shape down the meander of the path—and there beyond her loomed the other shape, clearly a man.

The Lady heard him too. She stopped, turned about. The man did not stop. He walked closer and closer.

Adiran stood, then climbed atop the bench for a better view. He'd seen this happen before, different versions of this. He wondered sometimes if the Lady had them meet out here just so it *might* happen. It seemed like there were plentiful other places around town that would have worked as well as this bench, places that were convenient to the midnight vendors offering sticks of grilled fish and mugs of sangria, for instance. But the Lady preferred the park.

The man was speaking to her. Adiran couldn't quite make it out, but he imagined her shaking her head *no*, and then her murmured *no*.

The man's voice grew more insistent. When he moved his arm to grab hers Adiran *did* see what came next, because there was this peculiar, unexplained flash of light that showed him. That, too, had happened before. The light was tinted golden and flared very briefly, like she'd scratched a match to life but an exceptionally bright one, right up by her face, but he'd never smelled the sulfur, so he still wasn't sure how she did it. It was another very good trick.

In that frozen second of illumination he saw the man's heavy face, his cravat and jacket lapels and the slope of one shoulder. The Lady had her back to Adiran. She wore a shawl with a long fringe.

Then everything plunged black again and Adiran heard a distinctive *snap*, and the man screamed.

Really screamed, high as a girl. He hit the gravel with his knees, keening and cursing, and the Lady walked away from him without another word, without any indication whatsoever of being rushed.

"There you are," she said to Adiran, as if he'd been hiding. "Shall we walk?"

"Yes," he said, and remembered to add, "my lady."

He jumped off the bench and stuck the knife back into the waistband of his trousers. He couldn't help a quick, backward look at the man, just to see if he had gotten up to follow them, but he couldn't see well enough to tell. Since the Lady strolled on in her tranquil, cat-footed way, he assumed the man was no longer a threat.

He wondered which of his bones she'd broken.

"Adiran," said the Lady in her velvet voice, and he recalled himself at once.

"There's a man," he said. "Staying with her."

"What manner of man?" she asked, not even sounding surprised.

"Tall, dark-haired. Gray eyes." He dared an upward glance at her. "One of you," he said.

She looked very deliberately back down at him. They were approaching a more open section of the park and he could see her face, because the trees had thinned and his eyes were swift to adapt to the wan city light.

That blond beauty, remarkable and foreign, and that gaze that was brown and black both, bottomless in a way that made him feel all queer inside when he held it too long, like he was staring into a mirror composed entirely of inside-out stars. Everything reversed, and strange, because in those moments he felt that he was grown and she was not, that she was small and charmed and needed his protection.

Then he blinked, and he was a Roma boy again, and she was the *gorjo* Lady.

"What is the man's name?" she asked.

He'd heard it, but it was another foreign thing to him, hard on his tongue. "Zan-du."

"And how long has he been there?"

"Two nights."

"Including tonight?"

"Yes."

"In the same room?" she inquired mildly.

"Yes," he answered, with some force.

She was silent, walking. He stubbed his toe on a rock and hopped a few steps, then went back and kicked it off the path.

"And today," he said, catching up, "she had another bleeding, a big one. Biggest I've ever seen. It took a very long while to clean her up."

"With the man still there."

"He was. He wouldn't leave her. They've been alone together a *lot*," he emphasized, in case the Lady had misunderstood his meaning. She seemed far too unruffled by his news, wrapped in her shawl, her lips gently pursed. "If they were of *my* tribe, they would have been forced to wed by now."

"Indeed," the Lady said, thoughtful, and slowed to a halt.

They were within a stone's throw of the front gates, which were always left open no matter the hour, so what was the purpose of them, anyway? The trees planted here were palms. Their fronds rustled with a breeze that never even made it to the gardens below, they grew so high.

Adiran and the Lady stood in the shadow of one of those palms. He watched the contrast of paler gray and darker gray swaying back and forth along the path and up her dress, slipping like a shroud over her shoulders and face.

"Thank you," she said, and he knew this was the end of their encounter. She held out a hand to him. He opened his and accepted the coins she gave him without glancing at them, without counting them or testing them, which was such a violation of all he'd been taught that it was a good thing none of his family was there to see. He'd be cuffed for certain.

But she looked at him with those black-star eyes. And he didn't wish to insult her by counting.

She smiled at him. "Go eat, Adiran. We'll meet another time."

He swept her a bow he'd copied from this cavalier he'd followed once for a whole day, just to see where the fellow went. Then he took off running, glad to be free again.

CHAPTER EIGHTEEN

For every Gift, a sacrifice.

It was a concept the *drákon* understood well, both those born of green fields and those born of the mountains. To embrace greatness required an understanding of it first; no true understanding could come without tribulation.

So these creatures who were ever encased in songs from metals and stars and stones no matter where they journeyed, heaven or earth, had themselves no voice.

These children of the beasts who survived the grotesque, involuntary agony of their very first Turn had peers, friends, brothers who did not.

And these animals who speared the skies in broken rainbows of color, whose radiance was the root of legend, whose splendor defied all mortal comprehension, were forced to walk the dirt with human faces, in human bodies, because their true selves were too awful and beautiful for humans not to fear.

What sacrifice, then, for she who could baffle Time itself?

Only one had this Gift.

The physical pain was just the preface of her story. The temporary loss of her blood, of her senses, were merely the beginning of what she would forfeit.

The soul of a dragon is a wild and untouchable thing. It shines gossamer, wholly pure no matter how sullied the body attached to it.

But for hers.

Hers became touched. Nipped. Small pieces and corners torn away, a little more, a little deeper, with each new Weave.

Such a soul would shine at first regardless. Especially hers: shy and wondering, marveling at every miraculous speck composing her miraculous life. Who might even notice a few minor fissures?

But Time itself could be a dragon, the most Fearsome Dragon of all, and it *would* have its way. Even one who might Weave around it must make offerings. Time would use its teeth to see to that.

So as this one creature, with her one Gift, aged and Wove, she had no notion that she was slowly allowing herself to be devoured. All the good in her, all the shy purity, digested and gone. Fragments of her caught up in its gums, and Time licked its lips and thought, *Yes, delicious.*

What soul she had left, those tattered pieces, grew sullied indeed.

CHAPTER NINETEEN

In the early morning somberness of September 26, 1788, mere hours after Amalia Langford dreamed about empty Darkfrith and a drawling girl, hours after she met her Gypsy boy spy to learn that fate had wiggled around her determined plans and sent the prince of the Zaharen to her daughter anyway, Lia experienced one last dream.

She'd returned home because she was weary, and she needed to mull the facts she knew. She did not go back to her bed but instead to the chaise longue in the Blue Parlor, the one with the rug that reminded her of sandy feet and fragrant sex and panting pleasure.

She missed her husband with a severity that felt like an actual knife to her heart. It closed her hands into fists so tight she'd later discover blood from her nails cutting into her palms.

As the predawn gray began to creep into the parlor, Lia abandoned the chaise longue, which was of stuffed satin and shockingly uncomfortable, and stretched out on that span of woven turquoise instead.

She didn't even think she'd closed her eyes.

The dream started high above her, floating, then

plunged without warning through her like a solitary leaf caught in a waterfall. It took her down with it, took her in water and light, and Lia realized that this dream wasn't like any of her others. In this dream, she could see.

She stood beside a lane of hard-packed dirt, with milkwort and grass trying to grow along its edges, but it was *hot*, so hot, and the grass had all wilted and crisped brown at its ends, and the sky was a bleached bone above her.

The sun beat down on the top of her head; she cast no shadow. The air and the grit and the dirt: Everything shimmered with heat.

A wasp buzzed past her. She turned around and there was the fence overgrown with dog rose, and dusty hedges poking through, and there was the gate, and there was the sign on the gate that read in very big, bold letters: DANGER, INFLUENZA. Only the A in DANGER was obscured, because there was a man's hand pressed flat over it, and that hand belonged to Zane.

He was wearing an outfit she didn't know, formal court clothing, a skirted coat and buckled breeches, truly splendid. One of his many disguises, she assumed; certainly they never ventured anywhere together that required such finery.

In the harsh light of the day he sparkled so radiant with silver and pale yellow she had to narrow her eyes to take him in.

"I had to," he said to her, glancing back at her, very calm. "Do you understand?"

Lia wanted to answer him but found she could not. She had no voice.

"I had to," he repeated, as if she argued. "She forced me."

He took his hand from the sign and left behind a bloody red handprint, a stain of a shape that actually did resemble a capital A, and he held out that dripping red palm to her.

"It was them or you, snapdragon. That's not a choice. She didn't leave me a choice."

Who? she tried to cry, but still made no sound. Terror had begun to climb acidic into her throat.

"She's not Honor any longer, you know. She hasn't been for years. Her name is Réz, and we should have let them have her as a girl, but we didn't, and they're all dead now."

He was a courtier who came toward her with that bloody hand, blinding silver and light, that calm, reasonable tone.

"For you, beloved," said her husband, his red fingers reaching for hers. "I killed them all for you."

Then she screamed.

CHAPTER TWENTY

I thought I should return to the apartments to say farewell to Lia. It wasn't as if I never meant to see her again, ever, but there was no question that I would be leaving, and I honestly wasn't certain how she would react to that. For two females whose Gifts shoved us both willy-nilly ahead in time—as differing as those Gifts might have been—we seldom discussed my future. I'd been living with her and Zane for more than seven years as their daughter. It was a convenient fiction for us, I suppose, but our story was beginning to show its age.

My age.

Most young women of twenty-one, human or *drákon*, would have wed by now and even borne children. At the very least, they would have been courted. There would have been balls or assembly hall dances to attend, teas and posies and flattering comments about the color of their eyes. Back in Darkfrith it seemed there had been a wedding capping every week between spring and autumn. More often than not, the grand ballroom at Chasen Manor hosted the receptions deep into the night. I'd been to some as a girl, and those I did not attend I could still hear, the music and laughter and champagne toasts wafting over the treetops of Blackstone Woods, right in through my bedroom window.

Those things were never going to happen for me. I had known that the instant I'd finished reading my very first letter to myself.

But I was going to have *something*. A December wedding, I guessed, which sounded passable. Better than a wedding, I would have a companion. A prince. And even though I'd told myself about it years earlier, my Weaves and my Natural Time had at long last caught up with each other, so now it had the weight of reality. The prince of the Zaharen had found me, had courted me, and if our courting had involved no tea or posies, my heart was stolen just the same . . . whether I liked it or not.

My suitor was a *drákon* who perceived me without flattery, who'd called me stupid and stubborn— perhaps not entirely without cause—and who liked me anyway. An Alpha who would ask me to marry him every single day for over a *year*. A dragon who'd fished me from a river and from the sky, and kissed me like he was starved for me, like I'd never tire him or bore him or aggravate him enough for him to step back and say, *No, wait, I was wrong*. Who was ready to claim me despite the consequences, because at last he realized that I belonged to him, even though I had known it since I was a child.

After all these years, I was no longer going to be alone.

So yes, I was leaving Barcelona and Lia. And Zane too, wherever he was. It wouldn't be without a measure of sorrow, but I was going.

I would be riding a dragon home.

Sandu had desired to come with me to the apartments, but I'd convinced him I was better off going alone. He had to go steal back his own belongings anyway, which he'd left in the belfry at the king's residence. We could meet up again at my *Casa de Cors Secrets*, whose secret hearts were about to lack one from their sum.

"Anyway, you said you were eager to get back," I reminded him, drawing a finger lightly down the intriguing bumps of his rib cage. "That every hour away from the castle mattered."

We were both in my bed, both disrobed this time, with the sheets drawn up over our heads. I smiled at him beneath them, a fellow conspirator tangled up in his limbs.

He trapped my hand, held it to his chest. "Yes. But suppose something happens? It's better if we stay together."

"What might happen? I'll get struck by a carriage while walking there? Horses run the other way from me. It's only Lia. She's gentle as a sparrow, I promise."

"Yes," he said again, and nothing more.

"Oh, no," I groaned, and buried my head against his shoulder. "Not you as well."

"Pardon?"

"I should charge a shilling every time I have to see that expression," I grumbled. "That dreamy, happy, ridiculous look men get woolgathering over her. I'll call it 'Lady Lia's Lovers' Lost Look.' You know her, don't you?"

"No," he said, turning his face away from me, gazing up at the sheet. "Not really. I met her briefly, back when I was first brought up to the castle. She and her husband were there. It's how we first discovered each other, the different tribes. Amalia and Zane found us in the mountains."

"She's very beautiful," I said.

"She was."

"Hmm."

His lips pressed into a smile. "Honor. I was *seven*." He rolled over to face me again, twisting the covers, yanking them down so that both our heads were exposed. "Perhaps she was beautiful, but *you* . . ." he leaned down, placed a feathery kiss upon the corner of my mouth, " . . . as it happens, are mine."

"That makes me the most beautiful," I insisted against his lips, unmoved.

"Of course."

It was a while yet before we left the bed.

In the end, Sandu had agreed to let me go back to the palace apartments alone. I think he sensed that there was more to my refusal than I was admitting, and was chivalrous enough to let things be. We parted ways at the door of the cathedral. After he bowed to me and walked off I lingered against the wall, my back to the limestone, watching him merge with the Others on the sidewalk and down the street, sending a flock of pigeons drowsing on a roof across the way into an explosion of flight. I watched for a good long while, until he turned a corner and I couldn't see him any longer.

The truth was, I didn't want him with me because I didn't know what Lia might say to him. If she might manage to convince him *not* to take me. She'd always been so determined to keep us here in Spain. She *was* beautiful, and damned clever; I dreaded the thought she'd be able to cite some ominous Future Dream and change Alexandru's mind.

But it turned out that Amalia wasn't at home. Nemesio answered the door for me—in my jittering state of excitement and dread, I'd forgotten my key— and grunted the news that the lady had left a half hour past after checking the morning mail, and had yet to return. No, he didn't know where. Yes, there was breakfast, but only if I hurried, because it'd been set out some time ago and the girl was about to take it back to the kitchen. If I'd wanted it warm, I should have been here for it when it was warm.

As his hulk of a figure clumped away from me down the corridor I realized there were some things about this life I would not miss.

And yet . . .

I'd spent so long here. I'd grown up here, in these rooms. And it had been nice. Mostly nice.

My bedroom was a chamber fixed in time, arranged and decorated according to the tastes of a fourteen-year-old maiden. I liked it still, it was true. The colors were restful, the gilt sang to me as prettily as it ever had.

But I was older than lavender walls and flowered curtains. I was old enough now to appreciate a plain square room with beveled windows, and precious gemstones glinting around a fireplace. A canopied bed with fur coverings, large enough for two.

I stood motionless for a moment at my doorway and simply took it all in.

I'll never have to sleep here again. I'll never have to stay trapped in here, afraid of my Weaves, ever again.

I found my valise and packed swiftly. It wasn't very large, and I could fit only three gowns into it, but I knew I'd have to hug it to me the entire time I was atop Sandu's back, plus his own satchel. Possibly he could carry them both in his talons or teeth, but I imagined that would be cumbersome. He'd already have a person sitting astride him for days. I'd hold the luggage if I could.

When I'd crammed everything in that I could and still get it closed, I went to my writing desk, pulled back my chair. I had a stack of paper and a penwork box I kept in a drawer, and to my great surprise the ink inside it was still wet.

I dipped the quill, brushed the tip of the feather under my chin, thinking, and then began to write.

Dearest Lia,

Thank you for my life. I know if Kindness and Grace dwell within me at all, they sprang from you. You have been a truly Excellent Mother. I pray you'll be pleased to know that it is through you I've found I can Love.

His name is Alexandru, and he is the Alpha of the Zaharen. You know him, and you know the castle. I hope you come to visit us there. ~~I hope you find a mate who~~
I hope you can be happy.

Your daughter,
—H.

It seemed acceptable. I wondered suddenly what Sandu would Read in it were he here, and was doubly glad he wasn't.

In our years ahead I was going to have to be very careful about my writing, I supposed. It was an unnerving thought, to realize that someone might know more of me than *I* did, just from a few scribbled words, even if that someone was my mate.

I sanded the note, folded it, and stood up to slip it under her door, or perhaps her pillow. But as I stood my hand brushed the stack of virgin paper before me; the sheets skidded sideways across the surface of the desk and ruffled down to the floor.

"Blast."

I bent to scoop them back up, careless. But as I bent down, I noticed one of the sheets wasn't virgin. It had writing on it. My handwriting.

I pulled it free of the rest and stared at it. A beam of sunlight falling across my hands made the letters appear bluish purple.

R.,

You are with child. Don't wait for Lia. Just go.

—R.

All the pages fell free of my numbed fingers, a soft papery rustle that blanketed the rug and the hem of my skirts, and in that brilliant splash of light, they shone like fresh fallen snow.

I decided not to tell him.

Perchance it wasn't true. Perchance it was true when I wrote it *then*, in the future, but it wasn't now; I was in a different ripple of time now. It seemed too enormous to comprehend. I felt no different than I had yesterday, or the day before, except for that nervous, thrilling energy that zinged through my limbs, and the more sensual awareness that I had been with a man, and so I actually *wasn't* the same.

Perchance it wasn't true.

But the dragon in my heart knew that it was.

Things had changed for us. That's what Future Sandu had told me. Things had changed, and Future Honor—Réz—thought our English parents would have cause to celebrate it, enough so that she would risk her life returning to the shire.

Gervase and Joséphine might celebrate a grandchild.

A flutter of panic began to bloom within me. It was too soon, I told myself. Too soon for this.

I hadn't wanted a mate, but I had one. I hadn't dreamed of drowning in love, but it appeared I was going to anyway.

But this. A baby, on top of everything else . . .

A strange laugh forced its way past my lips. I wasn't even certain whose child it would be, the prince who'd deflowered me or the one I was about to run away with. Did it even matter?

I crumpled the paper in my fist. I looked around, found a lamp that had been left burning, removed the glass and held the edge of the note over the flame until it caught.

The last smoking bits singed my fingers; I shook

them clear. The ash fell pale and feathery, dusting the table beneath in flakes.

A voice called from beyond my closed door; it was the maid. *"Senyoreta?"*

"Yes."

"Did you wish for a breakfast tray?"

I looked up. "Are there crumpets?"

A pause. "I'm sorry—are there what?"

"Never mind," I said, without turning around. "No breakfast today. I'm going out."

"Yes, *senyoreta*."

Before I left the room, I swiped my hand through the air above the ashes, and scattered the flakes to the floor.

CHAPTER TWENTY-ONE

Along the white-cliffed coast of southern France, not too distant from the city of Marseilles, was a series of caves that had once sheltered dragons, and then humans, and then eventually no one at all, because as the aeons had passed their entrances became submerged beneath the enameled blue Mediterranean. Accessing these caves now required the ability to swim to great depths, and to discern which sort of darkness between the limestone stalactite teeth might eventually lead to a space with a bubble of ancient air trapped inside it, and which might just lead to more water.

Within the greatest of these caves, one with an entrance tunnel that sloped sharply upward and so was spared the worst of the sea's invasion, was a cavern large enough for a tall man to stand fully upright. The walls were curved and covered in images: primitive handprints outlined in black and red, simple drawings of bison, horses, fish. There were even scattered depictions of what might have been, to one who didn't know better, curling snakes with talons and wide open wings.

And there was a box.

It was a modern sort of box, nothing natural to the cave. It was composed of oiled wood with gold metal hinges and brads, because she'd known that gold would never rust, not even under the sea. Inside the box was a silk bag with a drawstring cord, and inside the bag was a pendant, heart-shaped, made of silver. The silver was tarnishing, and there was nothing to be done about that. But embedded in it, as brilliant and evil as the day they had first been set, was a series of sky-blue diamond shards: the last known fragments of *Draumr*.

The box had been placed in the cave five years earlier, just because.

Because Lia had always known the future was an untrustworthy thing.

Because the gambler in her, the wily dragon, demanded a plan of last resort.

And because all the other pieces of the diamond, which had been in Zane's ring, had mysteriously vanished, and she would not risk these vanishing too.

Lia flew past the cave on her way to Paris. If she cocked her head and listened very hard, she could hear the lure of the shards, their soft broken calling to her that felt—for a perilous few seconds—like the *most urgent yearning ever*, even with miles of air and sea stretching between them.

She flattened her ears. She winged higher, putting more distance between her and the cave.

She'd retrieve the box on her way back.

He was dreaming.

Strange, because he seldom dreamed. He was not

the dreamer of the family; he was the more practical hand and voice, the procurer of life's necessities, of all tangible things great and small. But tonight he was dreaming.

He must have been, although to Zane's best recollection he was actually stealing through the chambers of the palace of Versailles, moving silently from room to room, because it wasn't yet dawn, and he could not reasonably summon his coach and depart before then without raising unnecessary conjecture.

It was never in Zane's best interest to arouse conjecture.

He'd been unable to sleep. His waking mind had become mired in a loop of exhaustive unpleasantness, of tactical arson and bullets, and how many men it would take to flush and ambush a sleeping English village, and how much coin it would take to ensure their utter silence, and what to do about the smoke that would rise and disguise what wasn't smoke—

He could not sleep. He needed to leave, and he could not sleep, and so he *thought* he'd been exercising one of his very best skills as a distraction: prowling.

He'd wound his way out of the wing of Unpleasant Cells, where most of the official visitors to the king and queen were housed. He'd passed, unseen, footmen nodding off at doorways, and hall-boys flopped about on beds of blankets, their livery and wigs and shoes all placed prudently near to their heads as they dozed.

Padded rugs were better for prowling than bare wooden floors, or—worst of all—marble tiles, so he'd been aiming for those, sliding from salon to salon, most of them unlit, looking close at paintings and sculptures, the intricate gilded friezes, mentally estimating the weight of the chandeliers, or the cost of the ivory and malachite inlay along the walls. There was an entire long gallery of mirrors that had been done up in nothing but real silver: silver chairs, silver pedestals and urns, silver tables, silver cherubs hoisting silver-dipped candles—if he hadn't been so rotten sure his luggage would be searched upon leaving, he might have lessened the unspeakable extravagance of the place a fraction.

As if anyone but the servants would have noticed.

He'd left the gallery of silver untouched. He was in another salon, one of those named after the Roman gods; he could never keep them all straight. He was standing stock-still and looking out the window at the starlit expanse of one of the gardens, and it was at that particular moment that Zane realized he was dreaming, because there was a mist of smoke against the panes, inexplicable smoke, not from a fire at all. It pressed against the glass and found a weakness, some chip in a panel, perhaps. And it poured into the salon and became his wife.

His wife.

He did not move. He only stood there and tipped his head and looked at her, lovely naked Lia, standing motionless as well with a particularly large and saccharine portrait of Diana with a stag hung behind her back.

The name of the room popped into his head. *Salon de Diane.* Of course.

"Awake?" murmured his wife, with an expression on her face he couldn't quite peg.

"Perhaps," he answered, careful. "You?"

"Oh, yes. Bad dreams."

"Snapdragon." He did awaken, then. She was here, *here*, and not held hostage by a murderous madwoman—

He went to her on his silent feet, his hands at her shoulders, gathering her hard into his embrace. And for a flicker of a second, everything was *right*, just as it had always been. She fit snug against him and her arms lifted to hold him back, and her hair smelled like wonderful summer roses, and he was so goddamned happy to just have her with him again he felt a burning prickle behind his eyelids that threatened to become something more, something entirely ill-suited to a hard-grown criminal.

But . . . there was a resistance to her he'd not felt before, or at least not for a very long while. A definite lack of the trusting pliancy that usually defined her.

It sent a chill down his spine and brought forth another unexpected thought: *She knows*.

Instead of acknowledging that chill, or even worse, that subtle menacing thought, Zane opened his hands upon the smooth flat of her back and took another breath of roses. Then he released her.

"Did you tell her you were coming here?"

Lia watched him steadily, her hands at her sides. She didn't bother to ask who he meant, and the chill bit into him deeper. "No."

He lowered his voice and spoke very quickly; he wasn't certain they were alone any longer; he wasn't certain of that at all. "Good. Listen. I need you to evaporate for a while. Whatever you do, don't return to

Barcelona. Go—go home to the beach house. I don't think she knows about it, we never told her, and—"

"Where will you be, Zane?"

The palace was still and silent, holding its breath, as soundless a place as he'd ever heard.

He took both her hands and drew her back to the wall, to the darkest of the shadows. A basalt bust of a crowned Caesar in a toga smirked at them from its pedestal.

"Zane."

His wife gazed up at him, ignoring the garish chamber and the bust and everything but him, and when she blinked at him—the slow, lazy blink of a predator arising—her eyes had gone to liquid gold.

"Amalia," he whispered, helpless.

"Where do you plan to be?" she asked again, cool and calm despite that gaze.

"Where I must," he replied.

Very deliberately, she freed her hands from his. "I had a dream."

"She is *here*," he all but hissed at her, desperate. "Do you understand me? She's here somewhere, lurking, and every day she finds me and dangles your life like a carrot on a stick in front of me, and god*damn* it, Lia, what do you *think* I'm going to do? She's a Time Weaver! She can be anywhere, any *time*. You'll never be safe from her unless I act!"

"No," she said.

"You don't know her now. You don't know who she is. This isn't your precious Honor, this is a beast named Réz, and all she wants—" He stopped himself, forced himself to draw a measured breath. He feared that his hands might be shaking with emotion and so clasped them behind his back, so she wouldn't see.

Lia only waited.

"I love you," Zane said. "You know that."

"I love you as well," his wife murmured to him. "But if you move to harm my family, I'll have to kill you. Surely you know that that would kill *me*."

He stared at her, dumbfounded.

"Where is the gain in that?" she added, composed. "I speak to the thief now, to the clever Shadow who never risks without gain. Your death would mean mine. I will not live in this world without you."

Love is a demon that destroys your soul. It eats and eats inside you, it hollows you out, and you'll do anything to keep feeding it.

He was breathing hard through his nose, unable to dig free the words to reason with her or bully her or just flat-out plead with her to go. Violence trembled at the edge of his fingers, half-formed, crazed notions, knock her out, trundle her away, keep her hooded, hidden, safe—

"Go to the beach house," she said.

He shook his head.

"You were right, she doesn't know about it. Go there, straight there, and I will find you."

He unlocked his jaw. "Absolutely not."

"Zane," she said, and smiled at him, still with those unholy glowing eyes. "I have a plan. But it won't work if you muck it up."

"I *never* muck it up—"

"If you go north, toward England, I'll know. If you go south, toward Spain, I'll know. If you go any direction but due west, I'll know. I'll take it as an act of war."

Shit.

"Please," said the creature with the unholy eyes, sounding just like his kindhearted and marvelous wife. "Please go west. If you do love me at all—"

"Stop it. Stop."

"At all," she continued firmly, "you'll listen to me now. You'll trust me."

He sank down into a squat with his back against the silk-and-velvet wall, unable to look at her any longer. He dropped his head into his arms and closed his eyes.

The palace, breathing, and then the sound of her kneeling down before him. Her fingers stroking his hair.

"Beautiful thief," she whispered. "My steady heart. I've missed you so much."

"You've a bloody odd way of showing it," he mumbled to the floor, "what with the threatening to kill me and all."

He could not see her smile but he imagined it, small and slightly sad. He felt her lips against his temple, cool as the night.

"And my God," he went on, aggrieved, not moving or relenting, "have you any idea how *hungry* I am here? How hungry I've been every sodding day?"

"Me too." Her lips found the top of his forehead; her hands slipped down to his shoulders. "I've been hungry too."

If he opened his eyes again she'd be back to herself. That's what he would believe. Back to her human self, with brown eyes, not gold, and he would lift his face and kiss her back, and then he would end up making love to his wife right here in the Salon of Diana, on the king of France's plush teal-and-orchid rug, and to hell with the entire rest of the world. He would.

Zane looked up. Lia knelt before him, her small smile still in place, her gaze that rich and familiar deep brown. Her palms cupped his cheeks.

He reached for her. He sank down the rest of the way to the floor and pulled her between his legs at the same time, all notion of restraint abandoned with the feel of her waist beneath his fingers, the teasing brush of her hair against his neck.

She tasted of summer, too; a soft evening in the countryside, a slow flowing river, nightflowers with exotic perfumes and petals that unfurled beneath the silvered light of the moon. He drew up his knees to better capture her, his fingers curving into her, urging her closer. Lia complied, her head above his, her lips stroking, retreating, her tongue gliding against his.

He cupped her breasts in his hands, his thumbs working at her nipples, teasing them into peaks. They were full and heavy and by heavens he'd grieved for this so much—grieved for her while they were apart, all of her, and now he *was* tearing some. Just some, faint moisture around his eyes that she found and kissed away with a breathless small moan of commiseration.

I love you, he wanted to say again, but he didn't need to, because every atom in his body sang it for him.

I love you, and her hands were at the buttons of his breeches, nimble fingers freeing him, and oh, she knew exactly what to do. Her stroking, her succulent lips, and he was arching into her, helpless once more, as she caressed him and kissed him at the same time.

Love you, as his magical wife crouched over him and lowered herself onto him, and Zane used the wall to brace them both as he held her at the hips and pushed up higher into her, his heels digging into the rug, straining for more.

More of her, more of this, this nearly unbearable sensation of Amalia wrapped around him, her legs spread wide over his, her face tipped back now, that breathless sound returning.

He knew her, knew her in every way. He knew exactly what she needed, and gave it to her, freeing one hand to find her place, his fingertips stroking, then gently pinching her, and when her movements grew more frantic and she clenched above him he covered her mouth with his other hand, muffling her cry.

But it did him in, too. As she shuddered and came down on him hard and deep one final time he lost control, and let the pleasure sling through him so violently it was closer to pain.

It was always like this, so very good. She was always so good, and he adored it, every shameless, unkempt, ravishing-her-in-the-king's-salon second of it. He adored her.

He turned his face to the side and brushed his lips across her nipple, a flick of his tongue that had it hardened again instantly, delightful against his face.

"We'll go to the beach house together" he meant to say, only it came out as more of a guttural gasp against her breast. "You and me. Right now. Forget everything else, everyone. We'll leave Europe and never return."

She bent her head to rest on top of his, and strands of her hair caught in his eyelashes.

"My lady." He brushed away the strands. "What say you? We'll start over. No one'll ever find us again."

She stroked a finger down his cheek.

"Peru," he offered, into her silence. "The Japanese Islands. Ceylon, Cape Horn. Wherever you like."

"Go to the beach house" was what she finally said, very soft. "Await me there."

"Whatever this plan is you have, I'm coming with you. You know that."

"No. I'm faster without you."

He pushed her back with his hands hard on her upper arms, scowling up into her face. Frescoes on the ceiling behind her depicted lazing men and voluptuous women, floating scarves entwining around them all like silken chains.

"Let us be serious a moment."

"I'm dead serious."

"As am I. You're not the villain here, admit it. If you've a plan, tell me about it. I'll make it better, you know I will."

"There's no time."

"Lia, you haven't seen her. Not like this. I swear to you right now, she's no one you can manage."

"She's my daughter."

He struggled to sit up higher. "Not any longer!"

"That never changes. Hearts don't change." She gave him that melancholy smile, lifting free of him.

"Now, wait—"

"Do you remember the turtles?" she whispered. "The baby turtles on the beach?"

"What?" he said, still holding her arms, absurdly close to tears again.

"I *will* meet you there." She leaned down for another kiss. "I love you so. Go west."

Before he could breathe another breath, before his heart could pass through another beat, she'd Turned to smoke. He was left cold and alone on the floor, watching the tendrils of the only being in his godforsaken life who gave a damn about him slither back through the windowpane and siphon up into the starred navy sky.

CHAPTER TWENTY-TWO

As it so happened, Sandu and I fit together very well indeed.

I smiled to myself as I recalled what he'd told me about the courting Zaharen couples, how they might take flight together to see how they'd fit.

I wasn't sure if he'd meant it literally, or if that was his charming, European way of not mentioning the word *sex*, but whenever I was atop his glimmering back, it felt like I'd been made to be there. We fit.

In a French port town named Cette we ate steamed mussels at a tavern perched at the edge of an empty beach, the Gulf of Lion spread out before us in a sparkling ultramarine blanket.

In Genova we found the astonishing Piazza di Ferrari, and admired the soft greenish brown hills backing away from the sea.

And in Bologna we spent the night, and that was the very first night that Alexandru asked me to marry him.

We were walking to the Neptune Fountain, which he had visited twice before and I, of course, never had. The streets were heaving with Others, almost as if there was a festival, although Sandu told me it was nearly always like this in the heart of the larger cities.

There were a few low-slung clouds above us, but mostly just the deep blue of a hazy night. Bologna offered imposing street lamps of molded iron and glass on nearly every block, as far as I could tell; their light condensed into one long, mellow pool along the boulevards. The prince and I strolled slowly through it. I was a little sore from the long day's flight, but mostly I was enjoying the sensation of simply being beside him, human Sandu and human Réz, arm in arm, just like all the other human lovers chattering and jostling around us.

The Neptune Fountain was a popular meeting place. People encircled it fully and still it loomed high above them all, the bronze god with his trident staring firmly away from the unruly masses gathered upon the steps below his feet, fish and mermaids squirting water from interesting orifices in high, glistening arcs.

We angled closer, Sandu easily parting the crowds with just a turn of his body, lean and graceful, guiding me forward. Men and women both stepped aside for him, and in the process he garnered more than his share of admiring glances.

Mine included. Less than an hour past, we'd been smothering our laughter atop the roof of a deserted warehouse, scrambling into our clothes. For our promenade tonight he wore the jade green velvet again, and with the coat buttoned closed I couldn't even see the splattered stains of my blood I knew had set near the waist. They wouldn't come out. I'd tried.

In my gown of silver foil print on primrose I liked

to think we made a smart couple. But between the two of us, Alexandru was the beauty.

The light from the oil lamps above accented the contours of his cheeks and lips and threw long-lashed shadows across his gaze. Beneath the shadows, his eyes shone looking-glass luminous. When he smiled and caught me close because I'd stumbled over an uneven paver, I swear I heard every female around us give a low gasp.

I understood. It hardly seemed fair to unleash him upon the general population.

But we were only in the great city for a single night, and I thought perhaps Bologna could suffer that.

I heard the bronze of the fountain well before we'd come near it. Bronze is a compound metal that has less of a song than a hum, which can be soothing, especially when combined with the tranquil splashing of water.

I didn't feel soothed. I felt awake, alive, delighted. I felt so filled with wonder and joy I couldn't seem to erase the smile on my lips.

I—that little lost runt of the shire—was in Italy. With Sandu.

It was the most tremendous thing that had ever happened to me, even if there was that small, disquieting niggle in my mind that could not stop remembering the note Future Réz had left me in my old bedroom.

I hadn't told the prince. I convinced myself it was because I still wasn't sure, and I wanted to be. When the time was right to tell him, I would.

Perhaps I wasn't entirely the dragon Réz yet. She was coiled around my heart, whispering *you cannot change this ending*, but Honor's old ways were proving difficult to break. Honor was a woman who was running off with a man after a whirlwind courtship that had lasted both days and years, and Honor liked to be sure.

Her reply to the dragon was simply: *Let me have this moment. Nothing is yet etched in stone.*

There was a nude god above us and a mass of malodorous people around us—no doubt some of them pickpockets, at the least—and the light was golden, and the fountain hummed, and at the edge of the stairs to the bottom pool Prince Alexandru slipped my arm free of his so that he might take my hand instead. We stood, both of us, facing the water, following the glittering streams that jetted and fell without pause, a miracle of some clever mechanical pumpwork we could not see.

I rested my head upon his shoulder. I closed my eyes, so that the light turned red behind my lids.

"Will you grant me the privilege," he said, in a voice low enough for just me to hear, "of becoming my wife, Réz?"

I sighed, so happy. "No, Alexandru."

"*How* many more times am I to ask?"

"I'm not certain. But when I am, I will tell you. Instantly."

Then *he* sighed. It was a small one, without frustration. His fingers tightened a fraction over mine.

"There's a word for this in English," he mused, still soft. "I can't quite recall it. I've made you a . . . a fallen woman. Yes?"

"Yes," I agreed, still smiling. "Thank you ever so much."

"It's been entirely my pleasure," he said in Romanian, and I turned my face into his sleeve and began to laugh.

❧

The journey back to *Zaharen Yce* took around a week. Had I not been with him, Sandu might have flown faster, but with me on his back I could tell he was taking care to ensure my comfort.

"The last thing I want," he said one morning in some watercolor-idyllic Austrian village, as we sipped our hot chocolate, "the very *last* thing, is to have come all this way and gone to all this trouble, just to end up with a mate who's little more than a distant splat against the earth. All because she wouldn't hold on."

"I do hold on," I protested. "Mostly." I sent him a sideways look. "*Am* I all this trouble?"

"Decidedly."

"No doubt you'd prefer someone who obeyed your every whim."

His brows began to climb. "How intriguing. Is that likely?"

"I don't know. I don't know the females of your tribe."

"Well, if you'd only mentioned the possibility before," he murmured, lifting his cup to his mouth. "I do wish I'd thought of it. What a lot of time and effort I might have been spared."

His tone was dry and his gaze was focused beyond mine, past the little courtyard of the boardinghouse where we planned to sleep through the day, past the neat garden of flowers and herbs and the white picket

fence that defined the edge of the yard. There had
been chickens picking through those flowers when
we'd first arrived; they'd all scattered to the winds.
Alexandru was looking at the mountains that rose in
the distance, blue shadows from here, a mere promise
of what was to come.

I set my cup upon its saucer, the taste of the chocolate abruptly sour on my tongue. I couldn't fathom
I'd not considered this before.

He was the Alpha of his tribe. By default, he would
be the greatest prize for mating. In Darkfrith every
single maiden, every one, dreamed of joining the
Alpha's family, even if they didn't like their choices
for doing so.

How much more aggressive might they have been,
all those females, knowing their chances of becoming
part of the head family would be limited to the seduc-
tion of a single male?

I tried to mentally summon any of them—faces,
names—and could not. I did recall a blur of voices
and gowns from that one disastrous Weave to the
ball, but otherwise it seemed like I'd nearly always
Woven to him when he was alone.

"Sandu. What *are* they like? The females?"

His gaze cut back to mine, the early sun glossing his
hair.

"Acquiescent? Submissive?" I persisted. "Comely?"

His mouth curved from over the rim of his cup. I
narrowed my eyes.

"Well? Am I going to have to fight them or not?"

"Fight them? Good heavens. Is that how it's done in
your tribe?"

"Sometimes. If the situation demands it. If there's a

boy—a male, and he's been dallying about with more than one girl—sometimes it becomes a battle of dominance. The Alpha female must win."

And oh, those Darkfrith girls. Those girls with their slanting looks and pretty pouts, and figurative claws. And fangs. Sometimes the battles were physical and sometimes they were more cunning than that, whispered rumors that tailed you, hushed giggles hardly suppressed behind lily-white hands.

Girls bigger than you, relentless girls homing in on you, the powerless. Pushing you down, pulling your hair, tripping you until you wept.

I remembered Wilhelmina and the particular pitch of her laughter as she stood over me before the silversmith's shop when I was eight. How light and trilling it sounded already, just like it would when she would be older, and courted by all the boys.

That was never going to happen to me again. I would never submit again.

I sat forward in my chair. "Is that the custom in your tribe? Do the females fight over the males?"

Alexandru stared at me, his expression arrested, the chocolate cup frozen in his hand.

I kicked at him. "Tell me. How many others?"

His lips began to pinch flat; his lashes lowered. I realized that he was laughing at me.

"I fail to find the humor in this," I said in frigid tones.

A babble of squawking came from the open door behind us; it seemed most of the chickens had fled inside. The *hausfrau* who'd taken us in poked her head out the door, her hair covered in a yellow kerchief, her eyes inquisitive hazel. Sandu sent her away again with a regal flick of his fingers.

"Réz." He looked full at me, set his cup upon the table. "There are no other females. You're the only one."

"What, never?" I demanded, skeptical.

That pinch returned to his lips, just a shade. "Perhaps not *never*. I am a male, and I have been alone for a very long while, and for all those years I did fear you an illusion, so I hope you might forgive me that much. But as far as I'm concerned right now, there has only been one female I've ever truly noticed, and who has ever truly noticed me. Only one. And she's the only one I'll ever notice again."

I regarded him silently. One of the chickens made it as far as the stoop behind him, released a piercing *bwaak!* at us before dashing back inside.

"Will you marry me?" Sandu asked.

"No."

He picked up his chocolate again, unperturbed, his gaze drifting back to those distant blue mountains.

❦

They traveled mostly at night, although as they soared closer and closer to home, he began to feel more comfortable remaining aloft during the early daylight hours. He made certain they kept high enough to remain a mirage if viewed from below; a part of him worried over it, chewing over the fact of their altitude again and again like a dog over a shabby bone. Logically Alexandru understood that it would hardly matter if she fell a hundred feet or a thousand feet; neither distance would mean a pleasant ending.

But the less logical side of him—this new and unknown side, which seemed rooted in nameless, churning emotions—thought, *Stay low, lower, she'll be safer that way.*

He'd lost count of how many times he'd twisted his head back to look at her, using his eyes to convince his mind that the insignificant weight upon his back was still there. She'd be sitting upright above his wings or else leaning forward on her elbows, her cheeks and nose pink with wind, her hands tight in his mane. He always found her hair first, that flip of coppery flame snapping out behind them like a bright pennant he'd won and was carrying home.

She'd wanted to hold the luggage, which was preposterous. It was fine in his claws; he was accustomed to transporting things in such a way. He needed nothing to distract Réz from her primary job: remaining on top of him.

He'd warned her before they'd begun that if he ever discovered her with her eyes closed, he'd land at once, city or countryside be damned, and he was sincere. Once, as they were following the lustrous polished line of the Danube, he'd turned his head and discovered her face to his neck with one eye closed and the other one open, the wind whipping her hair back and forth around her teasing smile.

Sandu found himself becharmed. Not merely charmed, because she wasn't merely charming. Becharmed, bespelled, whatever word might best suit this unexpected mixture of feelings that swept through him in a combination of tenderness and amusement and ferocious protectiveness. The closest sensation akin to it was how he felt about his position, his place as leader, but even that was born more of war and determination than love.

Miles above the earth, with the music of the wind and stars combing through his whiskers, he'd mull on that.

Love.

At times the clouds would engulf them in their acres of blue-cooled mist, and then, when looking back would make no difference because he wouldn't see her anyway, Alexandru concentrated on feeling her. Feeling her heat, and the pressure of her legs, and the small tuggings that came and went through her fists.

He couldn't do it for very long. The heat of her would translate almost instantly into darker, deeper thoughts of her body, and of beds and pillows and being hot inside her.

Never before had he known the peculiar discomfort of flying aroused. Sandu tried to avoid the cloud banks when he could.

In their hotel room in Óbuda, he'd come upon her in her boudoir without knocking, some thought at the edge of his tongue, something about the distance left to travel, not far now, and how to count the miles by the lakes below.

But she didn't notice his entry. She was standing before the cheval mirror placed in the corner, dressed in her chemise and stockings and nothing else. The chemise was white, with ribbons of cherry-red threaded through the neckline and sleeves, woven in a pretty pattern around the hem. The drawstring neckline was loosened, and two long strips of satin floated against her arms as she regarded her own reflection, pensive, both palms spread flat over her abdomen. Late autumn light filtered through the organza curtains behind her and lit every inch of her to a peachy glow.

The hotel was named the King's View, and Prince Alexandru was not unknown here. Composed of creamy brick and marble and overlooking the great river itself, it was the preferred lodging of traveling diplomats and aristocrats or anyone aspiring to either. The senior footman had recognized him as they'd ascended the front steps, and by the time they'd reached the threshold of the main doors the manager himself was there, bowing low with effusive greetings, accepting the coat and stick and hat Sandu had only just donned twenty minutes before.

"*Merci,*" Sandu had said, and then drew Réz gently forward. "*Ma femme, la princesse.*"

The manager transferred his attentions instantly, *how delightful, he had not realized, Her Grace honored them, champagne of course, and fresh flowers, the bridal suite was regretfully booked but the king's own rooms were free . . .*

During all this Réz only inclined her head with just the right degree of imperial condescension—did she speak French? he'd never even thought to ask—but Sandu thought he'd felt a stiffening in her posture, barely there.

He might have only imagined it. Looking at her now, so slim and girlish, with her hair curling wild down her back and her fingers pushed apart, she looked more elfin than dragon, a sprite wandered into the elaborately embellished royal suite of the best hotel in Hungary.

"*Princesse,*" he said softly, from his place in the doorway.

She looked up at once, dropping her hands. Their eyes met through the mirror glass.

"I hope you didn't mind," he said. "As one day, it will be true."

"One day," she agreed, and added, "I suppose I never thought of it before. The title."

"It can be a surprising thing," he conceded, feeling the smile that wanted to come.

Her gaze lowered to take in that promised smile; her own began to rise in answer. "Will I get a crown?"

"Holly," he reminded her.

"I like holly."

"Good thing. I fear there's not enough gold left in any of the mines for the other sort."

"But there are diamonds in the walls, and emeralds around your hearth. Those will do. Your castle twinkles with song."

He pushed off the doorway, giving a bow of acknowledgment. "I'm glad you like it."

Réz laughed. "It *is* noisy."

"We'll drown it out."

"How?"

"By making our own music, of course."

Her brows knit; the peached light shimmered through her shift as she turned to face him. "Oh, that was truly dreadful."

"My apologies. English is not my best language."

"Alexandru," she said, meeting him in the middle of the room, her fingers on his, her eyes deep as oceans, "that would have been dreadful in any language."

"I love you," he said, and in the sudden silence of the splendid chamber heard his own heartbeat, thudding hard.

"It's soon, I know," he said.

The windows had been left open a little. The organza puffed and fell like living breath, and beyond them a bell from a ferry on the river was clanging in clear, insistent tenor. The swell of air stirred her hair, lifted his own from his shoulders.

He pushed it back with one hand. "And perhaps you don't feel the same about me. Not yet. That's fine. But I wanted you to know."

She'd dropped her gaze again. He was left to look at the reddish brown crescents of her lashes, the straight line of her nose and lips that gleamed rose and tender gold. Her fingers remained curved loosely over his.

"Mate," he tried, and she glanced up.

"This is how we are," she murmured. "You said that to me once."

"I did?"

"I thought at the time you meant—something physical. But I understand you now. This is how we are. More than physical. More than animal. Two hearts as one, unable to part. This is what it means to be bonded." She shook her head. "I'd never guessed. I'd never come close to guessing how this might feel. You are the center of me. I think I . . . I think I wouldn't want to live without you." But the soft wonder of her voice had transitioned into something tinged more of indignation. She regarded him more directly, con-

frontation in her stance now, as if she dared him to re-
fute it. "I don't want to live without you."

"Perhaps I'll find you a crown of gold, after all,"
Sandu said, and to his surprise, they were just the
right words. Her edge of confrontation melted away
into the spreading light.

"No, I'll take the holly."

"And me."

"And you, *le prince*. Of course, you."

He lifted her hand for a kiss to shield his smile.

CHAPTER TWENTY-THREE

When the princess named Réz Wove away from the massacre at *Zaharen Yce*, she went ahead in time. Far ahead.

For a very long while, she was stuck there.

As a girl she'd already endured the experience of losing nearly a year of her life. She never recalled her trials as a sixteen-year-old, although she did live through them. At the age of twenty-five, she lost another six and a half years to the Dragon of Time, which took particular delight in devouring her then.

An enraged *drákon*, a screaming *drákon*, mother to a freshly slaughtered child, wife to a freshly slaughtered mate—in her involuntary Weave away from the dungeon of *Zaharen Yce*, she was especially delicious.

When she was thirty-two, she awoke one morning with nearly all the memories of her previous life restored intact. She sat up in her narrow, cotton-sheeted bed and realized that she was in Germany, that Germany was at war, and that she was English.

That she wasn't human. And it was not her war.

Réz attempted to Weave back. Over and over again,

she flung herself back in time, but she never did return to the scene of her family's demise. She never even managed to get close.

Zaharen Yce had turned its back on her. Whatever magic had lived in it before the pillaging, whatever welcome she'd once received, had all been revoked.

It did not have *life*, this castle. Not in the way the dragons did, or the forests, or even the lesser beasts. But it had a sort of memoried awareness, a sense of *being*, and of *having been*. Polarity, chemistry. Every block of quartzite, every single embedded gem, every grain of sand in the mortar . . . all of it, polarized like a magnet, drawing sweet, heavy magic to it, basking in it.

Until that day it did not.

Dragons may change the chemistry of stones; stones may change the chemistry of dragons. On that cold March day in 1791, the crimson flowing deaths of its inhabitants changed the chemistry of *Zaharen Yce* forever.

A smaller mind might describe the years that followed as accursed, for both Réz and her former home. She herself began to believe in witches and curses, in all manner of jabbering ghouls, although that might have been merely the onset of her madness sinking its first juicy tendrils into her.

The castle now existed as a hulking shell. Its polarity had been reversed, rejecting all magic, rejecting Réz herself. To her dismay and eventual fury, but for one solitary exception—when she was very old and used her considerable skills to trick the Dragon of Time, a trick she could only use once—she could not even return to it in its pristine state. She was tainted, *verboten*.

Even with trickery, she would never encounter her husband or daughter again.

Every Weave, another piece of her torn away, more blood, more anguish. Each one diminished her by degrees.

She devised a plan to write a letter to her younger self, a letter explaining what was to come. She'd done it before, long ago, and it seemed to be the best she could manage now.

But when she did, nothing changed. She would write to herself, mail it years before, and wait.

Nothing changed.

Write the letter, hide it in places Honor Carlisle might look.

Nothing ever changed.

Write the letter, send it to Lia, begging for help.

Nothing.

Réz realized she did not *remember* fixing this. She never *remembered* fixing it.

Somehow she had ended up in the wrong ripple of time, blighted. Alone. She could not change this ending.

Her years dragged on. To her credit, and with a great deal of unspoken, bitter turmoil, she attempted to live peacefully. She attempted to live in anonymity, far from England and Germany, far from her own brutal kind. But Réz was a wounded beast with a heart ripped in two, and a Gift that never ceased to carve away at her.

An empty womb and ever empty arms: Her ragged soul began to shrivel. So perhaps the madness was an inevitable thing.

Madness whispered to her in the voice of *Draumr*, that long-lost wicked diamond:

One lassst chance. Sssaaaave the Weaves, ssssaaaaave them. Go back and kill the English before they come. Before any of thisss ever sssstarts. Kill the English drákon *before they kill* him.

CHAPTER TWENTY-FOUR

Within the crystalline and dreamlike walls of the castle known as the Tears of Ice, no one called me *princesse*.

I moved through the hallways more an apparition than royalty, content to mostly observe for now, and that suited me. I enjoyed it.

There were footmen who followed me when they thought they should, and maids who found me formal gowns, *robes à la française* from God knew where or when, and helped me dress in them. Men and women either full human or else with faint emanations of *drákon*—carmine lips, translucent skin, movements a tad too swift or supple for ordinary Others—served me breakfasts and teas and dinners, and opened thick wooden doors for me, and brought me figs and wine as I gazed out from any of the crenulated terraces.

Over the centuries the quartzite had begun to melt. That's why the fortress was named what it was, for the frozen rivers of crystals that dripped from casements and corners. Viewed from any approach, it was a castle of sugar cubes that had been caught in the rain: sparkling pale and set improbably at the top edge of a very bleak crest, jutting out without concern for gravity or weather or even time itself.

Zaharen Yce persuaded anyone who viewed it that, just like the mountains, it had always been there, and always would be there, and the melting, glinting rivers down its walls would always flow.

Inside, however, its hidden heart was revealed.

The heart of the castle was more than stone walls, more than even the sumptuous furnishings or the ghost-colored bumps of diamonds studding every room and corridor. The heart was a constant hum of energy, ever present beneath all the metal and stone songs, all the murmured conversations and footfalls and noises of a place that held over two hundred residents.

It was hard to hear at first. In fact, for my first few days and nights there, I missed it entirely. I did get the sense of *something* beneath it all, some manner of elemental cohesion that eluded me, the newcomer, the woman who'd descended to the mountain upon the back of the Alpha.

"Just listen," counseled my would-be husband, as we lay in the big canopy bed at night. "Just still your soul and listen, Réz, and you'll riddle it out."

"Riddle what out?" I asked, fretful, because the hum surrounded me and the dragon inside me knew it, even if *I* heard only the more commonplace melodies of the hearth.

"Riddle out why you belong here." He smiled at me from his pillow, the firelight a dim burnish on the window glass behind him.

"I already know why."

"Yes. But beyond me, river-girl, and beyond even

the bond of our feelings. Beyond all that is this place. This sky and mountain, where our kind first were created. We're perched in the middle of it, right now, that invisible edge between heaven and earth. We're immersed in that ancient magic, the strongest magic known. It fills our pores and shines out of us, every one."

"Our *pores*," I said. "Egad."

His laughter was a rumble that shook the bed. He leaned closer with a sly, seductive smile, and the silky blue fall of his hair slipped from his shoulders to mine.

"Our every organ." His hand found my breast, a bare brushing of skin to skin that gave me goose bumps. His fingers began a downward slide, his hand turning over, the backs of his nails dragging lightly over my flesh. "Our every . . . little . . . bit . . ."

"Oh," I said, or something that only sounded like that, because by then he had found the most sensitive part of me, and it seemed like magic indeed, that he could touch me and stroke me and fill me with joy with just his hand.

How could I still my soul when he tormented me like that?

But it did happen. I think the first time I felt truly in harmony with my new world was the fifth night, when I stood outside on the terrace closest to our tower bedroom, a half-finished glass of wine in hand. We'd made love and then slept, and then I awoke and he didn't. I hadn't been able to fall back asleep.

The terrace was empty of anything but stone and a few cold, unlit torches. No doubt there were eager footmen lurking somewhere nearby, ready to spring into action and open more doors for me, but it was late, and luck was on my side. I had managed to elude them.

The wine was white, dry but not too dry, and the chill of the night only made it more fine. I stood beneath an endless silver ocean of stars; the mountains were silvered with them, jagged silver with glossy black shadows, and the gold ring on my hand shone silver too.

I transferred the wine to my other hand. I pressed the one that wore Alexandru's ring to my belly.

"Are you there?" I whispered. "Are you in this time, little baby, or no?"

My body gave no answer. The ring was a bright hard gleam against the woolen weave of my robe.

But . . . there was the something, rising up all around me. I held motionless, my breath caught, straining to gather it closer.

It was noiseless. It was infinite. It was an awareness, a light, better and brighter and more beautiful than even the frosted fall from the stars. I closed my eyes and let it warm me, let Réz the dragon lift her head and stretch her wings and sigh, *yes, yes, this is what we need*.

I opened my eyes again, and the range of mountains before me stretched up to claw the glowing firmament, and the air was thick with unvoiced music, and the magic bathed me, even my pores.

We had been born here. All dragons, from all times and places, first came from here, this soundless, slender breadth of Milky Way and rocky tors.

I'd been lost as a girl in a river, and lost in other ways ever since.

No longer.

"I'm home," I realized aloud, and *Zaharen Yce* offered her silent accord.

∽

Eight days passed. Eight days, nine nights. I moved from being an apparition in the halls to a creature of denser substance, one who felt she had a better right to wear the decidedly foreign, old-fashioned satin gowns that shimmered with crystals and beads and countless tiny sequins. To have meals served to her, or doors swung wide at her approach. I met the eyes of the *drákon* who moved through their lives around me and began to notice their patterns. Who spoke with whom. Who smiled, who did not. Which of the female nobles would regard me from over their fans, and which would turn their faces away and not regard me at all.

I didn't worry about them. Certainly I'd already assessed every eligible maiden of the fortress—and a few who weren't so eligible but looked daggers at me anyway—and decided I could defeat them all. I was small, yes, but ardently determined to hold my place, and perhaps the other females sensed this. Or perhaps it simply wasn't the Zaharen way to fight openly. No one challenged me. No one precisely welcomed me, either, barring the servants.

But it was fine. I was home, so everything was fine.

I toured the castle slowly, savoring each chamber or gallery or corridor, tracing my fingers along the diamond walls when I could, otherwise just listening, holding my soul in quiet. My favorite room, besides our bedroom, was the one Sandu had described to me back in Spain, the one that would host our wedding. It was called the Convergence Room, and I think it was one of the few places in the castle that really, obviously wasn't meant for humans. It was simply too yawning big and high.

That, and there were dragons painted upon the ceiling. Olden dragons, medieval, I guessed, roughly styled into the plaster but still brilliant with life. The stars painted in regular intervals between them shone with six points; it was a hidden heraldry, there for only those who knew to look up and discern it.

Alexandru had said there was no true wealth left to the Zaharen, but I found it difficult to believe. Every single room seemed to glisten with rare furniture and tapestries, huge paintings, gold-dipped chandeliers.

Ah, yes. The gold.

Like the diamonds in the mortar, gold leaf had been applied liberally practically everywhere but the water closets.

I'd not noticed it so much before in my Weaves, probably because my focus then was always Sandu— or else Weaving swiftly away again. Barring our plain tower room, gold sang and sang throughout the inner sanctum of the castle. Even in hallways with no natural source of light there would be some shimmery reflection against the ceiling from a window unseen, a door, some dusky polished glimmer to guide me on.

The most impressively gilded room of all was the royal Great Room, where the prince would sit and listen to the petitions of his people.

I sat beside him in that chamber of damask and gold one afternoon. I listened as he did to the farmers who'd trudged up the mountain to converse with him, the herders of sheep and goats, the hunters, the men who unearthed truffles from beneath the forest trees to catch the wild boars. Some of them were darker-skinned and some of them were alabaster pale, but all of them bowed to their prince, and spoke in words I nearly understood, their voices lifting and falling and ultimately bouncing away against the truly blinding, shiny splendor engulfing us. Remaining seated in the midst of it was a bit like drowning in a gilt pot.

Offerings began to pile up on a side table in a corner. Round wheels of cheese coated in wax, clusters of grapes, candied walnuts. Jars of blond honey, ropes of dried sausage. Saddles and blankets. Skeins of wool so floaty soft and beautiful I could not imagine spinning them into something else.

I kept looking over at it, in part because it puzzled me: Did this happen every time? All these lovely things, brought with reverent bows and deep curtsies? But also I stared because muted, natural colors offered my eyes wonderful relief.

By the end of that day the gifts from the Zaharen overflowed the table before us, and still there stretched a line of people beyond the doors, bringing more.

"They love you," I said, standing with my arms planted akimbo above my panniered hips, half-awed. A particularly fine chunk of clear quartz had been shaped and polished into a solid thick ball. The reflection across it showed me a pair of human-looking *drákon* in court clothing, copper and cream, blue and black, cast upside down.

"No," said the prince, standing before the table

with me. He brushed his palm against the small of my back; I barely felt it through the corset. "This isn't for me, Réz. All this is yours."

I sent him a dubious glance, squinting, because the wall behind him was of actual shaped gold leaves, layered like Spanish roof tiles from floor to ceiling.

"We don't need a wedding," he said, stepping closer, cupping his hands around my eyes so I wouldn't squint. His lips touched the tip of my nose. "You're here, you're one of us, already entrenched in our legend. You are Alpha, you're mine. So they'll pay homage to you. It's in our blood. It's how we are."

Alpha, *me*. It seemed both impossible and just what I'd always secretly, deliriously expected.

Oh, Réz was fully awake, and she was well pleased.

Our eight days brimmed with wonder. Our nine nights with a dark and magnificent passion. I took the time to find the meadow I'd call Sanctuary and began to hang the first of the crystal lustres from the trees around it, the ones that would lead me to my future. Sandu helped, reaching the taller boughs, sometimes boosting me up to his shoulders so I could get the highest ones of all.

I drank the wine and ate the food and submerged myself in this bright new gladness, this sense of home and love. Of hope for the very best of tomorrows.

Of course, none of that actually came to pass.

Instead, Lia showed up.

CHAPTER TWENTY-FIVE

It had been a very long while since Amalia had attempted a hunt. And it had been even longer since she'd flown in daylight.

Not that this was much of a hunt. She knew where she was going, just as she had known where to go to find Zane. She'd been to *Zaharen Yce* before, in her wilder youth, even though over a decade had passed since she'd been anywhere near the bald, snow-scuffed Alps that cradled the last of the original tribe of *drákon*.

She remembered the mountains. She remembered the taste of the wind, that icy snap of pine and glacier frosting her senses. The flash of the green and blue lakes below, the cold foaming rivers. Forests rippling over hill and dale in velvet colors without end.

The first of the dragons approached while she was still leagues away. He'd been a haze of smoke above a field when she first spotted him, but had swept near with a sudden velocity as soon as he was high enough to Turn to full dragon.

He was burnt red and orange, only a little larger than she. He arrowed close enough to force her to veer, which she didn't, because Lia knew better than to let his first challenge lead to her capitulation.

The new dragon veered off instead; she got a very good look at the crisscross pattern of his scales. No doubt he'd gotten near enough to realize her gender, as well. He didn't try to force her down again, but instead began to fly alongside her, his lips curled back and his eyes strangely scarlet.

Lia herself was dyed more of the heavens, cobalt and violet with pearled wings, golden barbs along her tail. In certain lights she knew she blended with the sky, but it was too late to blend, and she had no intention of slinking into *Zaharen Yce* anyway.

They flew as a pair. Another mile in and yet another dragon looped up to join them, a green one, all different shades of green, from ivy to peridot to glass.

The next one was bronze and rust, and the next silver and pink and black.

By the time she circled above the turrets of the fortress, she had an escort of no less than eighteen male dragons, and she didn't know where the hell they thought they'd all land, but she herself was going for the inner courtyard, because it was graveled and open, and she'd likely break only one of the fountains in her skid.

She broke two.

They were oversized and placed too close together, but she still might have avoided them if her escort had only realized what she was entirely about. Instead, a dragon with a yellowish back and an actual gray beard attempted to head her off at the last moment, and Lia was forced to duck beneath him, snapping at his flank. It shattered her concentration just enough to sacrifice that second fountain, which had featured a large bird or a dolphin, and was probably ugly anyway.

She left furrows of brown dirt easily nine inches deep, starkly visible against the crumbled white gravel.

With all four legs on the ground again she Turned to smoke, allowing the valise strung around her neck by a rope to fall free. She resumed her shape standing beside it, holding a hand to her eyes as the beasts above her Turned as well, one by one, slithering down in plumes to the courtyard.

The valise contained, among other things, a robe, which she removed and slipped on, ignoring the eyes of all the men materializing nude around her. She belted it, bent down, retrieved the nearly empty valise and let the rope drape over her arm.

"I've come to see my daughter," she announced in Romanian, her words clear and carrying in the thin, fragrant air.

From the dense pocket of shadows that concealed the main doors behind her, her name was spoken.

Lia turned around. Prince Alexandru—God, so grown, how many years had it been?—stood at the brink of the gravel, the light splashed just along the toes of his boots. When he moved forward into the sunlight and his hair went to indigo and his handsome face was thrown into sharp relief, she had a moment of vertigo so intense she had to ease a step back from him to preserve her equilibrium.

This place. The crushing magic of this place. How did any of them stand it?

"I must see her," she said, glad to hear her voice revealed nothing of her momentary weakness.

"Lady Amalia," murmured the prince again, and had the courtesy to offer her a bow, one complete with that unique Zaharen salute of curved fingers to his forehead. "Welcome, Noble One. Please come in. We'll speak inside."

"Yes," said Lia, holding her balance with a lift of her chin. "We will."

⌘

He was unsurprised to see she *was* still beautiful, this female who'd stolen the child Réz from the shire, and who'd summoned a faint tinge of unconscious jealousy in adult Réz's voice. Yet Amalia possessed a different sort of beauty than his beloved, more typically English, he thought, and in that sense, at least to him, more commonplace. She was lovely, yes, but Réz was extraordinary.

He knew they were unrelated by blood, except perhaps through some distant kinship probably all the members of the English tribe shared. But guiding her now into the cool, marbled vestibule of his castle, Alexandru imagined he glimpsed in Lia a distinct resemblance to the woman he'd left sleeping upstairs: the blaze of her eyes, the stiff column of her spine. It was nothing of color or size but entirely of attitude. Lady Amalia seemed prepared for battle, at least mentally.

It set a knot between his shoulders, one he couldn't shake off.

And it wasn't merely that, her straight back and her wary resistance to his smiles. She had music with her—issuing from that valise she carried, which she'd refused to hand over to him or any of the footmen— strange, dulcet music that both soothed and alarmed him on some deep, primal level, because he was very much afraid he knew what it might be.

Poison. All *Draumr* had ever been to his kind was poison in one form or another, and even though he knew it was broken and its power diminished, there was no question he felt it. Stronger, sweeter, more alluring than any of the other stones.

Aware of the servants stationed about, aware of the nobles trickling down the sweep of the main stairs on their way to breaking their fasts, Radu and Lucia and all the rest, staring, staring, Alexandru kept the cadence of his footfalls unrushed and exact. He led Amalia past the gradually bunching cluster of Zaharen aristocrats at the base of the stairs to the closest parlor, the East Room, and closed the door behind them. He was careful to do that, to keep his hand on the knob, to stand against the wood so she could pass, to listen for the soft *tick* of the latch to tell him it was all the way shut.

It took more willpower than he liked to simply lift his hand then and offer her a chair.

He wanted to snatch the bag from her.

He wanted to rip it open, and close his fist on the source of that sweet song.

He wanted to gobble it up.

Instead, Prince Alexandru waited for the Lady Amalia to take her seat, and then calmly, cordially, took his own in the leather armchair opposite.

The parlor was referenced by its wide bank of windows, which faced the courtyard and the rising sun; the walls and floors were streaked with light.

"You hear it," Lia said in English, not a question. She sat very prim at the edge of the cushion, her ankles crossed, her bare toes pressed into the rug.

He nodded.

"Good. I wanted you to. Where is Honor?"

"In our room. It's still early, you know. She likes to sleep."

"When will she be down?"

"I don't know." He managed another peaceful smile. "When she is."

Lady Amalia regarded him silently for a moment, a steely look entirely at odds with her charming, mussed appearance. Through the panes beyond her he could see a trio of groomsmen and a scullery maid encircling the remains of one of the broken fountains.

He felt as if the light was congealing around him, thickening solid as jelly. It was growing so thick he could hardly move it from his nose into his lungs. A sense of weight settled atop him, atop the restriction in his chest.

It was cold, pure dread.

"I have a letter for you," she said. "Two of them, actually."

He said nothing. She held him in that hard gaze for a moment more, then opened the valise. The sweet poison song of *Draumr* swelled.

He was leaning forward in his chair before he realized it. He was rising to his feet.

"Do not approach me, Your Grace," said Amalia, without looking up.

He stopped, again without meaning to. With a very

great effort, he dug his fingernails into the meat of his palms, and that woke him some.

He sank back into the chair.

Amalia stood, crossed to him. The sheet of paper in her hand fell open in folds.

"I mean you no harm," she said. "I hope you believe that. But what I'm about to do is . . . unprecedented. You are to read these two letters, Alexandru. You're to start with this one."

He took it from her, shook it out and lifted it to the sun.

It was from the English tribe. It was written in the form of a formal proclamation, dated over eight months past. The language was stilted, the script embellished with tails and curls so dramatic they seemed to swallow up the actual words.

But the message itself was stark enough.

Proposal for the Unification of the Drákon *Tribes*, he read.

One Alpha, two lands. Rule by proxy. Reasonable rights and privileges of the prince retained, all primary laws of Darkfrith to be upheld. Shared expenses. One rule.

One Alpha. Not two.

"Where did you get this?" he asked slowly, still reading. "I never received this."

"No, you wouldn't have. Apparently, they decided not to send it to you. Perhaps they realized the wording wasn't quite genial enough for what they really intended."

"Subjugation." He labored through a breath of the thick jelly light. "They mean to rule *Zaharen Yce*."

"Not just the castle." She sounded nearly sympathetic. "Everyone. Everything. Every last drop of blood in this land. Especially yours."

He was not surprised. He told himself there could be no surprise in this news, that in fact, the only actual astonishing part of it was that they had taken so long to reach this step in the deliberate, long-distance chess game they'd been playing with him since he was a boy. Stratagems and strategies, all the devious skills he'd learned in his short few years of rule, all for naught. He'd danced and sidestepped and tried to ever remain at least a move ahead of them but now, in the end, their patience was done. It was all going to come down to simple brute force.

Check, Sandu thought, detached, and opened his fingers. The proposal fell, a flat feather drifting, settling upon the rug between his feet.

It had landed upright. The true words of it glared up at him, bold slashes: *Give Us a Fight, Then, Boy. Let Us Destroy You.*

"Where did you get it?" he asked once more.

"From Réz."

His lashes lifted.

"Not the one you know. An older Réz. A different woman. I'd like to wait to show you the other letter, though. Until Honor is here."

The arched connecting door to the next chamber swung open, the flat china painted panels a sudden glare in a shaft of sun. "Honor's not coming."

They both turned their heads. Réz glided forward into the jelly-sun room, her eyes swift to his, then focused back on Lia. She seemed to have no trouble walking, not as he did, and the jelly was beginning to affect his vision as well; impressions of her came to him in quick, brilliant relief: December curls pinned up, a scintillating frock of robin's-egg blue. Pale cheeks, pale neck, pale chest. The puckered gauze that ended her sleeves matched the open petticoat of her skirts.

Her gaze, holding their deep rivers of emotion.

Apprehension, he thought now, so attuned to her. She was worried to see Amalia, even though her face was as smooth as a mask.

"I'm sorry to hear it," Lady Amalia was saying.

"Don't be. Réz is a far happier person than Honor was." She paused. "*I'm* happier, Lia."

"For now."

"Is that *Draumr*? There in that valise?"

"Yes."

"I thought you said you'd lost it."

Lia shrugged, watching Réz circle warily around her. "I lied."

Réz reached him, took his hand. Perhaps the dread had sunken into her as well; her skin felt like ice, chilling his bones.

"You won't separate us," she said. "If you came here to try, it's fruitless. Despite the diamond, there's nothing you can say or do. I swear to you, I won't go back."

Lady Lia smiled, a poignant smile, and with it Alexandru abruptly remembered the first moment he'd laid eyes on her, here in this very room, back when he'd been just a child and she a young stranger to his land, come to save the life of the human man she'd loved. How he'd been introduced to her but was too bashful to lift his gaze, until she'd knelt before him and took his hand, pressed a kiss to the back of it, something no one, *no one*, had ever done before. How the boy Sandu had looked up, astonished, and been struck dumb by just the smiling shape of her lips and the perfect lie of shadows on her face.

"No, *filla*," Amalia said gently, older, but perfect and shadowed still. "That's not what I want. There was never any going back."

❧

She had the prince show Honor the letter from her people, signed by Lia's brother and all the members of the Darkfrith Council, those gnarled, frightened old men. It shamed her that they would resort to this, shamed but did not amaze her. Lia'd always known the rulers of her tribe would place their own survival above all. A measure of bloodshed had never stopped them before.

It was her fault, some of it or maybe even all of it, and so she had to do what she could to mend these two families. Had she never come here with Zane so long ago, had she never fled the shire as a girl, had she never stumbled upon *Zaharen Yce* and written that very first letter to her parents, breaking the news of this unanticipated and undomesticated clan of dragons . . .

Perhaps it would have mattered. Perhaps not. It seemed unlikely the two groups could have continued to exist for much longer in utter ignorance of each other. The world was a shrinking place.

Honor held the proclamation between her finger-tips, pinkies extended, as if the page might fold over and bite her. She had that drowsy, cat-eyed look she sometimes wore first thing in the morning, indicative of a long Weave or a restless night.

Or not precisely restless, Lia amended to herself, her gaze shifting to the prince standing beside her, his arm curved about her shoulders.

It had been many years since Amalia had been around males of her own species. She'd never flown with the dragons of her shire; her Gift had come too late for that. She recalled being enamored of the village boys as a maiden, their shining skin and brilliant eyes. The way they'd work the fields in their shirt-sleeves, plowing, sowing, reaping, sweat darkening the cloth just enough to cling, to show off the un-bearably sensual concurrence of muscle and bone.

The same boys at her mother's social balls, dancing with their eerie grace, everyone fair, everyone gleaming, and the scent of lust in the air a near tangible mist.

Young or old, it seemed that *drákon* males seethed with the instinct to seduce, not merely sexually but intellectually, emotionally; without even trying, they could hit every pitch-perfect note. Unsuspecting females tumbled like skittles in their paths.

Poor Honor, because this male would be no different. Ebony hair, which didn't happen in her tribe, but the same sinuous elegance, the same instinctive sensuality that lured the eye and kept it there, appreciating every last detail.

The same lust too, she thought. Prince Alexandru and her daughter clung to each other like wool in winter static. If they pulled apart, Lia was sure she'd see sparks.

Useless to ask if they were already lovers. She knew

that they were, but even if she hadn't, she would have guessed by the intimacy of their postures, how they leaned into each other, how even shaken, he hovered over her, and even drowsy, she accepted it.

Honor, the timorous child who'd never relaxed enough to fully welcome physical touch, not even a buss on the cheek.

Oh, Lia thought, watching them, aching, *let this be true. Let what they have be real and true.*

Honor looked so vulnerable. She wore no paint, and her hair had been pinned into an uneven pile that tumbled down her back, and the style of the gown she wore was both too old for her and too young. A wedge of lace from her shift showed past the edge of her bodice, as if she'd had no maids to help her dress.

When she lifted her eyes to Lia's again, some of the sleep had vanished from her gaze.

"What does it mean?" she asked.

"Wait," said Lia. "There's more."

Then she gave them both the second letter, the one that sealed their fates.

CHAPTER TWENTY-SIX

Lia,

You don't know me. My name is Réz. I used to be Honor
Carlisle.

My Natural Time now is well ahead of yours. I'm older
than you, than I ever knew you to be. I live in what you would
call the former Colonies.

I'm trapped. My life has dwindled to a pinprick. I survive
in individual moments. I eat, I sleep. Every third day I walk to
the village market to wander the stalls and the chitter-
chatter colonists stare at me, five hundred forty-seven steps
there. Five hundred forty-seven steps back. I count the alien
insects that creep across my floor. I sleep.

I sleep.

Even awake, I'm so tired I don't have the power to lift the
carving knife I keep ready on the kitchen table, right there in
front of me, such a friendly shape. I can't even lift it to finish
this misery. Everything is gray and mud.

I cannot remember the precise day my life ended. I've tried so hard my head aches and my entire body trembles, but my mind is in tatters. So much about those years elude me now. But in the ~~sum~~ spring of ~~1792~~ 1791 the English are going to attack *Zaharen Yce*. They are going to kill everyone.

It's been decades since the assault on the castle, and as I've said, my life has dwindled. Details drift away from me. I'll tell you, though, I'll tell you what I remember most are the screams. Even as I pen this, I still hear them ~~how they~~

The weight of my daughter in my arms just before she was torn from me. Her head beneath my chin. Her hands around my neck.

I had a daughter.

~~I Wove away that day. I did not mean to I swear to God I never meant to i would never have but it happened and i couldn't stop~~

They're all dead. I cannot Weave back. Every time I try, I'm thrown here again. The best I may hope is to Weave sometime near you before it happens and post this letter. I'm enclosing something else, a declaration I stole from Darkfrith, the one time I was able to Weave there before they stopped me. I found it in the desk of the Alpha. I don't know when that was, but I know I never saw it before that day.

My tatty mind keeps thinking. I think and think, and the one phrase that never leaves me, that remains my constant miserable companion is this: *sanf inimicus*. And by the stars, Lia, sometimes that phrase seems more like *deliverance*.

The things in my head, Mama. The hobgoblin, nattering things.

Please. If you ever loved me at all, I beg you to please save my family.

—Réz
Last Princess of the Zaharen

&

"Would you like to know how it's going to happen?"

Lia's voice floated with casual nonchalance through the parlor, which seemed very hot to me. I did not know why the room had to be so hot; it was nearing winter, and the sunbeams slanting in held at best a tone of ambered coolness. Motes of dust danced through them, spinning their own small jigs.

I'd already read Réz's hobgoblin letter. Read it, absorbed it, let the horror of it pass into Alexandru's hands.

"How what will happen?" I asked, unable quite to tear my gaze from the motes. It seemed to me they were dancing to the unearthly poem of *Draumr*, keeping time with its funeral dirge.

"The manner in which they try to kill you," she said. "Your English parents, I mean. Would you like to know? It's in the late afternoon. It's summer in Dark-frith, and lilies are in bloom. There'll be a measure of laudanum in your tea. Your mother will hand you the cup. You're going to drink it. You speak of missing them—of your prince—and I believe you were even attempting to tell them about your daughter—"

"Our daughter," Sandu whispered, less than a sound, a scant parting of the air.

"—but the laudanum is potent, and you fall asleep first. They plan to behead you, which you may recall is our traditional method of handling *drákon* enemies. Your mother will cry, your father won't let her watch. They both agreed to it, though."

I wrenched my gaze back to Lia. The cooling sun put fire in her hair.

"I remember that," I said. A pulse of fright reached me, breaking past the numbed horror of the letter. "I remember Sandu telling me in the meadow . . . how I'd go to them, to tell them we were engaged . . ."

"In an effort," she continued steadily, "to soothe your mother's sensibilities, they plan to use an ax instead of the Alpha's teeth. It's really all very civilized."

"But I *live*." I jerked a hand toward the letter Sandu still held.

"Yes. You Weave away, even after falling asleep. You Weave back here, I assume. But the English know about you now, that you're aligned with the Zaharen. After you go to Darkfrith, they know, and they know also that you're *sanf*. The proposal for unifying the tribes is merely a ruse, one they decide they no longer need. They come here to destroy you."

"I'm *not*—"

"But you will be," bit out my second mother, a sentence so sharp it stilled even the motes.

I faced Sandu, desperate. "What does it say? Can you Read it?"

His eyes scanned the page again, gray and unfathomable. The funeral song of *Draumr* groaned between us, slinking and slithering around us, and it was all I could do not to go to him to pull him close. I'd gone hollow inside. I needed to feel him, his heat. His life.

"Nothing," he said at last. He looked up at me. "It says nothing else. I think it must be the entire truth."

"It *can't* be," I burst out. "That *can't* be our future! That can't be me!"

I didn't have to go to him; the prince came to me. He cradled me in his arms and pressed my cheek to his chest. I was breathing too quickly. The room began to blur.

The end, your end, the end, moaned *Draumr*.

"That is not going to be your future," agreed Lia, and with that single statement, *Draumr* suspended, an abrupt, waiting hush.

"Come stand before me, both of you," she said.

Like it had never desired to be anything else, the shattered diamond song swelled back to life, wrapped around Lia's command so that we had no choice but to obey it, because now it was lovely and long and persuasive.

She looked us over with a sigh. "I've had too much a hand in this, I think. I never meant to muddle things so. It happened. I knew you were destined to be with Alexandru, that it would enrage the English, and thought to circumvent it. I knew about the cathedral, Honor, and let it be, because it was in Spain still, and I thought, well, at least she's staying here. But perhaps, in attempting to avoid the future I dreamed, I've only caused it to happen. Had I left you in Darkfrith, had I let you grow up there, or been killed there—" She broke off, biting her lip. "Maybe none of this would have occurred. I honestly don't know." A hand lifted to her forehead; she seemed tired suddenly, thin and waifish. "The future has always been dark to me."

"Can you fix it?" I asked, and even to me, my voice sounded very small. I heard in it all the years of my childhood, all the yearning to belong, for Joséphine or Gervase to look at me and smile and soothe away my wounds, to take lasting note of me and all my turmoil and put it right like they never did.

Because Lia was also my mother, I realized. In all the ways that counted, she was.

"There is an answer," Amalia replied. "It is that you must never wed him. Never be with him. Never bear his child."

"No," snarled Sandu at once. He rocked forward a step but couldn't do more than that; *Draumr* had us fixed.

Lia transferred her dark gaze to him. "Réz cannot live here with you," she explained with awful kindness. "Réz cannot come to be. It's Réz they desire to obliterate, not you. The English will invade one way or another, my lord, but they'd let you live were she not your mate."

"She *is* my mate. It cannot be undone."

"I know. My dear friend, I know all about bonded hearts. So here is what will happen: You're going to leave *Zaharen Yce* forever, both of you. You're going to Weave ahead to the future, Honor. Far, far into the future, with him. And you'll never return."

My lips parted in dismay. There were so many things wrong with that plan, I could barely stammer out where to begin. "I–I can't! I can't Weave with another living thing! I've never been able to!"

"You will this time, though."

"No, but—"

"Honor," she interrupted firmly. "You *will*."

Wiiiiiill, throbbed *Draumr,* swooning deep. *Wiiiiiill . . .*

There were people outside in the courtyard. I'd only just noticed them. We were invisible to them, lost behind windows, but they moved slowly, languidly, as if they too were caught in the swooning net of the diamond.

"Wait," said Sandu, strained. "Wait a moment, please."

"Your Grace?"

"I . . . I thought I knew what love was," he said heavily. He looked at me, so dearly fierce, his face angled with light and shadow. He drew his fingers down my cheek, his gaze lost, absorbed. "If it means dying for her, I would. Gladly. Dying for them, for my people, I would. But leaving them. Abandoning them." He closed his eyes to shut me out; the lines bracketing his mouth deepened. "I'm sorry. I cannot."

Lia's tone turned astringent. "You would leave them for that love. To remain here is to doom them. If you choose that path, what lives in your heart isn't love but merely pride. I expected more from the male who won my daughter's heart."

I swallowed. The song was thick in my throat, blocking my own words, and I swallowed again.

Don't, is what I would have said, if I could have. Cowardly me, I would have pleaded, *Don't choose them over me. Please, please, don't choose them.*

But I said nothing.

Instead, Lia spoke for us both, and she was no coward. She was merciless.

"Everyone dies if you stay. I've dreamed it. Réz's letter reveals it. Is that the future you desire?"

Sandu looked like a man who was splintering in two deep inside, silently, invisibly. He was harsh, dark, and bright, his hands working into fists at his sides. He would not raise his eyes to mine.

"The English will come anyway," Amalia tried again, as if explaining a logic problem to a very young child. "They've been planning to for years, and ultimately there will be no preventing it. But if you are gone, they will take over in peace. I know them. Without the potential threat of your rule, your tribe will be treated with respect. Their ways and traditions will be honored, as long as they don't flaunt their heritage, which may sound severe, but it's better than annihilation. The very best you could hope for if you stayed, Prince Alexandru, would be to become a puppet leader, enslaved to Darkfrith and its Council. Otherwise, I suppose a few years from now you'll fight to your death, and your daughter's death, and destine what's left of your kin to disaster. You cannot win against them. I don't believe that the child I raised would fall in love with an entirely stupid man, so I must assume you're intelligent enough to realize that."

Now he looked at me, a hot and helpless look, and Lia saw that too.

"You have a choice this morning, my lord. You have a chance to seize destiny by the throat." She lifted a hand to the blurry figures in the courtyard.

"You can *save* them, *all* of them. Or not. I must wonder . . . what manner of ruler are you? What matters to you most?"

The *drákon* behind the glass were swimming in light, picking up chunks of fountain, putting them down again.

I asked her, too afraid to hope, "You've dreamed it that way? Everyone safe?"

If only, if only that bleak Future Réz would never come true—

"I will," she answered, with simple surety.

"All right," Alexandru rasped, facing her, expelling a breath. "Damn you, and let's do it."

"Turn around, both of you."

Draumr moved my feet for me. I felt Lia's hand push aside my hair, stroke the bare skin of my neck, the curve of my back that the gown did not cover. Her fingers burned like the sun.

There was a wedge of shift showing above the scalloped back neckline of Honor's gown, as well. Lia smiled at the sight of it, that girlish bit of lace against a border of sequins, a smile that felt like laughter and tears both.

The valise was at her feet. She bent down, removed the knife. It was one of Zane's, one he'd left for her protection, which was a dear and silly thought, but the edge was brutally keen.

"Don't move. You will not feel any pain." She closed her eyes, thought about it—*just the right place*—then pricked the flesh above Honor's shoulder blade with the honed tip.

Blood welled up, began a scarlet trickle down the slight curve of Honor's back to the edge of the gown. Prince Alexandru jerked in place.

"Be still," Lia snapped, a little appalled herself at the amount of it. She pressed a hand over the cut. Honor turned her head, made a soothing sound toward the prince, smiling up at him.

When they'd divided what was left of the wicked stone that had once been a wicked whole dreaming diamond, Lia and Zane had agreed that she would take the three larger splinters and he would have everything else, all the dust and smaller splinters and chips. Her three pieces of *Draumr* were narrow and pointed, almost like needles. She'd removed them from the pendant days before, torn them out atop a white limestone cliff with sensitive dragon claws, and she knew firsthand how sharp they could be. It wasn't difficult to press them deeper into the wound.

Two splinters to Honor, that diminutive creature of formidable talents. One to the prince, who'd shrugged off his coat and waistcoat and shirt without another verbal protest, only a fearsome scowl at the floor.

"No pain," Lia chanted softly, standing on her toes to reach the marbled crest of his shoulder, another small cut, another diamond needle inserted. "No pain."

She sank back to her heels, wiping the blood down the folds of her robe, faintly sick despite herself. She dropped the knife back into the open neck of the valise and took a breath.

This was the end. The edge of all her hopes for this

young *drákon* woman, her ambitions for her, right here and now.

"Neither of you will remember those pieces are there. The song will always be with you, but it never vexes you. You'll both heal and never even see the scars, or remark upon them. Do you understand?"

"Yes," said the prince.

"Yes," whispered Honor.

"Good. Listen."

∞

Lia was speaking. I was listening to her, admiring the serenity of her voice, that calm reassurance that had always seemed to be such a fundamental part of her. Whenever she spoke like that, in that tone, a tiny over-wound part of me deep inside began to relax, like a coiled spring easing loose.

She's so pretty, this Mama, I thought, watching her. *Not because she's* drákon. *Just because she is.*

Alexandru clasped my hand. I held the other over my stomach, and wondered why I felt so very fine.

"You will remember only what I say to you now," Amalia said. "Honor, you *will* Weave with your mate. You have that power. Do you feel it?"

"I do," I answered, marveling. And it was true, there was something new blooming inside me, something born of fearless Réz the dragon and my own more sensitive heart. It warmed through me, a magic stronger and better than any tug of Weave I'd ever felt before. It was potency without doubt, certainty without hesitation, a deep mighty sparkle in my bones. I was going to Weave with Sandu.

Finally, I was powerful enough to share my Gift.

"You will Weave to the future, generations away from now. You will spend the rest of your lives there, and you will never, never return to this time or any time near it. In fact, after this last Weave, you'll never Weave again. Can you do that?"

"Yes," I replied, smiling. "I can do that. Thank you."

She took a step back from us, her robe a puddle of silk around her feet.

"Your lives are ahead of you now, but don't ever regret what you had here. You will adapt to whatever the future holds, and in those years ahead, you will thrive. Do you understand?"

"Yes."

"Yes."

She nodded, and in her long hair and robe and the swelling amber sun, she looked a stern angel. "One last thing. You'll always be the child of my heart. Go, *filla*. Be happy."

Something was happening to me. It was a Weave, but it was open and brilliant, shining as bright as the hammered gilt walls of the Great Room. Within it stood my mate, the prince of the Zaharen, that blue-dark and elusive dragon of my childhood dreams. Only we were both grown now, and he was mine, mine as certainly as I was his. He looked at me unafraid, and in his eyes the light pooled and swirled and became twin delicate silver spirals of infinity.

"I love you," I said to him, as the coming wave of the tide lifted his hair, dissolving indigo into radiance. "Whenever we've been, whenever we're about to be, I love you. That's our constant. No matter what, it will never change."

Love you, he mouthed back, smiling, stepping closer to me, and the only reason I couldn't hear him any longer was the song that surrounded us, an intensely soulful and beautiful song that had become more than music. It was the thread and fabric of the Weave itself, binding us together. It soaked into me, seared through me in undiluted joy.

Love you forever, river-girl, Alexandru said silently, and hand in hand we jumped the wave and swept ahead to find our fresh ending.

⤜⤛⤛⤜

They melted away. It was like that, a melting, Lia thought, standing alone now in the studied sophistication of the castle parlor, her arms hugged to her chest to hold in the ache. She might have even glimpsed a flash of something like light in their final half-second before her. Better than light. It had texture, and feeling, and it had resonated of bliss.

Her very last sight of Honor had been of her blazing smile, aimed up at the young Zaharen prince.

But now they were gone. And there were, she reckoned, at least a dozen people pressed against the other side of the wooden door that led back to the main hall, holding their breaths, quiet as mice. She didn't know how much they'd heard or how much they might have guessed, but it wouldn't do to leave them unprepared. Their lives were changing soon, certain as the rising moon. Someone had to tell them.

She tightened the belt of the robe, picked up her valise, and walked to the door.

With her every step, she was bathed in yellow sun. And it felt good.

EPILOGUE

February 1789
Four Months Later

The ocean lapped at her dreams.

It was soft and ticklish, because the waves that hit the cove had to break through a long, bony reef of white and pink coral first, and the coral absorbed most of their force. By the time the waves broached the sugared shore they were little more than playful curls of foam, and bubbles left to swell and pop along the tide line at their retreat.

Beneath the waves would drift the sea turtles, peaceful in their rest, massive and silent and dark.

"What a smile," whispered her husband in her ear, his breath also a tickle.

Lia opened her eyes. She saw first the section of oak timber crossbeam supporting the ceiling above her, a thick shadow against the paler plaster, all of it tinted pearly blue with Caribbean moonlight. Then Zane lifted up to one elbow. His hair fell across his face, and he shook it back without looking away from her.

"You were dreaming," he said.

She rubbed a hand across her lids, languorous and warm. "Yes."

"The future?"

"Yes."

"And . . . ?" he prompted, a single eyebrow arching, the word a deliberate stretch of sound.

She reached up to capture a lock of his hair, twirling it around her finger.

"It's happy," Lia said.

He rolled atop her, trim and muscled, bunching the sheets between them. The tickle of his next words transformed into a slower, more sensuous caress against her lips.

"My dearest heart," her true love murmured, smiling his rakish thief's smile. "I could have told you that."

New York City, 1898

Paola and Lucy worked together at the shirtwaist factory, and had for the past nine years. Same shift, their machines bolted side by side, their heads bent at identical angles from seven in the morning until eight o'clock in the evening, scarred fingers shaping the stabbing course of the needle, Mondays through Saturdays and a half-day Sunday too, with only a single precious forty-minute break at three. They even pumped their floor pedals in mechanical unison, thump-*thump*-ta-thump, twenty-two shirts per girl per shift, or else.

There were times Paola feared she'd never be able to massage away the hot stony pain that yoked her shoulders. Still, they had it better than the girls on the night shift, who had to finish the same amount of work by the meager gas jets above the machines, set too high to be any sort of genuine help.

But the break:

Three o'clock, heads up, necks cracked, chairs shoved back. Three-oh-three, at the main door; a wait while the foreman sticks his fat fingers into their pocketbooks, rifling through their kerchiefs and pennies for any stolen scraps of lace. Three-fourteen, and if they had hurried they were at the edge of the park, moving at a brisk clip to their favorite bench, which was nearly always unoccupied because a prickly hedge had sprouted wild next to it and appeared to drape over its slats, discouraging all but the most determined of loungers.

Paola and Lucy were very careful to redrape the branches of the hedge back over the bench each afternoon before they left. The thorns were formidable, but not any worse than the sewing machine needles that would pierce clean through a hand in a blink.

And there they'd sit, eating the mashed brown bread and treacle from their luncheon tins, savoring the cigarettes Lucy stole from her father and smuggled to work in her bodice, which burned so harshly in Paola's throat it left her with a cough every time.

A good cough, because it meant she was outside, under the sun, even if only for these treasured few minutes. Out of the enclosed stench of the factory.

Even in the rain, even in sleet, they sat outside and smoked.

But today was merely damp, with late spring clouds puffing up dark over the edges of the trees, too far away still to soak this afternoon's break.

"Look." Lucy nudged her hard in the ribs with an elbow. "There she is."

Paola narrowed her eyes through the pall of blue smoke.

She walked alone, slowly down the park path, not seeming to mind the patches of wet and mud that pocked the sparse gravel, only stepping over them absentmindedly, like she missed them all without even trying. She was dressed well—she was always dressed very well, in garments much finer than anything the factory had ever produced. It had been clear from the instant they'd first noticed her, months past, that she was rich. Massively rich, society rich, the sort of rich that meant no holes in her stockings and no treacle for lunch, ever. Her complexion was unblemished, her hair such a bright, glinting red-gold it looked like actual strands of polished copper wound up in a fashionable puff beneath her hat.

Today she wore nearly all cream: a cream wool coat with black piping and pearled buttons from collar to hem; a cream felt hat with a wide, smart brim and the scarf hanging loose to wind around her neck. Cream gloves. Not a spot to be seen.

Paola nearly sighed with envy. Cream. The worst color on earth for practical wear.

Her coat was nearly shapeless, but it was clear anyway that the woman was heavy with child. She kept her hands in her pockets or else cupping her belly, emphasizing its roundness.

In Paola's village back in Sicily, a woman so clearly close to her time would have been confined to her home, wealthy or no. It would have been shocking indeed to see her out strolling through town by herself; people would wonder if she'd been hexed.

But this was not Sicily. This was America, it was the rolling acres of Washington Square Park, and although the woman had the sort of blazing, unreasonable beauty Paola had only ever seen in printed fashion plates, they'd never once witnessed anyone in the park bother her.

"And there," muttered Lucy, with another nudge, and jerked her chin toward a different path.

No, no one ever pestered the woman, and Paola suspected that *this* was the reason why . . . and the reason why she and Lucy took such pains to make it to the park each day by this time.

Because of *him*.

Like clockwork they would meet, the man and the woman, each drifting in from different directions, she with her daydreamy, pregnant grace, and he with a pace that was far more . . .

Paola frowned and drew at her cigarette, trying to think of just the right word.

Sleek. His pace was sleek, like the panther she'd ogled once at a traveling circus her grandfather had taken her to when she was a child, a fearsome trapped thing walking circles behind the bars of its pen.

The man moved like that panther might have, had it ever had the freedom of space, swiftly, fluidly, as if the soles of his shoes barely scuffed the earth.

She glanced down at his spats, instantly curious. Also spotless.

Beyond his sleekness, beyond the excellent cut of his trousers and coat—for he was surely the source of all that wealth—and the peculiar but oddly fascinating way he wore his hair—long like a girl's, tied back into a tail—was simply the overwhelming fact of his beauty. He was every bit the equal to *her*.

A true gentleman's pale skin, shining dark hair, his firm jaw and his wintry gaze that had caught Paola's once, had held her suspended and breathless and had seemed to cut through her more sharply than even the needles at work—

At her side, Lucy did release a smoky sigh. Paola waved her hand before them both to clear the view.

The man didn't see her today. He had eyes for one figure only. They came together at the joining of the two paths and touched hands, and then the man leaned down to her and kissed her right on the mouth, right in public. Not a peck, either. A long, full kiss, their bodies pressed close.

For the entire duration of it, neither girl on the bench either moved or breathed.

When they pulled apart again, both the man and the woman were smiling. She said something and he said something back; he offered his arm and led her to the next-nearest bench, where they sat together.

He unbuttoned the top half of his coat, reached inside, and withdrew a folded paper. A newspaper, she thought. They bent their heads together and began to discuss whatever they were reading.

"That," said Lucy suddenly.

Paola angled her gaze a fraction to regard her.

Her friend jerked her chin again at the couple, her gray eyes taking on a flinty cast.

"I want to be that loved."

Paola smothered her grin and returned to her cigarette, allowing her lids to sink not quite closed as she observed *le due bellezze pericolose*, the two dangerous beauties, inhaling the last sweet dregs of tobacco down into her lungs. When it was finished, she tossed the butt to the gravel at her feet and flicked the ashes from her skirt.

"*Cara*. We *all* want that."

The man and woman were rising. They were leaving together, just as they did each afternoon, walking leisurely now, because the woman was so very rounded.

They met a bend in the path and faded off behind the line of trees.

Lucy jumped from the bench. "C'mon."

Paola didn't have to ask where; they'd left their newspaper on the bench.

It was a morning edition, the usual blocks of tiny print telling tales of politicians and land barons gobbling up the world. But the page had been folded to hide most of the print. It showed instead all of an advertisement, a lavishly illustrated one.

"What, a ship?" said Lucy, studying it hard. "Are they taking a journey? What does it say?"

Lucy's mother had died of cholera when she was still an infant and her father had never bothered to send her to school; Lucy could not read. Paola's luck had run slightly better. She'd had lessons all the way until the age of nine, and even long words could be sounded out. She ran a finger down the scripted lettering.

"It is an announcement for an ocean liner going to Europe. The *Nikita Regina*, departing New York for . . . Liverpool, all cabins outfitted in the finest comfort guaranteed, turbine engines of the most . . . so-phis-ticated design. It leaves next week." She dropped the hand holding the paper to her side, staring out at the clouds.

"Oh," Lucy said, sounding deflated. "Well, it was a lovely fancy. While it lasted."

"Yes."

The sun was already starting to tilt against the tip-top crowns of the trees; in the long spring light the countless green buds of summer leaves to come flamed into perfect gold. Just beyond them a rainbow began to form, the colors growing truer and firmer as she watched.

A pair of birds soared through it, free as the wind, and for a very brief instant Paola allowed herself the luxury of imagining what it might be like, to fly like that, to sail through clear, enchanted colors and sky.

A lovely fancy, indeed.

❦

Did they live or did they perish?

Which ripple of time stretched through the dark sparkling universe with the most profound force?

In some, the *drákon* thrived, grew vibrant in their secret worlds, bred stronger and stronger and lived to dance with their particular mesmerizing elegance in and out of the human race, changing histories, changing destinies, all unseen by the lesser beings.

In some, war lived, and nothing else.

Réz and her prince leapt ahead into a future that had not been written. Their bonded hearts forged their way, and through war or peace, they loved. Réz was right: That never changed.

In the center of it all, the Dragon of Time opens his eyes and cranes his monstrous head, searching for his meal, never sated.

But in our deep spreading ripple, the *drákon* dance among us still.